Gracie withdrew her water bottle from its sling and took a long draught, pouring a little into her cupped hand for Minnie. As she replaced the bottle and looked around, her eye caught on a tree stump a few feet off to her left. She stepped over and looked down.

A symbol had been carved into the wood—a diamond shape with what appeared to be stick legs set above a pair of figure eights.

Gracie had jogged past the same tree stump countless times and had never noticed a carving. "Huh," she said aloud. "How long has that been there?" She frowned. "And what does it stand for?"

She peered at it more closely.

The edges were crisp, dug-out wood slivers lying on the flat surface of the stump.

The carving was recent.

And creepy.

Berkley Prime Crime titles by M. L. Rowland

ZERO-DEGREE MURDER
MURDER OFF THE BEATEN PATH
MURDER ON THE HORIZON

MURDER ON THE
HORIZON

M. L. ROWLAND

BERKLEY PRIME CRIME, NEW YORK

BERKLEY PRIME CRIME

An imprint of Penguin Random House LLC
375 Hudson Street, New York, New York 10014

MURDER ON THE HORIZON

A Berkley Prime Crime Book / published by arrangement with the author

ISBN: 978-0-425-26368-6

PUBLISHING HISTORY
Berkley Prime Crime mass-market edition / August 2015

PRINTED IN THE UNITED STATES OF AMERICA

10 9 8 7 6 5 4 3 2 1

Cover art: *Log cabin* © by Ev Thomas; *Dog* © by Sanne vd Berg Fotografie.
Cover design by Diana Kolsky.
Interior text design by Kristin del Rosario.

Penguin
Random
House

*For all the Search and Rescue volunteers
who routinely risk their lives
"So That Others May Live."*

ACKNOWLEDGMENTS

A heartfelt thank you to:

Nancy Chichester, Diane and Terry Hiebert, Dr. Barbara Law, Kathleen Law, Dr. Catherine LeGalley, Jeffrey Norwitz, Mark H. Rowland, Bonnie and Doug Towne.

My editor, Michelle Vega.

Anne McDermott.

"**D**AMN, that's a lot of blood," a man said, voice echoing in the large room.

"What the hell d'you expect?" a second man said. "Go get a bucket."

"Hey, got my hands full here! You get a damn bucket."

Footsteps receded.

The sound of sawing. A curse. The crinkle of heavy plastic.

Johnny Cash's deep bass sang from a radio somewhere nearby: "Now gettin' caught meant gettin' fired."

Banging and clattering from the other end of the room.

"Bring me two while you're at it," the first man yelled. "Gotta have something to put . . ." He stopped to sing along.

The man drew in a deep breath and belted out the chorus. "'I'd get it one piece at a time, and it wouldn't cost me a dime.'" He chuckled and said to himself, "One piece at a time."

Two buckets plunked on the floor.

"Hey," the man said. "One piece at a time. Get it? One piece at a time?"

"Yeah. I get it."

"IT'S friggin' *hot*," Gracie muttered, using a trekking pole to shove aside the bottom branches of a creosote bush. Dust and pollen billowed up around her, sticking to the sweat on her temples and making them itch. Pinching her nose to stifle a sneeze, she bent to scan the buff-colored ground beneath, spotting nothing but a powder blue plastic blob—a soiled disposable diaper tossed from a passing car. With the toe of her hiking boot, Gracie nudged the blue ball aside. Seeing nothing of interest, she stepped back and let the branches swing back into place.

Five members of Timber Creek Search and Rescue formed a ragged line stretching out across the Mojave Desert. Warren was guiding left off the sage-choked shoulder of the I-15 freeway with Jon Barton walking fifteen feet off to his right along the barbed wire right-of-way fence. Gracie walked on the other side of the fence with Lenny Olsen next to her and Carrie Matthews on the far end.

That morning, the searchers had responded to a callout for

an evidence search, leaving the Sheriff's Office substation before dawn, making the two-hour drive down from the Bavarian-style resort town high in the mountains a hundred miles east of Los Angeles, and out into the middle of the Mojave. Their assignment: Comb a mile-long segment of ground alongside the I-15 corridor for a Smith & Wesson Model 57 .41 Magnum revolver, black with a walnut grip, allegedly used in a triple homicide in the tiny desert town of Baker, and, according to a witness, tossed from a motorcycle of unknown make traveling west on the interstate in excess of eighty miles an hour.

Four additional county SAR teams were searching similar mile-long segments, three in front of the Timber Creek team, one behind.

Maintaining a cursory spacing of fifteen feet, Gracie and her teammates walked slowly westward, eyes scanning the ground in every direction. Using feet, hands, and trekking poles, they examined and poked around and beneath every bush, tree, and cactus, turning over every discarded fast-food wrapper, every empty Red Bull can, even scaring up an occasional jackrabbit to watch it zigzag away through the brush.

All wore the team's orange cotton uniform shirt, desert camouflage army-surplus pants, floppy-brimmed hats, thick leather gloves, and knee-high gaiters of black, ripstop nylon, worn over the tops of boots to stave off punctures from mesquite thorns or rattlesnake fangs. One or two of the searchers wore day packs containing internal hydration bladders, some a water bottle clipped by a carabiner to an outside loop with spare water inside their packs.

Gracie stopped and pried a damp strand of hair off her cheek. Squinting behind her Ray-Bans against the blinding glare of the midday sun, eyes burning from pollen and sweaty trickles of sunscreen, she looked around her.

The vast desert dwarfed the searchers—a hardscrabble floor of dirt and rock dotted with stubby clumps of creosote, mesquite, and sage, its mountains jumbled mounds of chocolate-colored rock lining the northern horizon.

On the asphalt ribbon of highway off to the left, pickups, minivans, and semi-trucks whooshed by in a steady steel stream—eastward toward Las Vegas, lured by dreams of easy riches, sex, or adventure, westward to the flash of Los Angeles and Hollywood, or slinking home with pockets empty and hopes of instant wealth dashed.

When seen only from a car whizzing along the highway at seventy miles an hour, the Mojave Desert appeared as an endless, boring wasteland, harsh, desolate. Closer exploration revealed a diverse plant and animal life—from desert holly to prickly pear, from roadrunners to cactus wrens, bighorn sheep to kangaroo rats.

Gracie loved the desert in the winter. But in the long summer season, when temperatures soared well past one hundred degrees, the Mojave was a superheated skillet, brutal, unforgiving, able to kill the naive and unprepared in less than two hours.

The sun blistered down on the searchers from a faded-denim blue sky, scorching bent heads and backs. A sudden gust of dry wind blasted them with grit and dust.

Gracie turned her back to the searing wind, anchored her hat with her hand, and waited for it to dissipate. Then she slithered down a rocky embankment to the bottom of a dry wash. "Have I said it's friggin' hot?" she said, lifting up one end of a section of blown vehicle tire and tipping it off to the side. She scanned the sandy ground in all directions, saw nothing of note, and slogged across the deep sand and clambered up the other side.

Jon's voice filtered up from the wash. "Only about twenty-two hundred fifty-three times." FedEx double-trailers roared past on the highway. "I love the smell of diesel in the morning," he said, reappearing out of the wash.

Fifteen years older and an inch or so shorter than Gracie,

Jon was a retired civil engineer, lean and fit, consistently surprising younger, less-experienced members of the team by outlasting them on the trail. Next to Ralph Hunter, the team's Commander and Gracie's best friend, she trusted Jon's physical capabilities and judgment more than anyone else's on the team.

Gracie laid her trekking poles on the ground. Straightening again, she stood with her weight on one foot, resting the other ankle, which ached from a break several months earlier. "I love evidence searches in the middle of the desert in the middle of the day in hundred-degree weather," she said, peeling her heavy braid off the back of her neck. She tucked the hair up beneath her hat and retrieved her poles from the ground. Looking over at Lenny on her right, she noticed the young man's cheeks were flushed, and the skin on his burly arms a bright red. "Hey, Lenny," she said. "Got sunscreen?"

"Forgot it." Lenny was one of the newest and, at nineteen, youngest members of the team. With a quick, wide smile, a wild thatch of straw-colored hair, and astonishing cornflower blue eyes, he was instantly likable, a good soul, by far the most exuberant on the team. But as time went on and the number of searches Gracie worked with Lenny increased, she was learning his youthful enthusiasm had a downside. Lenny was prone to carelessness about his own safety and equipment, often forgetting the most fundamental tenet of Search and Rescue: Don't Get Dead.

"Boy, you lookin' like a boiled mudbug, you," Jon called over.

Lenny grimaced. "Huh?"

"Crawfish," Gracie said. "A boiled crawfish."

"Okay, I get it," Lenny said. "I look at the sun, I turn red."

Gracie dug a four-ounce tube of Banana Boat SPF 100 from her radio chest pack and tossed it over to Lenny, who snapped it out of the air. "Next time maybe wear your long-sleeved shirt?" she suggested. "Keep those arms covered?"

"Yeah, okay," the young man said without resentment. He

stopped, removed his gloves, tossed them on the ground, and slathered the sunscreen over his broiled arms and cheeks. "How hot is it anyway?"

"Supposed to top out somewhere round a hundred and eight," Carrie called from the end of the line.

"Hunnert 'n' eight," Lenny said, lobbing the tube of sunscreen back over his head to Gracie. "That's not a temperature! That's an oven setting!"

"But it's a dry heat," Jon said, eyes gleaming with mischief behind his wire-rims. "It's so hot," he said in a voice loud enough for everyone to hear, "cows are giving evaporated milk."

"Here we go," Gracie said, then took a long draw of still-cold water from the hydration bladder inside her pack.

From the other end of the line, Warren yelled back in his deep, deadpan voice. "It's so hot, I saw a chicken lay a hard-boiled egg."

"It's so hot," Jon shot back, "I saw a chicken lay an omelet."

Chuckles drifted up and down the grid line.

Inexplicably charging, arms and legs thrashing right through the middle of a stand of sage four feet high, Lenny yelled, "By the time my wife got home from the store with the bread, it was toast."

Warren yelled again. "It's so hot, the squirrels are *fanning* their nuts."

Laughter.

"It's so hot," Jon said. "The hooker's—" He stopped.

"C'mon! The hooker's what?" Lenny asked.

"Later, Lenny. Mixed company."

"Bah-dum-bum," Gracie said.

More laughter.

The searchers moved slowly forward without speaking, eyes scanning the hard-packed ground, prodding beneath bushes, kicking over rocks, until Lenny broke the silence by asking, "Hey, Gracie, how far've we gone, d'ya think?"

Squinting back over her shoulder, Gracie could just make

out the overpass where they had parked the team's Suburban. "Half mile maybe. Maybe less."

"How much farther do we have to go, d'ya think?"

Gracie craned her head and looked up the highway. "Can't see the mile marker yet." She turned over a child's car seat with the toe of her boot and kept walking, eyes sweeping the ground. "We're not even halfway yet."

Carrie used her trekking pole to roll a sealed plastic bottle filled with what looked like dark brown tea away from the base of a creosote bush. She bent and picked it up to look at it more closely.

Petite, but physically strong, Carrie was the newest member of Timber Creek SAR, and not yet comfortable joining in the team banter. But there was no fuss with her, no drama. She was smart and competent, did her homework, and was ready for almost anything. As a result, even though Carrie had been on the team less than a year, Gracie trusted her to do her job thoroughly and do it well.

"What are all these?" Carrie asked, examining the bottle in her hands. "I've seen a lot of 'em. They look like iced tea or something."

Lenny guffawed. "It's trucker piss!"

"Ewww!" Carrie dropped the bottle and wiped her gloves on her pants. "What the hell?" She kicked the bottle away. "Really? Truckers do that?"

"And anyone else driving through the desert who doesn't want to stop," Gracie said. "Personally, it's my most favorite thing."

"Yum," Jon said. "Fermented redneck urine."

"Ugh," Carrie said, kicking at the bottle again. "Why can't they keep it to throw it away later? Or at the very least throw it out without the cap so it can dry out. That's just gross!"

"You really think we're gonna find this gun?" Lenny asked, whacking at the ground with his trekking pole for no apparent reason.

"Prolly not," Gracie answered.

"Then why do we have to do this?"

"The SO covering its behind." She looked over toward Jon, who had stopped several paces back and was using his trekking pole to poke at something black suspended from a mesquite tree branch a few feet off the ground. "Whatcha got, Mr. B?"

"Dunno yet."

"Hold up!" Gracie called to the rest of the group. "Jon's got something maybe."

"Is it the gun?" Lenny asked, trotting over.

Gracie walked over to stand next to Jon.

A black plastic trash bag, knotted closed, hung from the mesquite tree as if tossed from a passing car and snagged by the end of a branch. Its contents, a lump of something, hung at the bottom of the bag.

"What is it?" Carrie asked, walking up.

"No idea."

"Been out here awhile," Gracie said, leaning in for a better look. "Plastic's pretty dusty and degraded."

Gracie looked over at Jon, who was staring at the bag. She could see the layer of dust on his glasses. "Wanna do the honors of opening it?"

"I'm not gonna open it," Jon said, taking a step back. "You open it."

"I'm not gonna open it," Gracie said.

"You have seniority."

"You're older."

"You're younger. And tougher."

"This from the man who runs marathons in the mountains."

"Warren," Jon said to his teammate who was just walking up. "Get over here and open this."

Warren leaned both hands on his pole and studied the bag. "I'm not gonna open it," he said finally. "Let's get Lenny. Yeah. He'll open anything. Hey, Lenny. You open it."

With one eye closed in a grimace, Lenny stepped forward and edged the sharp point of his trekking pole into the black plastic and pulled it off the branch. The soft plastic, malleable from the heat, stretched and broke, spilling the contents onto the ground—a pile of human hands.

The entire group jumped back. "Gross! Damn!"

"What is that?" Lenny asked.

"Well, Lenny," Jon said, "It looks like a little clump of hands to me."

"Four, to be exact," Warren said.

"That's so gross," Lenny whispered.

Gracie looked over at him. His face had lost its color and his mouth was moving as if the 7-Eleven burrito he'd had for breakfast was about to make an appearance.

Her own stomach was doing its impression of Old Faithful, churning beneath the surface with the possibility of eruption at any moment. She breathed in through her nose, out again through her mouth, and then bent, elbows on knees, to examine the pile of hands more closely.

The skin was yellowed, tendons and bones showing white at the severed ends. The nails on two of the hands were painted with little palm trees. "Obviously two different people," she said. "One's a woman's."

Warren asked, "Is that a tattoo?"

"Where?" Gracie asked.

He pointed with the tip of his trekking pole. "The wrist there."

Then Gracie saw it, a portion of a tattoo, on the inside of one of the wrists.

Lenny took a careful step forward and leaned in. "Turn it over."

"Crime scene," Gracie said.

"Ya think?" Jon said with a wink in her direction.

"Were they murdered?" Lenny asked, his voice inching into its upper range.

Gracie shot him a look.

Lenny's eyes flicked to Gracie's. "What? I was just asking."

"Probably not going to make a big difference if we move something a hair," Jon said.

"Probably not."

"Somebody turn it over."

Nobody moved.

"Come on," Gracie said. "Who's got a trekking pole handy?"

"You," everyone answered in unison.

"Buncha wusses," she mumbled. With teeth bared, she nudged the hand with the tip of her pole so that it fell back, open palm to the sky, fully exposing the partial tattoo on the inside of the wrist.

Everyone leaned in.

Carrie pointed. "That's a skull and crossbones."

"And some kind of lettering."

"What's it say?"

"Hard to read."

"That's an *A*," Gracie said. "Then something else. Can't quite . . ."

She heard a faint click and looked over to see Lenny taking a picture of the hands with his cell phone. "Lenny," she said, straightening. "That turns up on social media somewhere and heads will roll. Yours. Mine. And ours."

"I wasn't gonna . . ." he said in a way that made Gracie think that was exactly what he was intending.

"I mean it."

"Okay! Okay."

"Everybody, listen up," Jon said. "You post a picture of something like this, of a victim, or anyone we rescue, on Facebook or YouTube or wherever and you're off the damn team faster 'n anybody can say, 'You're off the damn team.'"

"I got it," Lenny said, face even redder than before. "Sheesh."

"That applies to everyone, Lenny," Gracie said. "Me. Jon. Even Ralph." She looked around the group. "Everyone okay with me calling this in?"

Several heads nodded.

Unable to tear her eyes from the pile of hands, Gracie pressed the little microphone button on the HT radio in her chest pack. "Command Post," she said. "Ten Rescue Twenty-two."

"Ten Rescue Twenty-two," a male voice answered. "Go ahead."

2

GRACIE stood at the top of the steep driveway of her cabin, fourth from the top of Arcturus Drive, a giant panda mug of extra-strength Folger's Instant in her hands, looking out to where the sun, a glowing orange orb against a pink-pearl sky, hovered four fingers above the rolling hills at the eastern end of the valley. The morning air was still cool on her bare arms and legs, but the wind that blew her hair back from her face felt warm, carrying with it a hint of sage and pine.

She took a sip of coffee and puzzled for the umpteenth time over the severed hands the Timber Creek SAR team had found on the evidence search the previous week.

It was obvious the hands belonged to a man and a woman. But how were they related? Were they married? Brother and sister? Where did they live? Where had they worked? Did they have kids missing them and wondering what had happened to them?

That they had been murdered was a given.

But why?

Cut it out, Kinkaid, Gracie told herself with a shake of her

head. She knew better than to become emotionally involved with search victims, especially dead ones. But for the
past week, the puzzle of the severed hands had insisted on
wheedling its way into her thoughts as if with a will of
its own.

She took another sip of coffee.

Maybe it had been a family dispute. Or a drug deal
gone bad.

Gracie closed her eyes, trying to remember what the tattoo on the inside of one of the wrists had looked like. At the
time, she wasn't exactly concentrating on the tattoo on the
wrist, rather on the non-attachment of that same wrist to
anything else.

It had a skull and crossbones. And some kind of lettering. An *A*.

What else?

That was all she could remember: a skull and crossbones
and the letter *A*.

She assumed the hands had been lopped off to keep the
bodies from being readily identified. So where were the
bodies themselves?

By now, she figured, *gone with the wind*.

It was a grim fact that bodies left out in the Mojave, desic-
cated by the dry air and charbroiled black by the merciless
sun, torn apart and carried off by coyotes and other denizens
of the desert, simply didn't last very long. A few days. "Tops,"
Gracie said aloud. That was why it was the ideal dumping
ground for bodies and any spare parts lying around.

Quit thinking about it!

Gracie opened her eyes, took another sip of coffee, and
looked down at her dog, Minnie, sitting at her feet. Wind
ruffled her shining black fur. Her black nose was lifted to
the air and twitching. *What scents*, Gracie wondered, *is that
amazing nose catching that mine can't?*

She winced inwardly as her eyes traveled around the yard,
such as it was—after ten years, there were still mostly bare

rectangles of dirt and rock with a clump of bedraggled hot pink petunias near the steps leading up to the front door. The maroon paint of her Ford Ranger pickup parked at the top of the asphalt driveway was freckled with rust. But the Maltby cabin itself she admired with unabashed pride. The logs painted red, the trim and deck stained their natural cedar. A pair of antique skis crisscrossed beneath the east-facing window of the loft bedroom. The antique wagon wheel she had snagged at a Labor Day garage sale for $10.

A burst of hot wind hit Gracie, knocking her back a step. "Wow," she said. "Santa Anas, Minnie. Fire season's definitely here."

The dog responded with a single sweep of her feather duster tail along the asphalt.

With years of fire suppression and scavenging bark beetles dealing the final deathblow to millions of drought-stressed trees, the mountains lining the Timber Creek valley were a conflagration lying in wait. The opportunistic Santa Ana winds, blowing in hot and dry from the Mojave, whipped tiny sparks into whirling dervishes of fire. At the beginning of fire season, which, it seemed, began earlier and earlier every year, a clenched fist of low-level anxiety lodged itself somewhere behind Gracie's sternum and stayed there until the first real snow of the winter.

A low growl drew Gracie's eyes back down to Minnie, who now was sitting at attention, fur raised in a ridge along her back, head cocked to the left, ears pricked, eyes riveted on the road below the driveway.

Gracie's eyes followed Minnie's gaze to where a tall, lanky black man was just strolling into view. He wore a navy blue sweatshirt with the sleeves pushed up to his elbows, baggy khaki pants, and white tennis shoes scuffed to gray. A U.S. Navy baseball cap lettered in yellow—USS BEALE, DD-471—covered his short, gray hair.

Holding the man's hand was a girl, probably nine or ten years old, dressed in a pink butterfly-covered sweatshirt and shorts, white socks, and pink tennis shoes. Pink ribbons and butterfly barrettes held pigtails in place.

Gracie recognized the man as her new neighbor down the road. She had seen him only once since he and his wife had moved into the bungalow at the bottom of the hill, but was very pleased with the remarkable transformation that was taking place. Once owned by Mr. and Mrs. Lucas, local drug dealers, the house had been a blight on the neighborhood—faded red paint with visible patches of gray cement block, missing shingles, windows opaque with filth, and a trash-littered dirt front yard that turned into a mud wallow with the rain. Over the last several months, the small square house had been painted a sedate taupe with a glossy black front door and shutters. A new sod lawn had been laid and burning bush shrubs strategically placed. A cherry red Adirondack chair and pot of matching geraniums sat on the newly constructed front deck.

Tempted to sidestep out of sight behind her truck, but forcing herself to be a good neighbor instead, Gracie said with a smile, "Good morning."

The man looked up, his expression guarded, wary.

Minnie barked, the fur along her back bristling into a black ridge.

The man stopped. The girl cried out in fear, grabbing on to the man's hand with both of her own and backing out of sight behind his long legs.

"Minnie, no!" Mortified, Gracie grabbed ahold of the dog's collar. "Sorry. I've never heard her bark before." She pulled open the passenger door of the Ranger and ordered, "Get in."

Instantly contrite, Minnie hopped onto the seat.

Gracie rolled the window down and pushed the door closed.

The man and girl had continued walking past the bottom of the driveway.

"I'm so sorry," Gracie said, walking down the hill toward them. "I haven't had Minnie very long. I guess she's a little guarded around people she doesn't know." She stretched out her hand to the man. "Hi. I'm Gracie Kinkaid."

The hand that took Gracie's was as dry and light as an old leaf. "John Robinson," the man said in a deep voice, resonant with a pleasing lilt, the origin of which Gracie couldn't place. "This is my granddaughter, Acacia." The love and pride in his voice was unmistakable. He gave the girl's hand a little shake. "Acacia, say 'Good morning' to Miss Gracie."

The pigtails emerged from behind the man's legs. "Good morning, Miss Gracie." Barely a whisper.

"Good morning, Acacia," Gracie said, smiling and thoroughly charmed by the display of old-fashioned good manners.

For the next five minutes, Acacia peered out from behind her grandfather up the driveway to where Minnie sat looking out the window of the pickup as Gracie and John engaged in light, get-to-know-you talk about themselves, the neighborhood, and the quality of life in the mountains. Gracie shared that she was the new manager of Camp Ponderosa, a residential camp owned by a megachurch in Orange County, but that most of her life was taken up by her work on the local Search and Rescue team. In turn, Gracie learned that John, a retired attorney, and his wife, Vivian, a retired schoolteacher, had moved to the mountains from Pasadena for the quiet and fresh air. Reading through the lines, Gracie surmised that John and Vivian were raising their only daughter's daughter away from the blight and violence of urban Los Angeles.

Gracie glanced down at her watch. "Oops. I need to go or I'll be late for work. Nice to meet you. And welcome to the neighborhood," she said, shaking the man's hand again, pleased to see that the return smile had lost a little of its wariness.

"Pleased to meet you as well."

By the time Gracie backed the Ranger down the driveway and out onto Arcturus, John and Acacia had disappeared around the bend in the road.

CHAPTER

3

THE Ranger bumped up and over the rise in the gravel road, glided beneath the hewn-log archway entrance to Camp Ponderosa, and past the dilapidated caretaker's cottage known as the Gatehouse, which served as the camp office.

Gracie lifted her foot from the accelerator, coasting down a short hill and across the little bridge at the bottom, where months of summer heat had reduced the creek to a shining silver ribbon. Leaves on the cottonwoods lining its banks were already hinting at the brilliant yellows to arrive with the autumn.

Twenty feet past the creek, the woods ended with a large recreation field opening up on the left, a paved parking lot on the right. Straight ahead, in front of a tumble of boulders, wooden signs announced the camp's ten-mile-per-hour speed limit and LOADING/UNLOADING ONLY BEYOND THIS POINT. An eight-foot-high carved bear held another sign indicating the dining hall in Serrano Lodge off to the right.

The road itself continued on through to the rest of the developed ten acres of camp, past a small conference center, Mojave

Lodge, several smaller cabins, staff living quarters, and pristine, five-acre Ponderosa Lake. But it was the surrounding forest that Gracie treasured: two hundred glorious, virtually untouched acres of skyscraping ponderosa, Jeffrey, and sugar pine with an understory of live oak and manzanita, California granite boulders the size and shape of elephants, brimming with pygmy nuthatches and mountain chickadees, chipmunks and raccoons, and an occasional black bear lumbering down from higher elevations in search of water or a snack.

Gracie turned right at the carved bear, then swung the Ranger around to the back of Serrano Lodge—a two-story cinder block building painted a grayish brown to complement its surroundings. She parked near the back door leading into the kitchen, climbed out of the truck, and held the door while Minnie hopped out from her bed behind the front seat.

It was still surreal to Gracie that she was Camp Ponderosa's new manager. Three months before, a scandal at the camp had resulted in the firing of over half of its employees, including the manager, as well as the adventure programming company Gracie had hired to help run million-watt movie star Rob Christian's The Sky's the Limit camp, a summer adventure program for at-risk youth.

Gracie had spent hours meeting with the church's senior pastor, the congregational elders, and the accountants, after which she had been offered the job of managing the camp. She had jumped at the chance, surviving the frantically busy summer season by working sixteen-hour days and, more often than not, sleeping on a mattress in the empty room across the hall from her office.

Even though the fallout from the scandal had been short-lived, and despite the summer being a resounding success on all fronts, the emotional aftereffects of everything that had transpired, including multiple attempts on her life, had left Gracie feeling unsettled and wondering more than once if she needed a change of scenery, a fresh start somewhere else.

But Gracie adored Camp Ponderosa. As much as in her

cabin at the top of Arcturus Drive, she felt at home there, as if she truly belonged.

Gracie sighed and looked around. A well-fed western gray squirrel flipped its bushy tail from atop a nearby rock. Ten feet above her head, an acorn woodpecker hopped up the giant cinnamon-colored plates of a ponderosa pine. There was a crisp sharpness to the air that followed the first cold snap of autumn, a humming anticipation of winter as if the clear ringing of a bell still hung in the air.

"Come on, Minnie," she said to the dog sitting patiently at her feet. "Let's go see what Allen's up to." She crossed the faded asphalt and pulled open the rusty screen door.

Letting the door whack closed behind her, she settled Minnie on her bed in the hallway closet and walked into the well-lit kitchen.

Three of the walls were lined with stainless steel countertops, two enormous walk-in refrigerators, and a commercial dishwasher. The far wall held a swinging door leading out into the main dining room and two roll-up windows on either side, one for serving meals to camp guests, one for receiving dirty dishes. From a CD player on a shelf, Willie Nelson twanged about blue eyes cryin' in the rain.

In the center of the kitchen was an oblong butcher-block prep table. At the near end, Allen, the new head cook, was slicing through the tape on empty cardboard boxes with a box cutter, flattening them out, and piling them up for recycling.

To a fraction of an inch, Allen matched Gracie's height of five foot eight. Somewhere in his late forties or early fifties, the man was wiry without an ounce of fat, but with an extra pound in tattoo ink that seemed to cover every square inch of skin except his head and the palms of his hands. Allen wore a white short-sleeved T-shirt, Rustler blue jeans, and paint-spattered steel-toed work boots. Somber blue eyes. Forehead and cheeks deeply lined. Long salt-and-pepper hair braided in the back and coiled up beneath a hairnet. In Gracie's mind, it took a man without an iota of doubt—or care—about his masculinity to wear a hairnet. Allen was unflappable; his general expression and mild voice made it seem as if he had made peace with his existence in a hostile world.

Gracie had lucked out with Allen. Operating on a shoestring staff was the new normal at camp, at least until the following spring when occupancy rates would jump again along with the accompanying revenue. She had yet to hire a new maintenance director, but Allen had proven a maniacal worker, jumping in wherever and whenever needed.

The church had hired him away from another camp in the valley. Allen was an ex-con with a stint in San Quentin for a drug beef, but if a church-owned camp wasn't willing to hire an ex-con, who would? While in prison, the man had earned a college degree in sociology. Upon meeting Allen for the first time, Gracie had felt an instant rapport, yet there was a steeliness about him that both scared and reassured her. All she knew was that she would rather have Allen in her corner than not. Plus, considering her own tendency for dinners of cold pizza eaten while standing at her kitchen sink, a taste of Allen's lasagna and walnut brownies and she had been tempted to ask for his hand in marriage.

When Gracie appeared in the kitchen doorway, Allen glanced over his shoulder, then back down to the box he was flattening. "Mornin', sweet pea," he said.

"How are ya, stud muffin?" Gracie said as she walked over to the commercial dishwasher, slipped an apron over her head, and tied it behind her back.

Allen threw the flattened box on top of a pile on the floor. "As fine as if I had good sense, sugarplum."

Gracie sprayed a tray already stacked with dirty dishes with scalding water, sending a plume of steam billowing around her, then pushed it along the rollers into the stainless steel dishwasher, slid the door closed, and flipped the On switch.

She grabbed a towel and dried her hands. "Anything I can do for you?"

"Not a blamed thing. What'd you do last night?"

"Nothing much. Search and Rescue business meeting. Boring, but necessary. Then a beer after with some of the team at the Saddle Tramp."

"A beer?"

"A as in *one*."

"Tell me, buttercup, what do you find appealing about that Search and Rescue business?"

Gracie reached back to hang up the dish towel, then turned back, leaning against the counter. "It's never the same thing. Kind of like that Forrest Gump thing. You never know what you're going to get. Every mission is different, depending on who shows up, what the circumstances are. Could be a missing mountain biker or a downed airplane or a car over the side. Could be on San Raphael. Could be down in the desert. Could be snowing. Could be a billion degrees."

"And you like that."

Gracie nodded. "I do. Not always pleasant. In fact, sometimes it's downright unpleasant. But that's part of the job. I like the challenge. The variety. It's never boring. It's a way of life. Well, it's *my* way of life. Even though I'm only a volunteer . . ."

"No one's ever *only* a volunteer."

"Even though I'm a volunteer," she amended.

"Thank you."

"The team infiltrates everything I do, impacts every decision I make. It's who I am, how I see myself, how I define myself." She stopped, realizing she had revealed way more of herself than she would have deemed prudent to someone she knew well, much less to someone she had only recently met, an ex-con with unknown history, unknown connections, unknown friends. "Okay, then. Guess I'll go up to the Gatehouse."

"Thanks for sharing that part of yourself with me, Gracie. I know it's not easy for you."

Gracie frowned over at Allen. Sometimes he saw a sight more than she liked.

Beep! Beep! Beep! Her Search and Rescue pager shrieked

from the waistband of her shorts. She unclipped it and squinted at the tiny screen.

"Another search?" Allen asked.

Gracie nodded. "Missing juvenile." She clipped the pager back onto her waistband, then stood unmoving, undecided.

"So what are you waiting for?"

"There's a buttload of work to do in the office."

"You got a missing kid. Nobody's due in camp until tomorrow."

"Do you mind watching Minnie again? I could be out all night."

"Leave the little lady with me. I could use the intelligent conversation."

Gracie shot Allen a look. He stood, box in one hand, box cutter in the other. "Well, go already! We'll all survive without you for a day." He winked at her.

"Ha. Ha. Minnie's on her bed in the closet. She's got food and water." She lifted the receiver of the wall telephone, stopping again. How long would it take her to respond to the Sheriff's Office out of which Timber Creek SAR operated? Her twenty-four-hour SAR pack and everything else—radio chest pack, GPS, floppy hat, fleece jacket, leather gloves, water bottle—were ready and waiting in the bed of the Ranger. All she needed to do was change into her SAR uniform, which hung behind the driver's seat of the truck, then drive the twisting five miles down Cedar Mill Road and another four miles across town.

She dialed the number for the SO squad room and told the deputy who answered, "Kinkaid responding to the search. ETA twenty-five."

With a wave and a "Thanks, snickerdoodle!" she trotted out of the kitchen.

"Go get 'em, Tiger Lily" drifted down the hallway after her.

CHAPTER
4

From the time Gracie flew out of the back door of the camp kitchen to the time she turned into the parking lot of the Sheriff's Office substation, twenty-three minutes had elapsed.

Standing next to the Ranger in back of Serrano Lodge, she had pulled on her newly washed orange SAR uniform shirt, camo pants, and hiking boots while keeping one eye on the road into camp lest an unexpected visitor be treated to an impromptu peep show. With a quick stop at the office to tape a note and hastily drawn map on the front door to take any inquiries down to Allen in the camp kitchen, she careened out of camp and down steep, winding Cedar Mill Road at a hair-raising speed of fifty-seven miles per hour. Multiple stoplights and slow-moving traffic in town added another nail-chewing eleven minutes.

Gracie swung the truck into a parking space alongside the Sheriff's Office building—long, two story, painted off-white, and trimmed in dark brown. Grabbing up her radio chest pack from the passenger's seat, she walked over to where Warren was climbing down from out of the team's ton-and-a-half utility truck behind which, hooked up and ready to go, was the mobile Incident Command Post, or ICP—a donated travel trailer refurbished and equipped with everything the team could possibly need to manage a search: maps and white-boards, Incident Command System forms, laptop, copy machine and printer, office supplies, handheld radios and batteries, water and blankets.

Idling next to the utility truck was the team's Ford F-150 pickup pulling a trailer carrying two ATVs. Both vehicles and the Command Post trailer were white, emblazoned with the Department's signature chevron.

"Hey, Warren," Gracie said, threading her arms through the straps of her radio pack.

With graying rust-colored hair and a mass of freckles, Warren was a big man of few words and many talents, work-ing behind the scenes, doing whatever needed to be done for the team without thought or need for thanks or acknowl-edgement.

As Gracie clipped the radio pack on and untwisted the straps, she scanned the other vehicles in the parking lot. Her spirits drooped. Ralph Hunter's bright red F-150 pickup was nowhere in sight.

Ralph was Gracie's rock, the one person to whom she could talk, the one person she could rely on to always be there for her, to always care.

At least he had been in the past.

But several months earlier, Gracie had met Ralph's rare display of emotional vulnerability with not love and compas-sion, but pity. Ralph's response had been a cold fury and Gracie had been afraid she had lost her best friend forever. But Ralph had forgiven her and all was right with Gracie's world until, unwittingly, she had hurt him again. That time he hadn't forgiven her, freezing her out of his life and leaving her sick at heart.

Normally, Ralph clocked more hours and responded to more calls than any other member on the team except for

Gracie. He had been on the team longer than anyone else. His leadership and experience were the mortar holding together the disparate set of personalities on the team. But, in the past six weeks, he hadn't responded to a single callout, his absence from the last two team business meetings the topic of much speculation.

But Ralph not responding to searches or attending meetings because of a tiff with Gracie was an impossibility. He was too much of a professional to let personal squabbles get in the way of the job.

Something else is going on, she thought. He hadn't returned any of her calls about SAR business and the five times she had driven past his house, his pickup hadn't been parked at the top of the driveway. Ralph was a building contractor for high-end homes. Maybe his absence was as simple as his business picking up.

Worry and anxiety about Ralph pricked at Gracie. If he didn't show up for this search, she decided, she would drive over to his cabin and camp out in front until she found out what was going on.

Gracie jolted back to the present. If Ralph didn't show up for this search, managing the operation would fall to her. She looked around at the people and vehicles in the parking lot, taking stock of who had responded, thinking ahead to which assignment could be given to whom. Most of the core group—the diehards who showed up for almost every search—were there: Carrie, Jon, Warren, and Lenny.

"Kinkaid!" Jon called as he walked across the parking lot, backpack over one shoulder. "You in the ICP?"

"Unless you want it," she called back.

"Hell, no!"

Carrie emerged from the employee's entrance of the SO followed by two new team members, a married couple about whom Gracie knew nothing. Carrie conferred with the man and woman for a moment, then walked across the parking lot to hand Gracie a Dispatch printout of the original missing person call and a heavy Sheriff's Department radio. "Gardner's Watch Commander," she said. "He basically said, 'You're on your own.'"

"Of course he did," Gracie said, snapping the radio into her chest pack, perfectly content to conduct her own briefing, especially if it meant not having to deal with her nemesis on the Sheriff's Department, Sergeant Ron Gardner.

Carrie held up a half-inch-thick sheaf of paper rubber-banded together. "MisPer flyers?"

"Hang on to 'em until we get on-scene, will you?" Then she looked up and yelled, "Okay, everybody, circle up for a briefing."

When everyone had gathered around and the small talk had dribbled away to silence, Gracie said, "To those of you for whom this is your first search, welcome and thanks." She looked down at the Dispatch report in her hands. "Our MisPer is a missing juvenile. Baxter Edwards. Eleven years old. Blond over—"

"Hey, that's—" Lenny interrupted.

"—the same kid," Jon finished.

"That's two times in two months."

"Three."

"Months?"

"Times."

"Kid's a runaway," Warren offered.

"I thought we weren't supposed to be called out for runaways," Lenny said.

Gracie frowned. "I'm not familiar with him because I was—"

"Sitting at home eating bonbons," Jon interjected.

"Loafing," Warren added.

"Um, recuperating from a broken ankle?" Gracie said.

"Wimp."

"Slacker."

Gracie acknowledged the good-natured ribbing with a smile, and continued. "We're not usually called in for runaways, especially chronic ones. My guess is it's because of the boy's age and the fact that he's been missing for over twenty-four hours." Her eyes moved over the printout. "Anyway . . . physical description. Blond over brown. Four foot seven. Sixty-six pounds. Black glasses."

"He looks like Mr. Peabody," Lenny said.

"Mr. Peabody's the dog," Carrie said. "The kid's Sherman."

"Oh, yeah."

"Okay," Gracie said, forging ahead. "Last seen wearing woodland camouflage pants and jacket. Carrying a black backpack. Went missing from his home in Pine Knot sometime yesterday afternoon. Family's been out searching for him."

"Ain't that just peachy," Warren said.

"They'll have trampled all over any tracks," Lenny said.

"Grandmother finally called the SO this morning," Gracie continued.

"Why would they wait over a day to call it in?" Carrie asked.

"Let's just say the family doesn't like law enforcement," Jon answered.

"That's putting it mildly," Warren added in a low voice.

"They all live in a big, like, fortress in the woods," Lenny said, his blue eyes shining.

"Compound," Jon amended.

"Yeah. I heard they have an underground bunker and everything. Like on TV. They're . . . what do you call 'em?"

"Doomsday preppers."

"Yeah! Doomsday preppers!"

"Friggin' wing nuts."

"Hey, I watch that show."

"Let's stay on task here," Gracie said, shifting her weight to the other leg to ease her aching ankle. "A missing eleven-year-old is an emergency, regardless of whether he's a runaway or not. What happened with this kid the last two . . . three times?" She looked up. "Anybody know?"

"First time," Jon said, "Baxter showed up over the river and through the woods at Grandma's house a half mile or

so away from home. They don't all just get along. Kid told
the debriefing SAR member—that would be *moi*—he was
holed up at his fort the entire day. Close mouthed about
where said fort was. Second time, he was spotted walking
along the Boulevard by Maple. He was picked up by a deputy. Third time, who knows?"

"Third time," Carrie said, "janitor at the high school
found him scrounging in one of the Dumpsters for food."

"Okay then," Gracie said. "Warren'll drive the ICP up.
Set it up in the parking lot of the park next to the fire station.
Corner of Spruce and Clampett." She looked up. "Who's
driving the ATVs up?"

Lenny raised his hand.

"Good. You and Warren on ATVs. You both okay with
that?"

Lenny pumped the air with his fist. "Sweet."

"Okay, boss," Warren affirmed.

"Jon and Carrie. Since the family's uncooperative, we
won't be able to interview the parents. Grab an MPQ and
go talk to the RP, the grandmother." She looked down at the
briefing sheet. "Sharon Edwards. 1058 Oak Street."

Jon and Carrie scribbled down the information in pocket-
sized notebooks.

"At least until things get set up in the ICP, Warren is Comms.
Mr. Towne?"

Warren cleared his throat. "MAC10 talk group. I'll dis-
tribute radios to teams when we get on-scene. Those of you
who are new on the team and haven't had the radio training
yet, get with a more-experienced member who can show
you how to find the right channel."

"Standard safety message," Gracie said. "Wear hats and
sunscreen."

"I've got mine!" Lenny announced, holding up an enormous economy-sized bottle of generic-brand SPF 110.

Gracie laughed. "Drink lots of water. Even though it's
an urban environment, keep an eye out for snakes. Don't

forget to sign in. And out. Sheet's on the table in the squad room. See you all up there."

USING HER MOSTLY full water bottle and the heavy HT radio, Gracie anchored opposing corners of a large laminated street map of the mountain community of Pine Knot, then carefully sat down on the teetery secretarial chair, knowing from past experience it was prone to easily tipping backward. The last thing she needed was for someone—her favorite sergeant, for instance—to walk into the trailer and find her lying on her back on the floor with her legs waving in the air with girlish glee.

With colored sticky arrows, she indicated on the map the location of the Command Post, then the Last Known Point and Point Last Seen—both the Edwards family compound. "On Gorgonzola?" Gracie said aloud. "Who thinks up these street names?" Using a dry-erase marker and working her way out from the compound, she drew out search segments to which teams would be assigned, numbering them in order of priority.

She was aware of her heart pounding, feeling the pressure of multiple people standing around chomping at the bit, waiting for assignments, eager to be out in the field. The responsibility for the life of a child weighed heavily on her. A miscalculation in search segments or any other mistake might affect the outcome of the search—whether or not they found the boy alive.

Once everyone was in the field, then, maybe, she could catch up on filling out the myriad Incident Command System forms.

The trailer door opened and Warren stuck his head inside. "What do you need, Gracie?"

"A list of who's already here with what vehicles and what equipment and ETA of who's still on their way."

"On it." He ducked back out of the trailer.

"And ICP coordinates," she yelled after him.

"On it," Warren yelled back from outside.

Gracie dug into her black plastic file box, pulled out a stack of 204 forms, and began filling in the boxes with Case Number, Incident Name, Date, Time, Operational Period. Then following the search segments she had drawn, she began making search assignments.

The door flew open again and Warren climbed inside, tipping the little trailer with his weight. "On-scene personnel," he said, laying a list on the table next to Gracie. He pressed a yellow sticky note on top. "And coordinates."

"Thank you!"

Using the information Warren had just provided and the search segments she had drawn on the map, Gracie began making team assignments.

Four hours later, there was still no sign of the missing boy.

CHAPTER

5

ANXIETY had tightened the knot in Gracie's stomach. In another couple of hours, Baxter Edwards would have been missing for thirty-six hours. She would give it until then to call in help from neighboring teams—more ground pounders, a dog team or two, aviation.

Two hours into the search, Carrie and Jon had returned from interviewing the boy's grandmother, Sharon Edwards, and turned in a completed Missing Person Questionnaire, or MPQ. Immediately they had received another assignment, joining another team of ground pounders going door-to-door, street-to-street.

The MPQ had both brought new information and confirmed information already known. For only eleven years old, Baxter Edwards was impressively self-sufficient, never going anywhere without a backpack containing homemade snacks and water, but, it had been noted with a circled star, only water from the family compound, all other water believed to be tainted or poisoned by "the government." The boy was home-schooled, well-trained in survival, and very familiar with the area. Fights with the father were frequent, often physical, according to the grandmother, mostly because the father hated his son's preference of books to guns. The family was reclusive and, as had been already discussed, demonstrably hostile to law enforcement with prior run-ins with County Code Enforcement officials and inspectors. "Terrific," Gracie muttered.

Setting the MPQ aside, Gracie leaned over the map again, second-guessing the segments she had drawn, the assignments she had made, wondering whether she had missed anything, what she wasn't seeing.

The Command Post door was yanked open and Ralph climbed up the metal steps and inside.

Gracie straightened. "Ralphie!"

Ralph set the HT in his hand and two file boxes he was carrying on the table. He slid his black backpack off one shoulder onto the floor next to the chair.

When he straightened, Gracie's flooding sense of relief was replaced by alarm.

Ralph looked ten years older since the last time she had seen him. His face was gaunt, the color of dried clay. The blue-gray eyes were cold steel. And he had dropped five pounds, maybe more.

"I'm so glad you're here," Gracie croaked. She cleared her throat. "What happened? Where have you been? I've . . . I've—"

"What do we have?" Ralph asked, bending over the map. No "Gracie girl." No small talk. No gentle blue-gray eyes. No nothing, except detached professionalism.

Gracie stared at him for a moment, then, hyperaware of his presence, gave him an overview of what teams were in the field and what their current assignments were, which assignments had already been completed, which segments had been searched.

Ralph studied the map. "Everyone has an assignment?"

"Everyone except a new team member. Whitney. She got here about fifteen minutes ago. Can you believe it? She's wearing a—"

"Anyone else?"

Gracie stared at him again, but he didn't look up. "Me, I guess," she said. "Now that you're here."

"Okay." He straightened to scan the 204s Gracie had push-pinned onto the corkboard above the table. He unpinned one and scribbled Gracie's name on it. "You're Ground Three." He scanned the map. "Search Segment Seven. Piñon to Juniper to—"

"I know what streets," Gracie snapped, annoyed with his attitude, his unwillingness to forgive her, her own inability to know what to do about it. "I created the damned segments." She blew out a breath. "Sorry. Ralphie . . ."

"Take Whitney." He added the other woman's name beneath Gracie's on the form.

Gracie inhaled to protest, thought better of it, and said, "On it, boss."

"Map?"

"Yes."

"MisPer flyers?"

Gracie inserted the HT into the pouch on her chest pack and snapped it in place. "Yes." Then without another word, she gathered up her personal ICS forms, pens, and pencils, stowed them back in her file box, and used her foot to shove it out of the way beneath the table. Slinging her pack over her shoulder, she stepped out of the trailer, taking extra care to close the door quietly behind her.

She stood outside the Command Post, taking in a deep breath through her nose, and blowing it out through her mouth, resolving to wait until she got home to ruminate further about her estrangement from Ralph over a glass or two of Alice White Chardonnay.

Where the hell is Whitney? She scanned the parking lot and community park, finally spotting the woman standing in the open bay of the fire station next door, one tanned leg cocked off to the side, talking and laughing with a couple of young and healthy firefighters.

Gracie suppressed another surge of annoyance. In spite of being given the team's Policies and Procedures, which explicitly spelled out the code for both dress and field uniforms, Whitney had shown up for the search wearing her long, dark brown hair loose around her shoulders, multiple silver bracelets and necklaces and dangly earrings, a tight-fitting pair of white capri pants, and open-toed wedge sandals. To her credit, she was wearing the orange uniform shirt, but the top buttons had been left unbuttoned, revealing a dangerous décolletage.

Gracie pulled open the driver's door of the Ranger, leaned in to place the stack of flyers and the map on the console inside, and wondered why she was letting the woman bother her so much. Because there were standards and protocol to be adhered to and so far Whitney had ignored almost all of them? Because the valley had a small population base from which to draw its members and the team had to accept practically anyone it could get? Because Gracie felt proprietary about the team and Whitney was treating it as a social club? Or was it because the focus of this search had suddenly shifted to being a contest for who could garner the most male attention by dressing the sexiest and Gracie knew she was on the losing end? The sneaking suspicion that it was a little of all of the above added more prickles to her cactus mood. "Whitney," she called a little too sharply.

The woman looked over.

"You're with me. We have an assignment."

Whitney lifted a single finger in acknowledgement, tittered with the two men for a couple of seconds, then sashayed across the parking lot to the appreciation of her grinning male audience.

As Whitney walked up, Gracie said, "We're Ground Team Number Three. We'll take my truck. Throw your pack in the back."

"Oh, I don't have one yet. I got some of the things on the list though. They're in my car."

"Never mind for now," Gracie said. "I have enough in my truck for both of us."

Gracie climbed into the Ranger and started the engine, then watched as Whitney stood on her tiptoes to place her rear end on the passenger's seat, then drew her legs in behind. Gracie had seen another woman climb into the truck in exactly the same beauty queen way only a few months before. *What is up with that?*

The Ranger turned out of the parking lot. "Let's drive the perimeter of our search area," Gracie said. "Then we'll figure out the most efficient route to cover all the houses in our segment. Can you read a map?"

"Of course."

Gracie handed Whitney the map on which the outer perimeter of their search area had been marked with yellow highlighter.

Whitney tapped a long, elaborately painted fingernail on a front tooth. "Let's see." She turned the map one way. Then the other. "Hmmm. I think . . . Turn! Turn right here!"

Gracie turned the wheel right.

"No, left!" Whitney said with a giggle. "Left!"

Gracie hauled the wheel in the other direction. *They're gonna think we're schnockered.*

"I meant turn left right here!"

"It's all good," Gracie said, lifting her foot from the accelerator and inching the Ranger down the street. "Just tell me what's coming up."

"Uh, I don't know. I can't . . ."

"Have you located where we are on the map?"

"No."

"How about the park? The fire station?"

Silence.

Gracie steered the Ranger over to the side of the road and braked to a stop. "Let me show you. May I have the map?"

Whitney handed it over.

Gracie pointed. "Here's the park where the Command Post is. Here's where we are. On Spruce."

The woman flipped her hair back away from her face, crossed her arms, looked out the side window, and tapped the floor with the toe of her sandal.

"Okay, our boundaries are Piñon, Juniper . . ." She waited until Whitney looked to where she was indicating. "Shakespeare and Browning." She pointed. "We'll park the truck here and walk Juniper to Blue Jay. Then . . ."

"We're walking?"

"We're going door-to-door."

"Why can't we drive?"

"We're knocking on doors. Passing out flyers—"

"I can't walk in these shoes."

Gracie sank back in the seat and pinched the bridge of her nose against the headache looming there. "When we're done here, why don't you and I go out for coffee or something? Just to . . . you know . . . chat."

"About what?"

"The team. Dress code. What's required."

"What do you mean—'dress code'?"

Gracie stopped, unsure of how frank to be. She didn't want to piss Whitney off enough so she would quit the team. In as mild a voice as she could muster, she said, "Well, like what you should wear on your feet. Something more practical. Did you get a chance to read the Policies and Procedures?"

Whitney said something under her breath that sounded suspiciously like *boooring*.

"Hiking boots," Gracie said. "Tennis shoes at least, but, eventually, something sturdier. Sometimes we search in some pretty rough terrain." Whitney had heard this all before. "You need to wear long pants, heavy material, to protect your legs. Your hair needs to out of the way. I wear mine in a ponytail."

Whitney's eyes traveled over Gracie's thick auburn hair

pulled through the hole in the back of her black Sheriff's Department ball cap. Her pink lips pursed.

"Or a braid," Gracie continued. "You need to sew the patches on your shirt so people can identify you as belonging to the Sheriff's Department."

"Those uniforms are so masculine." Whitney flexed her feet and admired her shimmering turquoise toenails. "I'm not afraid to show that I'm all woman."

"It's not a matter of—"

"*I'm* proud of being feminine," Whitney said, looking Gracie up and down, one beautifully drawn eyebrow arched.

She's pressing on my last nerve, Gracie thought, and counted to five before saying, "This isn't a fashion show, Whitney. This is serious work. We're here to save people's lives. Not pick up guys."

Whitney's eyes narrowed into a glare. "I want to go."

"Go . . ."

"Home. I want to go home."

"Uhhh . . ." Gracie was flummoxed. "You can't. We're on a search."

"I'm not going."

"You're not—"

Whitney pushed her door open and slid off the seat to the ground. "I'm not going to walk around this neighborhood," she said through the open doorway. "It isn't safe. We could be attacked. And I told you I can't walk in these shoes." She slammed the door closed.

In the rearview mirror, Gracie watched her walk, hips swinging, down the middle of the street in the direction of the Command Post. "Okay," she said with a sigh. "So be it."

Now what? If she notified Ralph by radio that Whitney was on her way back to the Command Post, she would no doubt be summoned back there as well. The team protocol of not searching alone would dictate she either work in the ICP alongside Ralph, or be assigned to another team, which meant more delay, less ground covered, less efficiency.

Gracie pulled the Ranger away from the curb, drove to the corner of Piñon and Juniper, and parked.

Talking to strangers was one of Gracie's least favorite things to do on Search and Rescue, or anytime. But today a child was missing and knocking on doors was what needed to be done.

With flyers in hand, her day pack on her back, and a renewed sense of urgency, Gracie strode up to the first house on the block, a cottage painted green with white trim. In front were two yard butts—a man in overalls and a woman in a red and white polka-dot dress—surrounded by every imaginable yard knickknack—birds, mushrooms, rabbits. The wings of a Canada goose turned slowly with a lift of air.

Gracie hurried up the flagstone walkway and pressed the doorbell. "Sheriff's Department. Search and Rescue," she called in a loud voice.

The front door—flamingo orange—was pulled open by a woman with silver hair floating around her head like a sea anemone and pink glasses hanging from a chain around her neck. Wearing blue jeans and a purple plaid shirt, she smiled up at Gracie through the screen door. "Yes?"

"Good afternoon," Gracie said. "I'm with Search and Rescue. There's a boy missing in the area and we wondered if you had seen him. I have a flyer with his picture. Would you be willing to look at it?"

"Oh, my. That's tragic, isn't it? I'll be happy to take a look at it." The woman unlocked the screen door and pushed it open. "Would you like to come inside? I have pink lemonade."

Gracie smiled. "That's very nice, but no, thank you." She held out the flyer.

The woman put on her glasses and took the paper.

Only barely resisting the temptation to tap her foot, Gracie waited as the woman studied the picture, read the description below, then looked at the picture again. Finally, she shook her head. "I believe I've seen this young man around here from time to time, but not in the past week." She looked up at Gracie over the glasses. "Do you want this back?"

"No. You keep it. If you see him or hear anything you think might help us locate him, will you give us a call? The number's at the bottom there."

"I most certainly will."

"Thank you, ma'am."

"Mind the begonias on your way out."

Gracie stepped off the porch and fast-walked back up the flagstone walkway to the street.

Ten minutes later, Gracie was halfway up Blue Jay when Ralph's voice came over the radio microphone at her shoulder. "Ground Three. Command Post."

Here it comes. Without stopping, she thumbed the microphone button. "Ground Three. Go ahead."

"Ground Three. Return to base."

"Command Post," Gracie said into the radio. "Go to TAC." She tugged the HT out of its pouch on her pack and turned the little knob at the top to the TAC talk group in order to communicate with Ralph without the whole world listening in. She thumbed the radio mic. "Ground Three on TAC."

"I want you out of the field."

"Why?"

"You know damn . . . Standby one." Gracie knew that Ralph was counting to ten in order to not curse over the air, even if they were on a private channel. "Ground Three," Ralph said again, voice calmer, more even. "No one out in the field alone."

Gracie could just hear him say, *As you very well know.* She took in a deep breath to steady her voice and thumbed the mic. "It's door-to-door in a residential neighborhood. Nothing is going to happen."

"I want you out of the field."

"I'm already halfway through the assignment," she lied. "We need to find this boy."

Radio silence. From blocks away, Gracie could feel the

heat of Ralph's blood pressure inching upward toward nuclear meltdown.

Finally, Ralph's voice again. "Finish the assignment. Then back to base." Gracie couldn't imagine how his voice could get any colder. "Back to Primary."

"Copy," Gracie said. She dialed the radio back to the MAC10 channel, vision blurry with sudden tears. "I hate this, Ralphie," she whispered, wiping her eyes with the sleeve of her shirt.

For the next forty-five minutes, Gracie covered the remainder of her search area, walking up and down both sides of each street, checking in to the Command Post by radio at the half hour.

Several houses in her segment looked barely visited, much less lived in, vacation homes belonging to people who lived down the hill or out of state. Most were occupied though, the owners friendly, concerned, eager and willing to help in any way they could. Only one man refused to open the door, yelling at her from behind drawn shades to get her goddamned ass off his goddamned property.

At the edge of the man's yard, Gracie squinted down at the map, then up the street to where the Ranger was parked at the corner. Only four more houses and she would be finished with her assignment. And there had been no report from the other teams about the missing boy. The idea that, this time, Baxter Edwards wasn't missing by choice morphed into dread.

Gracie walked up to the next house, an Arts and Crafts bungalow peeking out from beyond a stand of tall pines, and up the front sidewalk, thick with pine needles, stepping over flat, yellowed newspapers with faded rubber bands.

Clearly it had been some time since the owners or anyone else had been there.

To be certain, Gracie walked up the steps, across the porch, and rapped on the screen door. "Sheriff's Department, Search and Rescue." No response. She knocked again.

Nothing. Pulled the screen door open and tried the front doorknob. Locked.

Cupping her hands around her face, she peered through the front windows. The blinds were drawn.

She walked to the end of the porch and peered around the corner, up the weed-choked gravel drive, which was blocked by a six-foot-high, gated wooden fence.

She squinted against the afternoon sun. Couldn't be certain. She walked back down the steps, around the porch, and back alongside the house.

The gate was closed, the latch open, the padlock unlocked.

Would owners meticulous enough about securing the house in other ways have left their padlock open? Probably not.

Sergeant Gardner had made the blanket decision that, unless specific permission was granted, searchers were never to enter property, unlocked buildings or vehicles if the owners weren't home. If she didn't have permission and entered the yard, she could be charged with trespassing.

Gracie trotted down to the end of the block, rounded the corner, and stood looking along the backs of the row of houses. From where she stood, she could see that, on the bungalow's property, a section of the high wooden fence had been replaced by a shorter chain-link, revealing the back of a carport and what looked like a motorboat on a trailer.

Gracie dithered only a moment before trotting back around the corner, up the block, and up the driveway of the bungalow. She pulled the gate open and slipped through into the backyard.

Just inside the fence, she stopped and looked around.

Most of the yard was enclosed by the wooden fence with a shorter, chain-link section along the back. On the left stood a storage shed. Next to it stood a gas grill covered with a green tarp. The driveway ended at a wide carport along the back, sheltering two trailers, one holding two snowmobiles, one a small motorboat.

The wind purred through the branches of the tall pines in the yard. A squirrel chattered a harangue from a branch directly overhead. Otherwise, all was still, quiet, undisturbed.

Gracie walked over to the shed and tugged on the padlock. Locked. She walked back to the carport, past the trailer with the snowmobiles, and clambered up onto the boat trailer. Shading the glass with her hands, she peered in through one of the side windows.

A pale face looked back at her.

WITH a yell, Gracie sailed off the trailer, landed hard with both feet, and wrenched her still-healing ankle. "Sonofa . . ." she hissed, staggering to regain her balance. Then she stood on her good foot, hands on her hips, and glared back at the boat.

The face staring back at her through the window had been a boy's, wide-eyed, afraid. There wasn't a doubt in her mind that it was the face of one Baxter Edwards, age eleven. *Thank God he's okay after all,* she thought. *Little bugger.*

In her best authoritative voice, Gracie commanded, "Sheriff's Department. Come on out of the boat."

Silence.

"Come on out of there. We both know I saw you."

A high, shaky voice carried out from the depths of the boat. "Don't shoot!"

Gracie almost smiled. In a milder voice, she said, "I'm not going to shoot you, Baxter. I don't even have a gun. I'm here to help you. Come on out of there."

Sounds of bumping and shuffling from inside the boat, then a black backpack with various accoutrements, including a metal pan, clipped to the outside, was heaved up and over the gunwale and landed with a clanking thud on the ground.

A very blond head poked into view, followed by a body, skinny to the point of scrawny.

The boy climbed out of the boat, jumped down from the trailer, and lay down, spread-eagled, in the dirt in front of Gracie.

"You can get up," she said. "You're not under arrest."

Baxter pushed himself to his feet and stood with his hands in the air.

The top of the boy's head barely reached Gracie's shoulder. He wore black, heavy-rimmed glasses and had white-blond hair with a giant cowlick sticking up in the back. His cheekbones and the bridge of his nose were spattered with freckles as if someone had flicked an almost-dry brush of burnt sienna paint across his face. He wore woodland camouflage pants and jacket, several sizes too big for him, and black lace-up boots.

His entire body trembled and the brown eyes that stared back at Gracie were wide with fear.

"Put your hands down," Gracie said.

The hands dropped.

"Baxter Edwards, I presume?"

The boy nodded.

"There are a lot of people out looking for you."

"I know," he squeaked.

"Your grandma, especially, is really worried."

He looked down at the ground and shuffled his feet. "I know."

"I was really worried."

He looked up at Gracie, as if really seeing her for the first time. "Why were you worried?" he asked, genuine curiosity pushing away the fear. "You don't even know me."

"I don't have to know you to be concerned about you, to want you to be okay."

He studied her uniform. "You really don't have a gun?"

Gracie held out her arms and turned in a complete circle. "I really don't have a gun. I don't even like guns. I'm Search and Rescue. We're affiliated with the Sheriff's Department, but we're not law enforcement."

Relief flooded the boy's face, his shoulders drooped, and he blew out an exaggerated "Whew."

"Come on, Mr. Baxter. What say we get ourselves out of these people's backyard."

The boy turned to pick up his backpack by a strap.

"That looks pretty heavy," Gracie said. "Let me help you with that." She grabbed the other strap and lifted. "Wow! This must weigh what? Twenty-five . . . thirty pounds? What do you have in there? Rocks?"

"Books," was the matter-of-fact answer.

"My name's Gracie, by the way," she said as they walked across the yard to the gate. "Do you need a drink of water?"

"Nah. I have some. Water's the number three essential ingredient for survival."

Gracie smiled as she pushed the gate open and held it open for the boy. "What are numbers one and two?"

He smiled back. "Air to breathe. Then shelter to stay warm and dry."

"That's exactly right," Gracie said, truly impressed. "You're pretty smart. Where'd you learn that?" She closed the gate.

A frown replaced the smile as quickly and completely as if window shutters had been slammed shut. He looked down at the ground and mumbled, "My grandpop. And my dad."

Ah, the dad, Gracie remembered. Sore subject. "How did you find this padlock? I want to leave it as it was."

"It looked like it was locked until I pulled on it." The window shutters were still closed and firmly in place.

Gracie fake-locked the padlock and, trying not to limp too much, walked out into the front yard with Baxter beside her. "I need to radio in to the Command Post," she said. "Let them know you've been located. You okay with that?"

Baxter shrugged a shoulder. "I guess."

Gracie noted the address on the front of the house and pressed the button on her radio mic. "Command Post, Ground Three."

Ralph answered immediately. "Go ahead, Ground Three."

"MisPer has been located. 218 Piñon Avenue."

"Repeating. The MisPer has been located."

"Affirmative. He's in great shape. Really knows his stuff."

When Baxter looked up at Gracie, she winked back at him and was pleased to again see sunshine peeking through a crack in the shutters in the form of a lifting of the frown.

"Copy," Ralph said, then, "All teams, return to base. All teams return to base. Subject has been located. Repeat. Subject has been located. Call in to confirm."

Gracie waited while the other teams called in, then keyed the microphone button and said, "Command Post, we're only two blocks from the grandmother's house. If you'd like, I can drive him there for debrief."

"Standby one."

"Let's sit down while we wait," Gracie said. They set Baxter's backpack on the ground in front of them and sat down side by side on the porch steps. Gracie ripped open the Velcro of her radio pack and pulled out an almost-empty pack of grape bubble gum. "Two left. Want one?" She held a piece out to the boy, stuffing the wrapper in a side pocket.

Baxter stared at the gum intently. Then he reached out and took it, unwrapping the little purple square as if it were a bomb.

In slow motion he put it in his mouth and began chewing. Then he looked up at Gracie and smiled.

He's never had gum before, she realized with amazement as she put her own piece into her mouth. "So what books do you have in your pack?" she asked.

"*The Sorcerer's Stone.*"

"That's a great book."

"Yeah. I know." The brown eyes sparkled with excitement. "I have *The Adventures of Tom Sawyer*, too."

"Wow. You must be a really good reader."

"Gran says I'm an excellent reader. What's your name again?"

"Gracie Kinkaid."

"Gracie Kinkaid," he said to himself as if cementing the name to memory.

"Which one are you reading now?" she asked.

"*The Call of the Wild.* But I'm only on chapter two. I have a little dictionary, too, so I can look up the words I don't know."

"Those are all really great books."

"Yeah, my gran gets 'em for me from the library. I'm not supposed to be—"

"Ground Three, Command Post," came Ralph's voice over the radio.

"Go ahead, Command Post."

"Watch Commander wants to talk to him at the SO."

Something close to panic flooded Baxter's face. "The SO?" he asked, voice rising even higher. "Isn't that the Sheriff's?"

"Hold on a sec," Gracie said, edging closer to the boy on the step. "We're only two blocks from the grandmother's house," she repeated into the radio, hoping Ralph would get the hint.

"Bring him back to the ICP. Per Watch Commander, he'll be transported from there to the SO for debrief. A deputy is already on the way to pick him up."

"I can drive him in. That's no problem."

"A deputy is already on his way," Ralph said in a tone that told her the issue was settled.

Why are they treating him like a criminal? He's going to clam up like a . . . clam. "Copy," Gracie said into the radio.

She looked down at Baxter. Beneath the freckles, his face had gone pale, and his eyes were round.

"You heard that, right?" she asked.

He nodded.

"We're going to drive in my truck to the Search and Rescue Command Post a few blocks from here. Then a deputy is going to give you a ride down to the Sheriff's Office. That's routine," she lied. "They just want to ask you some questions."

The boy's lower lip quivered.

"Would you like me to meet you there?" she asked. "Give you a ride back? Maybe to your gran's?"

"Yes!" Baxter said with such apparent relief that Gracie decided that's what she was going to do even if she had to slug it out with Sergeant Gardner to do it.

GRACIE AND RALPH faced each other in the Command Post trailer, both with arms crossed, feet apart.

"I got an earful from Whitney," Ralph said, the heavy black eyebrows merging into a single line.

"I figured."

"She quit the team."

"I figured."

"Because of you."

"I figured. Maybe that's not such a bad thing. I know we need every—"

"She said you cursed at her."

"*What!*" Gracie spluttered. "I did not." She picked the stale wad of gum out of her mouth and flung it into the wastebasket. "She just . . . made that up."

"So she was lying?"

"Yes!"

Ralph studied her for a moment, his face expressionless, revealing nothing.

"As I tried to tell you earlier," Gracie said. "She showed up here totally ill prepared. Hell's bells, she was wearing stupid wedgy-type sandals! She didn't want to hoof it door-to-door."

"Okay. I'm going to take you at your word."

"Well, gee. Thank you," she said, resisting the temptation to add, "That's mighty big of you since we're supposed to be friends" or "I would think so since you've known me for years and I've never lied to you before," or a half-dozen smart-alecky rejoinders designed to bleed off some of the hurt and indignation.

"However . . ."

"I knew I wasn't off the hook yet."

"You're a senior member of this team."

"I know."

"You know better than to go out on your own."

"Yeah. I know. I'm duly chastised."

"You think this is a joke?"

Gracie's face grew hot. She could feel the flush creeping up her neck. "No. I don't think this is a joke."

"What do you think would happen if everyone went off hotdogging on their own?"

"I know, Commander Hunter."

Ralph ignored her tone and the use of his formal title. "There are any number of reasons why it's unacceptable."

"I *know*."

"It breaks down chain of command. I could lose track of you in the field. Then we'd have to go searching for you instead. If you got hurt in some way, there might be no way for you to radio in."

"All right already."

"Do you think the rules don't apply to you?"

"Of course they do. If this really is what you're mad at me about, then I get it. I'm sorry. It was unprofessional. It won't happen again. *If* this is really what you're mad at me about. But if you're still mad at me because I hurt you, then can we please not pretend it's about stupid Whitney or the search and just talk about it?"

Ralph dropped his head so Gracie couldn't see his eyes.

"I miss you, Ralphie," she said, her voice cracking. "We're best friends. Can we please start acting like it?"

She looked back up at Ralph, who had lifted his head again and was looking at her with something as close to extreme pain as she had ever seen in the blue-gray eyes.

Then he turned around with his back squarely to her and began rolling up the laminated map. "We're through here," he said.

"Hey! No, we're not 'through here.'"

"Yes, we are." He dropped the rolled-up map into its cardboard tube and pounded the plastic end cap in place with the palm of his hand.

"What the hell? You're . . . dismissing me? Why are you treating me this way?"

"I'm not treating you any way."

"Yes, you are. You're acting like a jerk."

Ralph turned around to face her again, his face mottled red. "Everything, all the time, is not about you."

"What the—"

The Command Post door was pulled open and Warren stuck his head inside. "'Bout ready to head on back to the SO, boss?"

"Thirty seconds," Ralph said.

"Copy that," Warren said. "Hey, Gracie. Nice find."

"Thanks," Gracie said, forcing a smile.

Ralph opened the long overhead door above his head, set the map tube inside the cupboard, and dropped the door closed with a bang.

Gracie stared at Ralph's back for a moment, said, "I'm outta here," and stepped out of the open door of the trailer.

GRACIE FED QUARTERS into the SO soda machine and pressed the button for Fanta Orange. She grabbed the can that plunked down, walked around the corner and down the hallway.

At the sound of Sergeant Gardner's voice inside the squad room, she stopped.

"Look up at me when I'm speaking to you, boy," he said. "Where have you been the last thirty-two hours?"

"I refuse to answer on the grounds it may incriminate me," came Baxter's high voice.

Gracie snorted a silent laugh and leaned against the wall next to the door to listen.

"You're not under arrest," Gardner said. "Although, you probably should be. I want to know where you were. What you were doing. If you damaged any property."

No response.

Gardner's hand slammed down on a flat surface. "Look at me when I'm talking to you!" Several seconds of silence, then the sergeant said in a low voice, "I don't have time for you, you little punk. And neither do my men. They've got more important things to do than run around looking for you."

Right, Gracie thought. *Like it was you who was doing the running around.*

"Keep this up and I will arrest you," Gardner said. "That what you want? You wanna end up in jail? A loser like your old man? Or like his old man? Buncha losers. The lot of ya."

"Sir!" Baxter said in a loud voice. "My father served in the United States Marines! As a veteran of Operation Desert Storm, he is worthy of your respect!"

Gracie's mouth fell open.

"My grandfather served in the United States Marines! As a veteran of the war in Vietnam, he is worthy of your respect." A split second later, he tacked on, "Sir!"

"So you *can* talk," Gardner said. "You listen to me, you little—"

Gracie pushed off the wall and rounded the corner into the squad room.

Cream-colored walls were lined with maps, bulletin boards, cubbyhole in-boxes. A black chalkboard filled an entire wall. A shelf serving as a desk ran along the three remaining walls. In the center of the room sat a twenty-foot-long wooden conference table and chairs. Baxter sat slumped in a chair at the near end of the table, hands deep in the pockets of his pants, angry tears tracking his face, and glaring at Sergeant Gardner.

A foot away, Gardner leaned over him, hands flat on the table.

The hair on the back of Gracie's neck bristled. Everything about the man proclaimed pugnacity. Bully. Six foot two. Red hair buzzed to nonexistent. Beefy, hairless, freckled arms. Barrel chest made even bulkier by the bulletproof vest worn beneath his putty-gray uniform shirt.

When Gracie entered the room, the sergeant looked up, then straightened and growled, "What are you doing here, Kinkaid?"

Gracie set the can of orange soda in front of Baxter, pulled out the chair next to him, and sat down. She mildly folded her hands in front of her on the table, looked up at the sergeant with eyes as wide and innocent as she could manage, and asked, "Doesn't a parent or guardian have to be present during the questioning of a minor?"

Gardner's slits-for-eyes narrowed even further. Then he leaned over so that his mouth was inches from Baxter's blond head. "I don't want to see your face in here again. Do you understand me?"

"Sir. Yes, sir!" Baxter said with such open hatred in his eyes, it frightened Gracie. If only an hour before she hadn't seen the boy completely different, congenial, excited about reading J.K. Rowling and Mark Twain, she, too, would have thought he was nothing but a sullen, bad-tempered little punk on the fast track to prison.

The sergeant picked up a manila file folder lying on the table. "Get him out of here, Kinkaid," he said. With a final slap on the table with the file, Gardner strode out of the room, slamming the door behind him.

"**B**RANDY, you're a fine girl." Gracie sang softly along with the radio. "What a good wife you would be." She edged the Ranger out of the Sheriff's Office parking lot and into traffic on the main boulevard.

She glanced over at Baxter, who sat unmoving in the passenger's seat, staring out the window. Since Sergeant Gardner had left the squad room, the boy hadn't spoken a single word.

The song ended and Gracie turned the radio volume down.

She guided the Ranger around the curve in the boulevard. Through the trees on her left, Timber Lake flashed by, glittering cobalt blue.

Gracie glanced at Baxter again. "They're not all bad, you know?" she ventured.

The boy made no indication he had heard her.

"Law enforcement, I mean. Deputies. Cops. I've worked with them, mostly Sheriff's Department, quite a bit through Search and Rescue. Not that my opinion is that important, but I like, or at least get along with, the vast majority of them.

I understand that you're afraid of cops. I'm not sure why. Maybe your experiences so far haven't been very positive."

She looked over again to see if she received any response. The boy didn't move.

"Baxter," she said. "Sergeant Gardner is a class A jerk. I don't like him either." She added under her breath, "to put it mildly." Then to Baxter again: "I'd hate for one experience to taint your view on law enforcement forever. There are some nice ones out there. They're not all the enemy. In fact, most of them aren't."

Baxter looked at Gracie, then turned back to stare out the window.

"I mean it."

Gracie punched the radio button away from an ad about erectile dysfunction.

". . . multiple brush fires," a male announcer said.

Gracie turned up the volume again.

". . . just before four p.m. yesterday afternoon, west of the community of Shady Oak. Officials are investigating whether the fires, started within a quarter mile and hours of each other, are related in any way."

"Shady Oak," Gracie said aloud. Picturing the map of the area in her head, she mentally calculated that the fire was miles away on the other side of the valley's southern mountain range.

Still, she leaned over and looked out the window. There was no smoke visible above the mountain ridgeline. Not even haze. The sky was a clear, perfect cerulean blue.

She sat back in the seat again, glanced over at Baxter, then back at the road. "I need ice cream," she said suddenly and made a U-turn in the middle of the boulevard.

That got the boy's attention. He looked over at her. "What are you doing? Where are we going?"

"We're getting ice cream."

"Why?"

"We need a reason?"

Gracie swung the Ranger into the entrance of the Dairy Queen.

"I don't think I'm supposed to have it. Ice cream," Baxter said.

Gracie swooped around into the drive-through line and stopped behind a banana-yellow Volkswagen Beetle. "Why not?"

A shoulder lifted. "I dunno."

Gracie glanced over at Baxter. "Ever been to Dairy Queen?"

"No."

"Well, then, it's about time." At his face, she added, "You can have anything you want. It'll be our secret."

A car horn drew her attention to a white Subaru station wagon driving past. Acacia smiled from the passenger's window, waving both hands.

Gracie tooted the truck horn and waved back. "Hi, Acacia," she called out the open window.

Baxter craned his neck to watch the Subaru turn out of the parking lot onto the main boulevard, then he swung his head around toward Gracie. "You know those . . . ?" He used a racial slur that made Gracie sputter, "Do . . . I know those . . . *what*?"

The boy repeated the word. "I heard some new ones had moved into the valley."

The yellow Volkswagen crept forward. Gracie lifted her foot from the brake and let the Ranger inch ahead. "Baxter, that's not a good word. You should never use it. Never call anyone that."

"Everyone calls 'em that."

"Everyone who?"

"My dad. My grandpop. Uncle Win. It's in *Tom Sawyer*."

Gracie cleared her throat, buying herself a little time. Choosing her words very carefully, she said, "Well, without getting into a literary discussion about Mark Twain's use of the word"—she took in a deep breath—"I think it's wrong to use it nowadays. Or ever. Very wrong."

"Why?"

"Well, that's difficult to answer in something shorter than a book." She thought for a moment, mentally sifting through a litany of ethnic epithets. Finally, she said, "It depersonalizes. Denigrates. Do you know what that means?

"No."

"Words or labels like that make, or try to make, people less than they are, less than human."

"Oh." He turned to look out the window again.

"A better word to use would be *black*. Or *African American*."

Another shrug. "Okay."

THE RANGER TURNED right onto Oak Street. Gracie leaned forward to peer at the house numbers. "Your grandma's is 1058, right?"

"That's Gran's house up there," Baxter said, pointing several houses up the block. "The green one."

The house was an undistinguished cracker box with gray wood showing through patches of weather-beaten forest green paint. The bowed front porch held a lone rocking chair and a bedraggled potted fern. The yard itself was bare dirt and rocks adorned with a few scrubby piñon pines.

Gracie pulled to a stop behind an old, rusted-out blue Honda Civic parked on the side of the street. When she shoved the truck into Park, Baxter made no move to open the door. Instead, he sat staring down at the empty container from the Georgia Mud Fudge Blizzard Treat in his hands.

"I can take your empty cup," Gracie offered. She took it and stuffed it into the plastic grocery sack serving as a litter bag. She peered into his face. "You okay?"

No answer.

"I'm sorry, Baxter. Sergeant Gardner shouldn't have said the things he did about your dad. That was mean and uncalled for."

Several seconds passed, then Baxter looked up at Gracie. "But it's true."

"Well, I don't—"

"My dad *is* a loser!" Baxter yelled. "And so's my grand-pop! They're both sons of bitches!"

"Baxter."

"That's what Gran calls 'em. That's why she doesn't live with them anymore. And why she doesn't want me to live with them anymore either. She wants me to live with her. She wants to adopt me. But they all say no."

"They?"

"Grandpop. My dad. Mom Michelle. And—"

The front door of the house opened and a woman stepped out to the edge of the porch, shading her eyes with a hand and peering at the truck. Wearing long silver hair pulled back from her face, a denim shirt, and ankle-length patch-work peasant skirt with leather sandals, she was, Gracie guessed, in her early sixties.

"That's my gran," Baxter said, pushing open the door. "I gotta go."

"I'll come and say hi," Gracie said, pushing her own door open.

"Hi, Gran," Baxter called as he jumped down from the truck. "It's me."

At the sound of the boy's voice, the woman was off the front porch and running across the yard, arms held wide open, a look of pure joy on her face.

She dropped to her knees in the dirt and threw her arms around the boy. "Don't ever do this to me again. I was so wor-ried about you!"

"Sorry, Gran," Baxter mumbled. He pulled away and ges-tured back toward Gracie. "This is Gracie. She's on Search and Rescue."

The woman looked up and saw Gracie standing at the edge

of the yard. She pushed herself to her feet and crossed the dirt, both hands outstretched. "Thank you," she said, taking Gracie's hands and shaking them both. "Thank you so, so very much."

Gracie smiled back at her. "You're welcome, Mrs. . . . Edwards?"

"Oh, please. Call me Sharon." Behind a hand, she whispered, "Changing it back to my maiden name." She gestured back toward the house. "Would you like to—"

The sound of squealing tires drew everyone's eyes back down the street to a dark green pickup truck roaring toward them.

"It's my dad!" Baxter yelled. Grabbing up his backpack, he sprinted toward the house.

The pickup left the road, bumped up into the yard, and skidded to a stop in a cloud of dust, blocking Baxter's way.

The boy changed direction, heading for the trees at the side of the yard.

The driver erupted from the truck. Gracie's brain registered only snippets of information. Shaved head. White shirt. Red suspenders. Bared teeth.

"Lee!" Sharon screamed, running across the yard in an attempt to intercept the man. "No!"

Lee easily caught up with his son. "You stupid goddam little sissy girl!" he yelled. He drew back a hand to slap the boy.

"Stop!" Sharon screamed, pushing in between Lee and Baxter.

The blow meant for the boy landed on the side of the woman's head and she fell to her knees.

Gracie yelled and jumped forward.

"No!" Baxter pummeled his father with his fists.

Lee lifted the boy up by the shoulders of his jacket and shook him like a rag doll. "Your stupid stunts is gonna bust us!"

Gracie leapt right onto the man's back, threw her arms

around his neck, and hauled back with all her strength. "Let! Go!"

She made no more impression than a flea. Lee swung an elbow back, catching her in the face.

Pain. And a burst of white light.

Gracie dropped and fell back full-length onto the ground.

"I hate you!" Baxter screamed. "You're a loser! I hate you!"

"You goddam—" Lee yelled, lunging after the boy.

"Lee, stop!" Sharon screamed, pushing herself up from the ground.

Head whirling, Gracie sat up. She swiped at her nose with the back of her hand. In a daze, she stared at the bloody smear, then over to where Sharon was crouched over Baxter, shielding him with her body.

"Stop protecting him!" Lee grabbed Sharon's arm and pulled her away. "Time he acted like a man!"

Gracie put a hand on the ground and tried to stand up. Her world reeled. She sat back down.

She was only vaguely aware of a second man, as big as a bear, running across the dirt.

"Get him outta here, Win!" Sharon screamed. "Or I'm callin' the police!"

From behind, Win grabbed ahold of Lee's arms and dragged him back across the yard.

Lee fought to free himself, growling like a cornered wolverine.

"Goddammit, Lee!" Win said in an incongruously high voice. "Cut it out! We gotta get. Your ma's gonna call the cops." With one arm across Lee's chest, the huge man lifted him completely off the ground, walked back across the yard to the truck, and practically threw him into the passenger's seat, slamming the door. Then he walked around to the driver's seat and climbed inside.

The engine revved. Wheels spun. Dirt and gravel sprayed. Tires screeched on pavement. The truck sped off and disappeared around the corner.

Gracie sat in the dirt, head hanging. Blood dripped from her nose, bright red flowers in the fawn-colored dirt.

The sound of Baxter crying drew her eyes up and across the yard to where Sharon was on her knees beside the boy, arms around his body, voice soft, comforting.

A Steller's jay squawked a ruckus from a pine branch somewhere above her head.

Gracie looked back down at her blood puddling in the dirt. "What the hell just happened?"

CHAPTER
8

GRACIE stood in front of the mirror in the Gatehouse bathroom, glumly inspecting her face by the dim light of its single wall sconce. The right side of her nose was plum-purple with a twist of Taco Bell napkin protruding from the nostril. Her upper lip was as puffed out as if a cotton ball had been stuffed beneath. Dried blood was smeared across her cheek. "Lovely," she said to her reflection. "Simply lovely."

"Should have sidestepped that Mack truck, doodlebug."

Gracie's eyes slid over to Allen leaning against the doorjamb, arms crossed and displaying to their full glory solid fields of tattooed peacock feathers and solar systems. "Hardy har," she said. "Ow."

"Got ice?" Allen asked.

"Freezer trays were empty."

The man disappeared from the doorway.

The front foyer door slammed, setting the little bell hanging above the door to tinkling. Outside in the parking lot, Allen's old Bronco roared to life and drove away.

Gracie withdrew the blood-soaked piece of napkin from

her nostril. "Ow, ow, ow." A line of blood trickled down her upper lip. She dabbed at it with the napkin. "All ready for the prom."

She leaned on the sink, staring into the mirror, contemplating her lame loser looks, which then progressed to an analysis of her life and how maybe it was time for a change, although what change, she had no idea. "Something," she said to her nose. "Anything."

The front office door slammed again and the little bell did its thing. Quick, heavy footsteps on carpet and Allen reappeared in the doorway. He held out a sandwich bag full of frozen peas and two white capsules. "Tylenol."

"Thanks." Gracie washed down the painkillers with a swig of water from the faucet. She used her thumbs to shape the peas into a concave bowl and placed the bag on the side of her face. "Owowowow!" She blew out a long, slow breath. "I need to sit."

Allen stepped aside to let her pass, then followed her down the carpeted hallway to the Camp Manager's office in the back.

With a groan, Gracie eased herself down into the chair behind the desk. "I feel as if I aged fifty years in the past hour." She bent forward to peer at a little pile of pink squares in the middle of the blotter. "What are these?"

Allen placed a pile of purchase orders beside the pink squares, then dropped into a metal folding chair on the opposite side of the desk. "Telephone messages. People freaked out that Timber Creek is burning down."

"The fire's down the hill," Gracie said, aware that her tone sounded suspiciously like a whine. "On the other side of the mountain." She leaned back in the chair, closed her eyes, and rocked. "All right. Thanks. I'll call 'em all back. Give them a reassuring talking-to."

"So, you gonna tell me what the heck happened?"

"No."

"Suit yourself."

Seconds passed.

"Some creep was whaling on his boy. Or trying to until the grandmother got in the way and got whaled on instead. I got in the middle. Well, not really in the middle . . ."

"On purpose?"

"What do you think?"

"Did you stop it?"

"I'd like to think I helped. Maybe a little."

"Then it was worth it, right?"

"I guess."

"So quitcher whining."

Gracie stopped rocking and looked over the peas at Allen. "I wasn't—"

He winked at her.

She shot him a look and started rocking again.

Allen leaned forward, resting his arms on his knees. "So what happened? I want details, girlfriend."

Gracie lifted her foot up onto the desk, saying by way of explanation, "Ankle's bothering me." Skipping the Whitney fiasco and her argument with Ralph, she described the search for Baxter, finding the boy inside the boat, Gardner's bullying tactics, the boy's use of a racial slur, the father's enraged attack. "The grandmother wouldn't let me call the cops." She shook her head. "Doesn't want to press charges. The guy just gets to drive away." She stopped, staring off into space.

"Earth to Gracie," Allen said.

Gracie retrieved her focus. "Sorry," she said. "I was indulging myself in a little mental castration."

"Well deserved."

"The big man who pulled the dad away? The guy's brother-in-law, I think?"

"Yeah?"

"I've seen him before. Maybe even met him. He's kind of hard to forget. Pretty much the size of Alaska. But I can't place him. My head's still jangling from getting my bell rung. My . . . uh . . ."

"Clock cleaned?"

"Yeah, that."

"I've heard of the family," Allen said.

"Edwards."

"They're the ones. Something ain't right there." He rubbed his palms together. "I know you didn't ask for my advice, but I'm givin' it anyway. Stay away from that crowd. They're bad company."

"Well, unless I run into 'em between the Wonder Bread and the mayonnaise at Stater Bros., I have no intention of seeing any of them again. Ever." She glanced down at her desk. "I gotta get to work. I'm way behind on paperwork."

Allen pushed himself to his feet. "Need anything? Give me a call."

"Thanks."

Allen disappeared up the hall. "Later, lovebug."

"Later . . . whatever." She dabbed her upper lip with a fingertip. "Ow."

CHAPTER

9

WITH dark eyes sparkling, Rob smiled his perfect, golden smile. Then he lowered his head and kissed Gracie. Hands pressed flat against her lower back, he lifted her body against his.

She closed her eyes and tilted her head back. Rob kissed her ear, tongue brushing the lobe and raising goose bumps along her arms. His hands wandered across her back, over her shoulders, the curve of her hip, fingers caressing, teasing. His soft lips moved down her throat, her shoulder, moving to her stomach and lower.

"Holy cow!" Gracie shot straight up in bed and tossed back the sheet. "Holy cow!" she yelled again, tipping herself off the camp mattress that served as her bed and ending up on hands and knees on the wooden floor, heavy hair draping both sides of her face. Her nose and upper lip throbbed.

Gracie shook her head slowly as if she could dislodge the images of Rob swirling inside her head. The feel of his mouth on hers, the warmth of his hands on her body was so vivid, she wouldn't have been the least bit surprised to look up and see him sitting in her bed.

A faint whine drew her eyes to Minnie, who sat in the darkness six inches away.

"Ohhh, sorry I scared you, little girl," Gracie said, reaching over to stroke the silky head. "Scared my friggin' self."

She pushed herself to her feet and padded barefoot downstairs to the kitchen with the dog on her heels.

A glance at the clock above the doorway told her it was 5:18 a.m. "Too early to be up. Too late to go back to bed." In the mudroom off the kitchen, she scooped a cup of dry dog food from a giant bag next to the back door and dropped it into Minnie's silver dish.

Back in the kitchen, she grabbed up the teakettle, filled it with exactly the right amount of water for two giant panda mugs of coffee. Then she smacked the kettle back on the stove and turned the burner on.

Hands gripping the edge of the stove, she stared at, but didn't see the blue flame. "Yeeesh," she whispered. "That was real. Bad idea to watch a Rob movie. Very bad. Idiotic."

Because just like that, Rob Christian was back inside her head. And her heart.

Rob Christian—British megastar, whose life Gracie had saved on a nightmare search the previous Thanksgiving, the man whose mere proximity set her body aflame from head to toe, the man with whom Gracie had played emotional cat and mouse until the last time she had seen him, when she had realized with a sudden onslaught of self-awareness that she was in love with him. She had left him still sleeping. No note. No explanation. Her inability, or unwillingness, to answer his calls and e-mails in the days following had apparently angered him so royally she hadn't heard from him in the months since. The mouse had gotten away. Or had he been the cat? Gracie didn't know and really didn't want to explore the question.

Fed and happy, Minnie pranced back into the kitchen.

"You ready to go out, little girl?" Gracie walked into the living room, pulled open the sliding glass door, and let Minnie out to do her morning doggie duty down in the fenced-in backyard.

Gracie had been able to tamp down to numbness her feelings for Rob. Or at least she had fooled herself into thinking so.

Now, with a single dream, months later, the feelings had roared back to the surface, knocking her feet out from under her.

Back in the kitchen, the kettle wound up to a whistle. Gracie scooped two heaping spoonfuls of Folgers Instant into the panda mug and stirred in the crystals. "So what am I going to do about him? Call him? E-mail him? How about nothing?"

A tinny piano played "Für Elise" on her cell phone charging on the counter.

Gracie looked up at the clock again. "Who's that this early in the morning?"

She made no move to answer the call. Anyone she wanted to talk to knew she had no cell coverage at the cabin. Unless she performed aerial gymnastics on the northwest corner of the deck railing, the good old-fashioned landline was the only way to have an intelligible conversation when she was at home.

The cell phone stopped ringing. Seconds later, the phone on the counter rang.

Gracie took a sip of scalding coffee, leaned over, and checked the caller ID. Three-one-three area code.

"Evelyn." Once again, her mother had forgotten about the three-hour time difference between Michigan and California.

The phone kept ringing.

Gracie took another sip of coffee, relishing the liquid caffeine surging through her body. "To answer or not to answer." It wasn't like she was doing much of anything else at the moment. She grabbed up the receiver. "Hello?"

"MoMo is dying!" her mother wailed.

Gracie blinked. "What?"

"MoMo. He's dying. It's vascular disease. The doctors don't give him very long."

Gracie set her mug on the kitchen table and sank down onto one of the ladder-backed chairs.

"You need to come to Detroit," her mother continued in a quivering voice. She blew her nose loudly, then said, "He wants to see you."

Quick! Think of an excuse! "I can't. I . . . have a dog now." *Yeah, that's it. A dog.*

"Put the dog in a kennel, for Christ's sake! It's a dog, not a child."

"And I have a job now, Mother. A good one. I'm managing a camp. I can't just take—"

"So take the time off. It'd only be a couple of— Stop it, you naughty girl!"

"Wha . . . ?"

"No. It's that stupid Corky. Ridiculous creature. Take the time off, Grace Louise. Surely you can do that for Morris."

Memories rushed back. Morris. The man her mother had married two years after Gracie's own beloved father suddenly, without note or explanation, had left them. Morris. The man who had inherited an eleven-year-old tomboy filled with anger and resentment. The man who had beaten her and her half siblings. The man who had pressed the glowing end of a cigar to the soft skin of her ribs. The man whose toupee Gracie, years later, had shot off with a shotgun after he had broken her mother's arm. The man who, in the ensuing verbal altercation, her mother had defended, so wounding Gracie that she had quit her high-paying job as an ad exec, sold her house, given away her belongings, and traveled two-thirds of the way across the country to Timber Creek, California.

That man was dying.

"Surely you can do that for Morris," her mother had said.

What Gracie wanted to do for Morris was help him along a little by chucking him out of a tenth-floor window.

Reminding herself that her mother was losing her husband, Gracie took in a deep, cleansing breath. "I really can't, Mother. I have a group in camp until tomorrow and another one coming in on Saturday after lunch. I have to be here." She tacked on, "I'm really sorry."

Beep! Beep! Beep! The shrill tones of her SAR pager filtered down from her loft bedroom.

"I have a callout," Gracie said. "I need to hang up now."

"A what?"

"A Search and Rescue callout. My pager just went off."

"I thought you had quit that nonsense."

"Nope."

Phone to her ear, but barely listening, Gracie took the stairs to the loft two at a time. She grabbed up the pager from the bedside stand. Squinted at the tiny neon screen.

MISSING JUVENILE. SHORT TEAM. TRACKERS ONLY.

"Shit, Baxter. Not again."

"What?" came Evelyn's voice over the line.

"Mother, I have to go. I'll talk to you later."

"I'm buying you an airline ticket."

"Don't. Please."

"I'll send you the information."

"Mother. No."

"I won't take no for an answer."

"Gottagobye." Gracie thumbed End, listened for the dial tone, pressed Talk, dialed the number for the SO squad room, and said, "Gracie Kinkaid. ETA fifteen minutes."

GRACIE LOOKED LEFT. Then right. Then left again. No traffic coming. She stomped down on the accelerator and zoomed out onto the boulevard, the main artery running east and west the entire length of the Timber Creek valley and along the southern shore of Timber Lake.

She checked her watch. To haul on uniform shirt, pants, socks, and liners and lace up her hiking boots, run downstairs, check that Minnie had enough water out back, gather up her gear, run out to the truck, back down the driveway, and career down Arcturus to the main boulevard had taken her less than seven minutes. "Record time," she said aloud. "And now . . . hardly any traffic. For once, I won't be the last one there." With only those with tracking capabilities responding, she might even been the first. In fact, she might be the only one to show up. One never knew.

She watched the speedometer inch upward to sixty, then held it there. As the Ranger glided around the curves leading into town, Gracie mentally planned what steps she would take upon her arrival. Park. Run into the SO. Grab a sign-in sheet. Sign her name. Jog back to the SAR storage room. Grab the Pelican case with the HTs. If Warren wasn't there— he wasn't a tracker— grab the keys to the Suburban off the hook on the wall. Run outside and across to the SAR—

Beep! Beep! Beep!

"Really?" Gracie said. "They called it off?" She unclipped the pager from her waistband and read the screen. "All SAR stand down. Juvenile located."

"Well, crap. I'm already here." She braked and turned right into the SO parking lot. "And no one else is here yet. Boo." She pulled into a spot and stopped, leaving the engine running. Rather than going into the SO and risking another run-in with Gardner, she called the number for Dispatch on her cell phone. When Gracie identified herself as Search and Rescue, the woman confirmed that the missing juvenile was indeed Baxter Edwards.

"What happened?" Gracie asked.

"He went missing from the parents' yesterday evening," the Dispatcher told her. "Grandma reported him missing early this morning. He showed up at her house about ten minutes ago."

STUFFING THE TRUCK keys into an outer pocket of her pants, Gracie walked into the Stater Bros. grocery store.

Still in field uniform—orange shirt and camo pants, short, black
gaiters over hiking boots, baseball cap with the Department
chevron on the front and her name in orange script on one side,
she felt as conspicuous as a jack-o'-lantern at an Easter egg hunt,
swiveling heads and drawing curious looks as she sauntered the
aisles.

She picked up a jumbo jar of Folgers Instant, another of
Jif creamy peanut butter, plus three six-packs of PayDay
candy bars and took her place in line in the express aisle
behind a middle-aged woman with an enormous derriere,
wearing pants so tight she looked as if she had been dipped
in white pant. Trying to look everywhere except at the
woman's dimpled backside, Gracie dumped her groceries
on the conveyor belt, picked out a pack of grape bubble gum
from the impulse-buy shelf, and threw it on after, then
focused on the rack of magazines at the end of the aisle.

Her eyebrows shot up. Her jaw dropped.

On the front page of the *Star*, in living color, was a picture
of Rob, dressed in a tuxedo and looking as dazzlingly
gorgeous as ever. On his arm was a young woman—blond,
equally gorgeous, and bursting out of a slinky silver dress
that looked as if it had been created with less fabric than the
hand towel in Gracie's kitchen.

Beneath the picture, headlines screamed, ENGAGED!

"He's getting married?" Gracie yelled.

The woman with the painted-on pants turned around,
and said, "A tragedy, right? My heart's broken."

The groceries moved forward.

Gracie snatched the magazine out of the rack and riffled
through it, looking for the accompanying article. She found
and scanned it.

According to the article, Rob had indeed, just the day
before, announced his upcoming nuptials. Farther down in
the column, her own name jumped out at her. "What the—?"
She read: *When asked about his alleged romance with*

Grace Kinkaid, the woman who rescued him the previous Thanksgiving, Christian responded, "She's a terrific girl."

"Girl!"

"Fifteen sixty-two," the young, male cashier said in a bored voice to the woman in line ahead.

"She'll always hold a special place in my heart," Gracie read. *"We're still very close. She's like a sister to me."*

"Sister!" Gracie wadded up the entire tabloid down to the size of a basketball and tossed it into the wastebasket beneath the register opposite. Then she grabbed the rest of the tabloids on the rack and stuffed them in after.

"Hey!" the cashier hazarded. "You can't do that."

"I just did," Gracie growled. She dug a twenty and a ten out of the side pocket of her pants and slapped the bills on the belt. Gathering up her groceries in her arms, she squeezed past the enormous derriere whose owner was still fiddling in her purse, and stalked out of the store.

"A sister?" she stormed. "Three months ago he tells me he loves me. Now I'm his friggin' sister?" She strode across the parking lot, practically spitting nails from her mouth. "What the hell? What the *hell*!" She stopped next to the Ranger, cradling the groceries with one arm and anchoring them with her chin, and hauled her keys out of her pants pocket.

Something slammed into Gracie from the side. With an "Oof!" she bounced off the truck window, slid along the fender, and crashed down onto the nubbly asphalt. PayDays and gum smacked the pavement. The Folgers and Jif rolled in opposite directions across the parking lot.

"Uhhh," Gracie groaned, prone on the asphalt. "Hell's b— . . ."

"So it is you, you bitch," a husky female voice spat.

Gracie squinted up to see someone standing over her, silhouetted against the sky. "Well, I'm certainly glad you shoved me because it was me," she grunted, trying to sit up, "And not because it was someone you didn't know." Brushing the stinging grit from the palms of her hands, she pushed herself to one knee, then to her feet.

Standing before Gracie, poised to charge like a bull in front of a matador's cape, was Mrs. Lucas, former neighbor, the bane of Gracie's existence for years, the wife of the valley's most notorious drug dealer, who, thanks in part to Gracie, now sat in jail down the hill awaiting trial.

If possible, the woman looked even worse than the last time Gracie had seen her. Raccoon eyes. Sunken cheeks covered with scabs. Teeth brown at the roots. Dull, dark blonde hair pulled back into a stringy ponytail. Skeletal arms poking out from a loose-fitting black T-shirt. The only thing that hadn't changed was her dirty, yellowed toenails hanging off the ends of her flip-flops.

The woman bounced on the balls of her feet, clenching and unclenching her fists.

Tweaking, Gracie thought. *Probably meth*. She could prove to be even more volatile, more dangerous than normal. "Nice to see you, too," she said.

"You called the goddam cops," Mrs. Lucas snarled in a voice, phlegmy and low register from too many years of too many cigarettes.

Gracie didn't even pretend not to know what she meant. "You shot my dog."

"'Cuz you called the cops."

"So you admit you shot her."

"I ain't admittin' to nothing! You called the fuckin' cops!"

"You shot my dog."

"Prove it."

"I followed your tracks."

"Don't prove nothing. If it did, ya woulda had me arrested." Tears formed in her deep-set eyes. "They took my kid."

Gracie had known the county's Child and Family Services removing the Lucas boy from the home was a possibility, even a likelihood. But she had never received confirmation of that happening.

She looked over the shorter woman's shoulder and noticed a crowd of shoppers gathering around in a ragged semicircle. Gracie looked back at the woman in front of her. "I'm truly sorry about that," she said even though she really wasn't. The child was better off anywhere other than with his methamphetamine-using mother and drug-dealing father. "I'm getting in my truck. And I'm driving away. Have a super day."

She looked around on the ground for her keys, spotted them behind the front tire, and bent to retrieve them.

Mrs. Lucas head-butted her in the ribs.

Gracie hit the ground again, this time with the other woman on top of her, screaming and kicking with her feet and flailing with her fists.

Sirens wailed in the distance.

It was all Gracie could do to grab the woman's forearms and fend off the blows. When Mrs. Lucas, mouth gaping, aimed her teeth at Gracie's knuckles, she threw the smaller woman off to the side, rolled up onto her knees, and straddled her, pinning her to the ground, hand on her wrists. Enraged, the woman roared even more loudly, kicking Gracie from behind with her knees and trying to buck her off.

Its siren winding down, a Sheriff's Department unit rolled to a stop a few feet from Gracie's head, with a second unit right behind. She looked up as Deputy Montoya, whom Gracie used to refer to as the Cute Deputy because she could never remember his name, emerged from behind the wheel and rounded the front of his unit.

"I can't . . . let her go," Gracie yelled up to him, out of breath. "She's trying . . . to kill me!"

CHAPTER

10

GRACIE grabbed a can of beer from the refrigerator, popped it open, threw two Extra Strength Tylenols into her mouth, and swallowed them down with half the beer while standing in the open doorway. She wanted—needed—something stronger, a *lot* stronger. "A triple, no, a quadruple vodka martini. Extra, extra dry. With two of those big, fat olives. Five big, fat olives." But since she had no vodka, no dry vermouth, and no olives, a Coors Light would have to do. She held the ice-cold can to the grape-sized bump above her eyebrow. Then to her nose. Then her upper lip. "Ow," she whispered.

It had taken three burly deputies fifteen minutes to fully subdue Mrs. Lucas and secure her, handcuffed and screeching verbal abuses, behind the cage in Montoya's unit. Timber Creek's big story for the week.

"Yes," Gracie had told Deputy Montoya. "I'm refusing medical attention."

"You sure? You look a little . . ."

"Rough?"

Montoya smiled, showing a row of straight, very white teeth below the black mustache. "Roughed *up*. You sure you don't want to press charges?"

"No. Yes, I'm sure. No, I don't." Gracie had looked over to where Mrs. Lucas was using both feet to try to kick out the side window of the Sheriff's unit. "She needs rehab, not a jail cell."

Gracie closed the door of the refrigerator and leaned against the kitchen counter. "Damn, what a sucky day. And it's only . . ." She looked up at the clock. "Nine fifteen? That's all?" She looked at the beer in her hand. "Oh, what the heck. It's five o'clock in . . . Nairobi." She downed the rest of the beer, rinsed out the can, and threw it in the recycling container next to the back door.

She grabbed a year-old bag of frozen corn from the freezer and placed it along the right side of her face. Looking over with one eye, she noticed the little red light on the answering machine blinking, and punched Play. "Grace Louise." Her mother's voice filled the room. "I bought you a ticket."

"Nooo!"

"First class."

"Really? First class? She must want me there bad."

"Out of Ontario. That's the right airport, isn't it? Early Wednesday. Arriving Detroit Metro about ten o'clock. Returning the next afternoon.

"Fast trip."

"I have your e-mail address somewhere. I'll have them e-mail you the itinerary." There was a long pause. "Thank you."

"Not much choice, have I? You already bought the ticket."

"This means a lot to . . . well, to me."

Setting the corn aside, Gracie drew her laptop out of her day pack sitting on the kitchen chair, set it up on the table, and checked her calendar. "Move stuff around a little. Get Allen to cover. Again. But I guess that'll work."

While she was on the laptop, she opened her e-mail and wrote a cursory note to Rob: *Congratulations on your upcoming nuptials.* Typed in, *Love, Gracie.* Backspaced over that and typed instead, *Really. I'm happy for you.* Signed off with just, *Gracie.*

She placed the cursor over the Send button. Hesitated. Exited the document without saving it and closed the laptop.

Stripping off her clothes, she hung the uniform shirt and pants on hangers in the mudroom with gaiters tucked into hiking boots neatly below, ready for the next callout. She donned sweatpants and T-shirt fresh from the dryer.

Back in the kitchen, she stood in the middle of the floor feeling pent-up and jittery, yet at the same time drained, the aftermath of that morning's double dose of adrenaline. Every part of her body seemed to hurt—knees, elbows, nose, eyebrow, wrists, ribs. "Even my hair. I want to talk to Ralphie." She dialed Ralph's number. As she listened to it ring on the other end of the line she wondered if he was screening his calls, refusing to pick up when he saw it was Gracie calling.

The answering machine picked up. After the beep, she said, "Hi. It's me," forcing herself to sound upbeat. "You'll never believe what happened to me already this morning. Well, maybe you would. Um . . . I wanted to let you know I'm going to be gone for a couple of days. Wednesday and Thursday. Flying to Detroit. My . . . um . . . stepfather . . . the asshole with the cigar, remember? Anyway, he's pretty sick. Dying, as a matter of fact. My mom bought my ticket. Going first class! Woo-hoo! Anyway, I'll be unavailable for a search for those days. And . . . um . . . I wanted to talk to you about the training next weekend. So, give me a call when you can. Please." She almost hung up, then added, "I hate you being mad at me. I miss you."

She disconnected and walked out through the living room sliding glass door and out onto the deck, where Minnie stood waiting, tail wagging.

In the shadow on the western side of the house, the air was as crisp and cool as spring snowmelt. Gracie lay down on the chaise longue and contemplated the panorama laid out before her—a mosaic of green dotted with brown overlaid with a cloudless blue sky. With relief, she noticed there was still no ominous plume of smoke from what had been officially named the Shady Oak Fire rising up over the mountains to the southwest.

"So Rob is getting married," she said, laying her head back and closing her eyes. He was out of her life. For good. Somehow the thought left her with a gaping hole in her chest and a heavy lump of bread dough in her stomach at the same time.

What right, really, did she have to be angry or upset or anything with him for marrying someone else? She answered her own question aloud. "None. Nada. Zero. El zippo." He had asked her. She had said no. He had moved on to someone else. "Really, really fast."

Gracie lifted her head and noticed Minnie standing at the railing, head through the slats, looking down and wagging her tail.

She pushed herself to her feet and walked over to lean her elbows on the railing above the dog and looked down to the street below.

John and Acacia were walking up the road, the girl skipping ahead of her grandfather.

"Good morning!" Gracie called down to the pair.

Acacia looked up and waved. "Hi, Gracie!"

"Good morning," John said with no accompanying wave or smile.

"Someone is watching you and wagging her tail. Acacia, would you be willing to give a little dog a second chance? I think Minnie would really like to be friends."

The girl looked back at her grandfather, then back up at Gracie. "Okay."

"Oh, good. I'll bring her down to the end of our driveway so you can be properly introduced."

By the time John and Acacia rounded the sharp curve in the road and reached the bottom of the driveway, Gracie was

standing there with Minnie, leashed and on "sit" and "stay,"
the end of the dog's tail brushing a semicircle of asphalt clean.

With John watching and a little coaxing from Gracie,
Acacia reached out and petted Minnie's head. Within two
minutes, the girl was sitting on the driveway with her arm
around the dog, who was wriggling with happiness.

John eyed the lumps and bruises on Gracie's face. "You
run into a door or something?"

"Something like that."

"We're having burgers on the grill for dinner," Acacia said.

Happy to change the subject, Gracie said, "That sounds
like fun."

"Can you come over?" Acacia looked up at her grandfather. "Can she come over, Oompah?"

"No, that's okay," Gracie said quickly.

"Please?"

"Sure," John said, giving Gracie a sidelong look that
belied his words. "Why not?"

At exactly one minute to six that evening, Gracie pushed
the doorbell of the Robinson bungalow, holding Minnie on
her leash and arms laden with store-bought potato salad and
a bottle from her cold stash of Alice White Chardonnay.

With appreciation, she marveled again at the complete
transformation the house had undergone in the past few
months and the most recent addition—an American flag
hanging from a black pole tipped with a gold eagle, its wings
outstretched.

A woman answered the door. Slender and long limbed, she
would have been taller than Gracie if she hadn't been sitting
in a wheelchair. One side of her face drooped as if smudged.
Her hair was silver, cut short in a neat, no-fuss bob. A long
pink linen dress covered her legs. She wore neatly tied white
Keds on her feet. "You must be Gracie," she said with a smile.

"Yes. Vivian?"

"That's me. Come in. Come in." The woman reached
forward to unlatch the door, then, with the flip of a little

switch at her fingertips, rolled out of the way for Gracie to walk through and into the living room.

The hand Vivian held out was chocolate brown and warm, like her eyes.

"I'm pleased to meet you finally," Vivian said in a voice that was low and mellow with the hint of a Southern drawl.

No doubt the source of Acacia's good manners, Gracie thought.

Those same good manners prevented her from mentioning the lumps and bruises on Gracie's face. "And this must be Minnie," Vivian said, reaching down to stoke the dog's head with her fingertips. "I know someone who's going to be ecstatic to see you. She's talked of nothing else since she got home." Although her words were somewhat slurred, the woman spoke with the careful diction of a schoolteacher.

Gracie turned around and surveyed the living room. Polished wood floors, matching love seat and chairs, television set, shelves with books.

Vivian rolled past her into the middle of the room. "Well, come on in," she said, eyes twinkling. "We don't bite."

Gracie laughed. "No. It's just the last time I saw this room . . ." The last time she had seen the room, it was a drug dealer's lair, the foulest, filthiest house she had ever seen, furnished with guns and ammunition, with a booby trap for a welcome mat. "Let's just say, it's hard to believe it's the same house. It's beautiful."

"Why, thank you, Gracie. We got the house for a song, mind you. John did much of the work himself. He's very proud of it."

"As he should be." Gracie held out the wine and potato salad. "These . . . are for you. Nothing fancy."

"They're perfect." Vivian patted her knees. "I have a built-in table." With the bottle and plastic container on her lap, she swung the chair around and rolled out of the room and down the hallway. "John and Acacia are out back."

Gracie followed Vivian past two bedrooms, a tiny

bathroom, and into the kitchen. New countertops and floor, crisp double-cell shades on the windows, walls and cupboards freshly painted white, new white refrigerator, stove, dishwasher, and sink. The entire house down to the width of the doorways had all been efficiently redesigned and reconstructed with great care, everything raised, lowered, widened, or removed for someone in a wheelchair.

Vivian wheeled out the back door and down a ramp into the backyard, a work in progress with sawhorses and wood planks, a wheelbarrow and piles of gravel.

Near the back door sat a pint-sized picnic table covered with a red-and-white-checkered tablecloth and set with white plastic plates and utensils. Standing at a propane grill, wearing a chef's apron that said, KISS THE COOK, John acknowledged Gracie's appearance with a lifting of the spatula and returned to flipping burgers.

John's cool reception didn't particularly bother Gracie. Aloofness or even animosity with no previous emotional investment on her part rolled off her back. Until he made it hers, whatever was going on with John was his problem.

"Minnie!" Acacia cried. Dressed in bright yellow, with pigtails bouncing, the girl ran over, ball in hand, and accepted the leash from Gracie. For the rest of the evening, girl and dog were inseparable.

During a meal of hamburgers accompanied by corn on the cob, baked beans, and the potato salad, the conversation was light, general, during which Gracie learned that, three years before, Vivian's twenty-six-year career of teaching high school had been cut short by a stroke. Also that Acacia was the only child of their youngest daughter, living with her grandparents for a year, an experiment to see how she fared in an environment less urban than Pasadena. Sensitive, art and nature loving, the girl seemed, so far, to be thriving in the mountains.

As Vivian scooped Neapolitan ice cream into paper bowls, she asked, "So this Search and Rescue work is your job?"

"No, that's all volunteer," Gracie said. "I work as the manager of a residential camp, Camp Ponderosa. On the west end of the valley. You should come visit sometime. It's beautiful. Lots of big trees with its own little lake."

"That would be lovely. Wouldn't it, John?"

Her husband gave a noncommittal grunt and dug his spoon into his bowl of ice cream.

"Volunteerism is a noble and necessary thing," Vivian said.

Gracie winced. "I don't think of it as noble."

Vivian gave her a look. "Don't kid yourself, child. Isn't some of what you do dangerous?"

"Sometimes. But you know what the job entails when you sign up for it. We train often and hard. Rescuer safety is always the number one priority."

"What types of things do you do?"

"We search for lost kids, mountain bikers, hikers, downed airplanes, vehicles over the sides. We also help with evacuations. If the Shady Oak Fire comes up to the valley, we'll help with that."

"Lord forbid," Vivian said. "You think that will happen?"

"There's really no way to tell right now. It's always a possibility."

"Something to think about, John," Vivian said.

No response from her husband.

"It's always good to think ahead of time about having to evacuate," Gracie said as a gentle suggestion. "What you would or wouldn't take."

"My, yes, I suppose it is," Vivian said.

"Because I don't trust myself to remember everything in the moment of crisis," Gracie said, "I keep a list on the refrigerator. If I have only five minutes to get out, what would I grab? If I had fifteen minutes. Thirty minutes. Two hours."

"We don't need any advice," John said, sending her a sharp-eyed look as he pushed himself to his feet and started gathering up the dirty dishes. "We know about fires. We've lived in Southern California for forty years."

"Land sakes, John," Vivian said, gently chiding her husband. "Gracie has some knowledge and ideas. So why don't we listen to what she has to say? Go ahead, Gracie. What would you grab if you only had five minutes?"

Shooting a look at John, who was walking into the house, hands loaded with dishes and food, Gracie said, "Essentials. Minnie first. Then my laptop and my strong box of important documents and valuables. Fifteen minutes, I'd take photo albums. Sentimental things. If I had two hours, I could remove everything I care about. Everything else, including the cabin itself, is replaceable."

"That's an excellent idea." She looked up at John, who had reemerged from the house and was walking back down the ramp. "We'll make out our own list tomorrow, won't we, John?"

Another noncommittal grunt.

"Now, where is it you're from, Gracie?"

"Grosse . . . , um, the Detroit area. I'm flying home in a couple of days. Family stuff."

Acacia, who had left a half-eaten bowl of ice cream to throw the ball up in the air for Minnie, bounced over to stand next to Gracie. "Who's taking care of Minnie, Miss Gracie?"

"I . . . hadn't gotten that far yet. I—"

"Can I take care of Minnie? I want to take care of her." She turned to Vivian. "Nana, can I? Please?"

"I—" Gracie tried again.

"I don't see a problem with that—do you, John?"

"What do I know?" John said, scrubbing the grill with a brush. "I'm just the cook."

Vivian just chuckled and seemed to be amused by her husband's surliness.

With much good-natured back-and-forth between the two women, Gracie cleared the rest of the food from the table and, back in the kitchen, rinsed the dishes and placed them in the dishwasher. As the women sat on the front deck, Vivian in her wheelchair and Gracie in the red Adirondack chair, John puttered around the yard, hand-edging the lawn, pulling nonexistent weeds along the wooden fence, unobtrusive, but obviously keeping a protective eye on his wife. From what— or whom, Gracie couldn't guess.

Acacia threw a tennis ball for Minnie on the front lawn, then, as Gracie discovered later, settled quietly on the bed in her room, sitting cross-legged on the spread of pink and yellow flowers, watching television with Minnie curled up at the end of the bed as if she belonged there.

It was pleasant and peaceful in the little house at the bottom of the Arcturus hill. As the sun dropped to the horizon at their backs, chilling the air, stretching the shadows longer, and turning the sky overhead incandescent opal, Gracie and Vivian chatted and laughed, the conversation as easy and comfortable as a pair of old slippers. As they talked, birds chirped their evening songs in the background and an occasional car drove by—three in an hour—the cranberry-colored Equinox that was a part-time neighbor's up the street, a maroon sedan that Gracie guessed was someone for the vacation rental two houses up from her cabin, and a rust-pocked white pickup truck with a hole in the muffler.

The evening was the most enjoyable Gracie had experienced in years, certainly one of the most serene. Vivian might be trapped in a broken and infirm body, but she was a wise and old soul infused with a calming spirit.

It was fully dark when Gracie walked with Minnie back up the steep curving road to her own little cabin. The night sky was bursting with stars—large and brilliant, with the Milky Way slashing across the zenith. As she walked, Gracie realized she was filled with something unfamiliar, something resembling contentment.

As she stepped up onto her front porch, she heard the telephone in the kitchen ringing. Unlocking the door, she let Minnie run inside ahead of her, trotted into the kitchen, and grabbed up the telephone on the counter. "Hello?"

"Ahhh!" A man's voice screamed in Gracie's ear, sending a shock wave of adrenaline down to her fingertips.

She slammed down the receiver.

CHAPTER

11

WITH Minnie at her heels, Gracie jogged along the long, flat plateau studded with California juniper and piñon pine, accented with clumps of sage and yellow rabbitbrush, and stretching south from the hill above her cabin over a mile to the community of Pine Knot. The midafternoon air was warm and light, the sky China blue infinity. But, at over seven thousand feet, the Southern California sun scorched Gracie's bare arms and the top of her head and she mentally chided herself for knowing better than to have gone out for a run without a hat.

Gracie breathed in, breathed out, keeping time with her footfalls in a rhythm that would carry her for miles.

At the sound of the man's scream on the telephone the night before, Gracie had slammed down the receiver, then prowled back and forth in front of the counter, eyes riveted on the telephone, waiting for—daring—it to ring again. But a second call never came.

Further increasing her frustration and angst, the caller ID had displayed only *Timber Creek, CA*. She told herself that the odds were it was a prank call, logically shrugging it off as some idiot teenagers dialing numbers at random for their sick idea of a fun time. But the call had left its mark, obliterating the feeling of contentment from dinner and conversation with Vivian Robinson, piercing her psyche and leaving her more shaken than she would have imagined. She had lain in bed for hours, unable to sleep, the sound of the maniacal voice reverberating inside her head.

A hair-trigger jumpiness had continued into the next day. Running up on the plateau, she still felt destabilized, vulnerable, afraid.

And that pissed her off. "Royally," she said aloud, and ran faster.

When Gracie jogged, she only occasionally looked around to check that Minnie was running along behind her. In the past several months, the little dog had learned to heel, black nose inches from Gracie's right foot. When Gracie trotted forward, Minnie trotted forward. When Gracie stopped, Minnie stopped, sitting down at her feet and looking up expectantly. Gracie had experimented with removing the leash to see how the dog acted with acres of rolling hills and woods and not a person in sight. The first time, Minnie had bounded around, tail wagging, running with her nose to the ground after a scent here, swerving after another there. But she had stayed within calling distance. So faithful and predictable was her behavior that Gracie had taken to running with the dog off leash all the time, carrying it along, wound around her own waist, in case it was needed.

At the perimeter fence of the community high school, Gracie circled around and headed back along the plateau toward home.

She glanced back over her shoulder.

No Minnie.

She thudded to a stop and turned around. "Minnie? Where are you?"

No dog.

Visions of coyotes and mountain lions rose in Gracie's mind. Alarm clutched her throat.

"Minnie!"

The only sound was the sighing of the wind.

"Minnie!" Gracie yelled again. Louder. Sharper. "Come!"

A fly shot like a bullet past her right ear.

Gracie's eyes darted from tree to bush to tree.

Then, twenty feet back, Minnie sauntered out from behind a giant piñon pine, its top domed like a massive umbrella.

Thank God! Gracie pointed to the ground next to her feet. "Come here," she commanded, the sternness in her voice belying her relief.

Minnie trotted up, wagging her tail, pink tongue lolling out of the side of her mouth.

"You scared me, little girl," Gracie said, reaching down to stroke the black fur, hot from the sun. "Don't do that."

Gracie withdrew her water bottle from its sling and took a long draught, pouring a little into her cupped hand for Minnie. As she replaced the bottle and looked around, her eye caught on a tree stump a few feet off to her left. She stepped over and looked down.

A symbol had been carved into the wood—a diamond shape with what appeared to be stick legs set above a pair of figure eights.

Gracie had jogged past the same tree stump countless times and had never noticed a carving. "How long has that been there?" she wondered aloud, frowning. "And what does it stand for?"

She peered at it more closely.

The edges were crisp, dug-out wood slivers lying on the flat surface of the stump.

The carving was recent.

And creepy.

The hair on her arms prickling, Gracie straightened and looked around again. She had been fretting about wild animals, forgetting completely about the infinitely more frightening, more unpredictable and therefore more dangerous animal—the two-legged kind.

The plateau was on national forest land, open to anyone. In all the years Gracie had been jogging up on the plateau, while she had seen signs of other humans—a gum wrapper, a cigarette—they had been rare and weather-beaten. She had never actually encountered a single other person. It had simply never occurred to her to be afraid for her safety. She realized with a jolt that out here, a half mile from the closest building, essentially unarmed as she was, a man alone could attack, overpower, kill, and dispose of her body in any number of ways and no one would ever be the wiser.

Note to self, she thought. *From now on, carry pepper spray.* And maybe jog somewhere more populated.

But Gracie loved the plateau for its solitude, its feeling of remoteness, its peace. The thought of never running there again left her feeling bereft. "It's just a stupid carving," she said to herself, then, "Heel, Minnie," and looked behind her.

Minnie wasn't there.

Fear constricting her throat, Gracie swung around, spotting Minnie twenty feet away, standing at attention, staring into the trees on the right, ears pricked, a ridge of bristled fur running down her back.

"Minnie, come," Gracie commanded in a stage whisper.

The dog's tail began to wag slowly, then she trotted off into the trees.

"No!" Gracie started after her. "Minnie! Come back here!"

Minnie had disappeared.

Gracie stopped and listened. Nothing.

"Minnie!" she called again, and walked ahead several more steps, feet scrunching on the stony ground.

Then she heard a single yip followed by the whispering of a human voice.

What felt like tiny spiders ran up Gracie's arms, making all the hair stand on end.

She took a step forward, pressing her foot toe-to-heel on

the ground. Another step. And another until she reached the edge of the plateau where the ground sloped downward in a series of gentle hills, heavy with brush and trees.

She stopped again, leaning forward, straining to hear something, anything that might indicate where Minnie had gone and who was whispering and why.

"No, Minnie," she heard a high voice whisper. "Go away."

Gracie blew out a shaky breath. "Baxter?"

Silence.

"Minnie! Come!"

The dog appeared from within a thick clump of brush and sticks piled up against a mountain mahogany tree and climbed up the hill to where Gracie stood. "Good girl," she said, patting the dog's head. "Hi, Baxter."

On the hillside below, some branches waved, then a neat foliage-covered hatchway was moved to one side and Baxter crawled into view. The boy stood up and looked up the hill at Gracie. He was wearing the same camouflage pants as before, but, instead of the jacket, a black T-shirt.

Gracie crossed her arms and rested her weight on one leg. "What are you doing here?"

The boy shrugged a shoulder. "Hanging out."

"Did you walk all the way here?"

"Yeah."

"From your gran's?"

He nodded, then pointed back in the direction of Pine Knot. "It's not that far."

"I guess it probably isn't. Does your gran know where you are?"

"No."

"She's not worried when you leave like this?"

"No. I dunno. Maybe."

Deciding an interrogation wasn't going to break down any barriers, Gracie switched tactics. "Is that your fort? Can I see inside? It looks pretty cool. I don't know the secret password, but the sun's kind of hot and I forgot my hat."

Baxter shrugged again. "Okay." He dropped down to hands and knees and crawled back through the opening in the pile of brush.

With Minnie on her heels, Gracie slithered down the slope, then, following Baxter's lead, dropped to her hands and knees and crawled through the opening.

Just inside the entrance, she sat back on her heels and looked around.

A camouflage tarp had been fastened over a framework of branches, and in turn covered with interwoven branches forming a shady enclosure, cozy and cool.

In the semidarkness, Baxter sat cross-legged on an inexpensive, three-season sleeping bag laid over a thick cushion of pine boughs on a level shelf of ground. Several water bottles, books, and a flashlight lay on the ground nearby.

Minnie pushed past Gracie and lay down on the bag next to the boy.

"This is cool, Baxter," Gracie said. "You build it all by yourself?"

He nodded. "We learn about survival and stuff like that on Saturdays."

"I'm impressed."

No response.

"So, you've had this awhile?"

"A little while."

"What do you do here?"

"Read. Practice my compass. Study my map. Mostly read."

"Aren't you supposed to be in school?"

"I'm homeschooled," Baxter said, reminding Gracie she had learned that tidbit of information from the Missing Person Questionnaire on the search. "Mom Brianna teaches us."

"Your mom's name is Brianna?"

He nodded. "But Gran teaches me lots of stuff. She has this really cool globe of the whole world. It's kind of old, so some of the countries aren't right. And she has a map of the United States. She made me memorize the name of every state and every capital. Now I'm learning all the state birds. And the flowers. And the trees."

"Wow. That's a lot."

"The California state bird is the California valley quail. The flower is the California poppy. The tree is . . . uh . . . I can't remember."

"The redwood, I think."

"Yeah. The redwood."

"That's very good, Bax," Gracie said, thoroughly charmed. She moved over to sit on the sleeping bag, clasping her hands in front of her knees.

"Mom Brianna gives me boring stuff. Math."

"I thought your mom's name—"

"Gran gets me fun books to read from the library," the boy said. "I can't read 'em at home. Grandpop doesn't permit it. So I read 'em when I'm at Gran's. Or here."

Gracie smiled. "Your gran is pretty great, I think. Don't you?"

"Yeah."

"Seems like most kids your age have their noses stuck in their iPods or iPads or smartphones or whatever."

"Grandpop won't let us have electronics."

Not all bad, Gracie thought. She looked around the hideout, then back at the boy, who sat with his arms wrapped around his knees, head bowed, staring through his legs at the ground.

"You can't keep running away, Bax." When he was silent, she added, "I know it's . . ." *Impossible living with a violent butthole father.* ". . . really hard living with your dad . . ."

Baxter snorted at the understatement. "And my grandpop, too," he said. "And my uncle Win. And some of my cousins. Like *Jordan.*"

"They all live with you? At the compound?"

"Yeah."

"You said your gran was going to adopt you. Has she started the process yet, do you know? Filed any papers?"

"She told me it might take a long time." Then with a

bitterness beyond his years, he said, "I don't think it'll ever happen."

Gracie put a hand on Baxter's arm. "It'll happen, Bax," she said. "Things will get better. You just have to wait them out." Knowing exactly how it felt to live with a violent parent, she added, "I'm sorry."

"That's okay, Gracie. I know you want to help me."

Gracie smiled at the bent head. "Hey, when's the last time you ate something?"

"I dunno. Breakfast, I guess."

"You hungry?"

He looked up at her. "I guess."

Gracie gestured over her shoulder with a thumb. "My cabin's not very far from here. Why don't you come home with me? We'll give your gran a call. Let her know where you are and not to worry. I'll fix you something to eat. Then I can give you a ride home."

"Um, I dunno. I don't think I'm supposed to."

"Supposed to what?"

"We only eat what we make ourselves."

"Really." Gracie stared at the blond head and wondered what the hell was going on in that home, in that compound.

"Sooo, it'll be another of our little secrets. I make a mean PB and J."

"What's that?"

Gracie blinked. "Peanut butter and jelly. In this case, it's probably 'and jam.'"

A pause, then a lifting of the shoulder. "Okay."

GRACIE HUNG UP the phone in the kitchen and called out to Baxter in the living room, "Your gran said I was supposed to bring you home to the compound no later than five o'clock."

"Okay," the high voice answered.

Gracie hung from an arm from the kitchen doorway and looked into the living room.

With Minnie sitting at his feet, Baxter was standing motionless in the middle of the room, arms at his sides, staring at the shelves running along the far wall crammed full with books.

Gracie ducked back into the kitchen, opened the refrigerator, and scanned the contents: a shriveled slice of week-old pepperoni pizza, five cans of Coors Light, an almost-empty jar of Smucker's strawberry jam, four bottles of Alice White, an unopened half gallon of 2 percent milk, a half loaf of whole wheat bread, and three unopened packages of PayDay candy bars.

Pathetic, Kinkaid.

She pulled the bread and jam from the refrigerator and a knife from the drawer. She was lifting a paper plate from the cupboard when a soft knock sounded from the mudroom.

Minnie bounded through the room with a bark and sat down in front of the mudroom door, ears perked, eyes fastened on the back door, tail wagging.

Gracie pulled the door open.

Acacia stood out on the porch, this time dressed in lavender right down to her lavender tennis shoes.

Minnie ran out to greet her. The girl crouched down and put her arms around the dog, letting her cover her face with sloppy doggie kisses. "Hi, Minnie," she said, giggling. "I missed you, too."

"Hi, Acacia."

The girl stood up. "Hi, Gracie. I'm here for Minnie's walk."

"Sure. But come on inside for a sec first. There's somebody here I'd like you to meet."

The girl followed Gracie through the kitchen and into the living room.

"Acacia," Gracie said, "this is Baxter. He's a friend of mine from . . . Baxter, this is Acacia. She's a friend of mine, too. She lives down the street."

Gracie looked from the blond head to the black one and back again, wondering how this was going to play out, fascinated, but half-terrified that Baxter was going to use another racial slur, causing all hell to break loose in the little house at the bottom of the hill.

The boy and girl stood six feet apart, staring at each other as if they were from different planets.

Finally, remembering her manners, Acacia said, "Hi, Baxter. I'm pleased to meet you."

Baxter looked at Gracie, as if for reassurance, then back at Acacia. "Hi. Um, pleased to meet you, too."

"Acacia has come to take Minnie for a walk," Gracie said.

"Wanna come with me?" Acacia asked Baxter.

Gracie held her breath.

"Didn't Minnie just . . . ?" Baxter looked at Gracie, caught her head shaking a fraction, looked back at Acacia, lifted a shoulder, and said, "Sure."

BAXTER SAT SLOUCHED on the living room couch, munching on a Jif and strawberry jam on whole wheat sandwich. A half-drunk glass of milk sat on the sea chest serving as a coffee table.

Gracie sank down at the opposite end of the couch. Minnie hopped up and curled up between them.

"This is good," the boy said, taking another bite. "She's nice."

"I'm glad. And she is. Very nice."

"What's her name again?"

"Acacia."

He took a sip of the milk. "That's a weird name."

"It is unusual. I think it's pretty. An acacia is a kind of a tree. We better get you home, don't you think? Finish your sandwich and we'll go."

"Okay." He took another bite and looked past her at the bookshelves, a not-very-subtle look of longing on his face.

"Would you like to borrow a book to read?" Gracie asked. "Or two?"

Mid-chew, Baxter looked up at her. "Can I?"

"Sure. You can read it. And then we can talk about it if you like. Like with your gran. Would you like that?"

"Yeah!"

Gracie studied the boy for a moment, then pushed herself to her feet. "Well, let's take a look." She scanned the shelves, painfully aware that she hadn't a clue of what was appropriate reading for an eleven-year-old boy. "*Treasure Island*," she said, pulling the book from the shelf. "That's a good one."

"Do you have any about black people?"

Gracie threw Baxter a look over her shoulder, then turned back to run her eyes along the titles. She drew out a hardcover she had bought for a nickel at a garage sale. "*Maniac Magee*," she said. "It's about a boy who's an orphan. He lives in Pennsylvania and . . . Well, you read it. We'll talk about it."

Baxter shoved the rest of the sandwich into his mouth and said, "Okay."

Gracie's hand hovered over another book, then she pulled it out. "Ever heard of *Uncle Tom's Cabin*?"

Baxter shook his head.

"It's about slavery in the United States. It was written in the 1800s and helped start the Civil War. Some people say it stereotypes blacks. But it changed our country's history, so I think it's worth reading." Gracie stepped over and laid the books on the sea chest in front of the boy.

Still chewing, Baxter leaned forward and studied the cover of *Uncle Tom's Cabin*.

"I have a couple of others you can have when you finish these," Gracie said.

A smile transformed his face, making it younger, more vulnerable, brighter. He swallowed with a loud gulp and said, "Okay! Thanks, Gracie!"

* * *

GRACIE TURNED THE Ranger into a gravel driveway leading back through a forest of rolling hills and tall pines, and
stopped in front of a green metal gate blocking the entrance
with a sign announcing, NO TRESPASSING.

"Thanks for the ride," Baxter said, pushing the door open.
"I'd ask you to come in, but we're not supposed to have
visitors."

"Oh, that's okay. I—"

"The ground is booby-trapped. Trip wires and stuff
like that."

"Good to know!" Gracie said and peered ahead out of
the windshield.

"Thanks again for the books. I'll take good care of them."

Gracie smiled back at Baxter. "You're welcome again.
I'm leaving early tomorrow for a couple of days. Maybe I'll
see you when I get back, okay?"

"Okay." Baxter reached back to where Minnie lay on the
mound of gear behind the seat and petted the dog's head.
"Who's going to watch Minnie?"

"Acacia. I'm bringing her down to their house later on
tonight."

"She's lucky," Baxter said. "I'd like to help watch her for
you. But, Gracie?"

"Yup."

"I like you."

"Well, thanks, Baxter. I like you, too."

"You don't treat me like I'm stupid."

"Who treats you like you're stupid?"

"My dad. My grandpop."

"And Jordan?"

"Yeah. And Jordan." He picked at a frayed patch on the
knee of his pants. "They tell me I'm stupid. All the time. Call
me a mama's girl and a sissy." He looked over at her. "You
don't think I'm stupid, do you?"

"Not a bit. In fact, I think you're pretty doggoned smart."

The brown eyes sparkled back at her. "I gotta go." He reached back and patted Minnie's head again. "Bye, Minnie. You're a nice dog." Then he climbed out of the truck. "Bye, Gracie. Thanks for the ride."

"Bye, Baxter."

The door closed with a click.

Gracie watched the boy circumvent the gate and disappear down into a ravine. Seconds later he reappeared on the other side, turned, and waved.

Gracie waved back. "Wow," she whispered to herself. "I could grow to love you, Baxter Edwards."

CHAPTER

12

"I'M lost?" Gracie growled, staring out the tiny side window of her rented Chevy Spark. "I'm friggin' *lost*?"

On her way to the hospital in downtown Detroit from the airport, she somehow, somewhere had taken a wrong exit from the interstate and, for the last fifteen minutes, had been wandering aimlessly through a maze of sagging houses, abandoned buildings, and overgrown vacant lots. Driving a car the size and consistency of a sardine can instead of her truck had only contributed to her general crankiness at having to spend the next twenty-four hours in a city. Not just Detroit. A *city*. Any city.

"I hate cities," Gracie said aloud as if in confirmation, then swerved at the last second to avoid dropping a tire into a ten-inch-deep pothole in the middle of the road. She swooped back into her own lane and grabbed up the Detroit street map provided by the rental car company, glancing at it between takes of the mélange of cars and trucks and pedestrians up ahead.

Finally, after almost taking out a stray dog, she swept the

car around the corner onto a side street, pulled to the curb, and stopped. She frowned down at the map. "Where the hell am I?" She squinted at the minuscule lettering. Blinked. Held it closer to her face until she realized it was the map that was slightly blurred and not her vision.

Driving along I-94 toward downtown, Gracie had felt as if she were on the Paramount Pictures studio tour and had walked from one movie set onto another. In less than four hours, she had been transported from Southern California's Inland Empire—hot and arid with palm trees, orange bougainvillea, and pink oleander set against a backdrop of the San Gabriel Mountains, capped by a cloudless blue sky—to southeastern Michigan, where the air was pleasantly warm and humid, the land a flat cross-hatching of asphalt and cement, punctuated by lush green hardwoods and angular office buildings, opaque windows reflecting the slate-colored sky.

"What street is this?" Gracie said as she glanced back over her shoulder at the sign on the corner. "Benson."

She studied the map, finally pinpointing exactly where she was—miles from where she should be. She tossed the map on the passenger's seat, sighed, and looked around.

The Motor City, once healthy, industrious, and thriving, had been decimated by years of recession, the decline of the auto industry, the resulting mass exodus of half its population, its former glory obscured by the creeping scourge of poverty, blight, drugs, violence, and virtual anarchy.

The street on which Gracie was parked was lined with dilapidated houses staring out through broken or missing windows. Mournful. Depressed. And depressing.

Several times over the last decade, Gracie had been back to southern Michigan. But she had never engaged, emotionally or mentally, behaving and talking like an automaton at family holiday gatherings, existing in suspended animation until the minute she could reboard the plane and fly west again.

I should never have come, she thought and sagged in her seat.

On the road ahead, a gray squirrel ran across the pavement, some tasty morsel in its mouth.

Gracie rolled down her window. The rush of air was moist, laden with the heady smells of fields and trees and grass. The street ahead was lined on both sides with massive, stately elm trees. Across the street from where Gracie sat, side-by-side vacant lots were bursting with milkweed, goldenrod, and purple asters. The hum of traffic had faded to a murmur behind the twittering of birds in the branches overhead and a dog barking from several blocks over.

Somewhere above Gracie's head, a cardinal called, startlingly loud and sweet, instantly recognizable, transporting her back years to her childhood. She leaned her head out the window, searching the leaves above for the flash of brilliant red, never realizing before this how much she missed the sound.

Gracie pulled her head back inside the car with a sigh. She reached her hand over to shift into Drive, then stopped. Halfway up the block, another animal trotted across the street. She leaned forward and stared out the windshield. Gray fur. Long tail. Easy lope. "That's a coyote!" she said and laughed with pure delight.

Suddenly conscious of the eerie beauty within the ruin, she lifted her foot from the brake and let the car roll forward. Meandering through the neighborhood, she looked around with increasing interest and the realization that what she was witnessing was a transformation in progress. The natural world was reclaiming what once had been a city, replacing brick with oak, redbud, and maple, cement with grass, and glass with roses, daisies, rabbits, and even coyotes.

Gracie turned from one deserted street onto the next and whispered to herself, "This is just awesome."

GRACIE STOOD IN the middle of the brightly lit hallway of the intensive care unit. Her face felt flushed and hot. Clammy fists clenched and unclenched. Looking in through the wide doorway of the hospital room, past a blue-patterned curtain pulled partially closed, she could see the end of a bed and two swollen bare feet encased in what looked like black casts.

Her arrival at the hospital had peeled back the scab of a deep-burning rage. Feelings she had worked so hard to tamp down and suppress had roared to the surface. Her heart was pounding so loudly in her ears, it took her a moment to comprehend that a young Asian nurse standing next to her had asked her a question.

"What?" she asked.

"Can I help you?"

Gracie squeezed out a tight smile. "No. Thanks." She took in a breath and gestured to the room. "This is . . . where . . . the room . . ."

Almond-shaped brown eyes smiled up at her. "We're here if you need anything," the woman said, and walked away down the corridor.

The nameplate to the right of the doorway identified the patient in the room. RODGERS, M.

At the request of her mother, hoping for a deathbed reconciliation between her husband and her estranged daughter, Gracie had flown two thousand miles, rented a tin can for a car, driven a circuitous route to the hospital, and now could go no farther

She turned away from the doorway.

"Grace Louise?" A tremulous voice stopped her.

She hesitated for a moment, then turned back and stepped inside the room, dark except for a single light bar at the head of the bed and the glow of the late afternoon sun through the large casement window.

Morris was sleeping, mouth open, head sagging off to one side, looking mildly ridiculous in a green hospital gown short enough to reveal swollen knees. An oxygen tube from his flat nose and multiple IVs from both hefty arms ran to no less than a half-dozen blue screened monitors crowding both sides of the bed.

Perched on the edge of a chair on the other side of the bed, barely visible amid the stands and equipment, was Gracie's mother.

When Gracie walked in, Evelyn rose unsteadily to her feet.

Gracie hesitated, shocked at how old her mother looked, as if she had aged twenty years in the last year.

Evelyn's hair, dyed to a dark auburn the same as Gracie's, was pulled into a short, neat ponytail at the back of her neck. As always, she was dressed exquisitely in a tony, bright red bolero jacket, gold braiding at the neck and cuffs, black slacks, bowed flats. But her face was pale, haggard. Worry lines dug into the corners of her mouth, the meticulously applied makeup insufficient to fully hide the sunken cheeks, the bleak, despairing eyes.

"Hello, Mother," Gracie said.

In short, fast steps, Evelyn hurried around the end of the bed and up to Gracie, putting her arms around her waist and clinging to her as if she were a life preserver.

Gracie was amazed that the top of her mother's head only came up to her chin. She hadn't remembered her being so short. It had been a long time . . . years . . . forever . . . since they had embraced.

"I'm so, so glad you're here," Evelyn mumbled into Gracie's shoulder. Then she stepped back and, taking her daughter's hands, gave them a little shake and nodded toward her husband.

With feet that felt like lead, Gracie stepped over to the bed and looked down on the sleeping man.

In spite of their tumultuous history, in spite of his horrible, abusive behavior, and in spite of the despicable things he had done, Gracie felt a pang of something, perhaps even sympathy. The man was a human being. And he was dying. "Morris?" she said in a quiet voice.

Morris opened his blue, rheumy eyes and turned his head toward Gracie. "What the hell do you want?" he asked, voice deep, harsh. He turned his head toward his wife. "Goddammit,

Evelyn! What the hell is she doing here? I don't want her here! Get her out of here!"

Evelyn fluttered nervously over to the bed, smoothing Morris's hair back from his wide forehead, straightening his hospital gown. "She's here to see you, MoMo. All the way from California. She wanted to see you. She cares about you."

"Bullshit!" Morris glared back at Gracie. "She's nothing but a greedy little witch, sucking up at the last minute, trying to weasel her way into some of my money."

Gracie felt her heart petrify to stone. She put both hands flat on the bed and leaned forward until her face was inches away from Morris's. "You're a sonofabitch," she said in a raspy voice unrecognizable as her own. "You're mean and you're hateful. You made my childhood a living hell, you worthless piece of shit."

Morris glared back at her, chest rising and falling, nostrils flaring with every inhalation.

"And," Gracie said, her entire body trembling, "I don't want a single penny of your goddam money!"

"Get the hell out of here." Morris's voice rose to a hoarse croak. "Evelyn! Get her out of here!" He struggled to lift his head from the pillow, but couldn't.

Gracie spun around on her heel, her head whirling. She put a hand on the doorframe to keep herself from falling, then stumbled out of the room.

Her mother's footsteps came up behind her. "Grace Louise. Please stop."

Gracie stopped and turned around.

"He's in pain," Evelyn pleaded, placing a hand on Gracie's arm." He doesn't mean it."

"Of course he means it," Gracie said. "Pain doesn't have a damn thing to do with it. He's always been this way, Mother. And you've always covered up for him. Always defended him. I'm leaving."

"But where . . . where are you going?"

Gracie stopped again, anger blowing out through her lips like steam from a valve. "I don't know."

"Stay at the house. I stay in a little room here in the hospital. But you stay at the house. I'll see you tomorrow?" A question, not a statement.

Gracie looked over at Evelyn, a frightened little bird, frail, soon to be alone. "Okay, Mother," she said. "I'll stay at the house." She blew another long breath. Suddenly exhausted, she said, "And I'll see you tomorrow."

GRACIE PUSHED THE door open and looked around what had once been her bedroom.

Gone were the Sierra Club and Greenpeace and Defenders of Wildlife posters, an entire wall of pasted-on wolf and mountain lion and wildflower pictures cut from magazines, the little oval rag rug she had woven at camp, the glass-top case holding carefully hoarded treasures: a tiny bird skull, a sloughed-off blue racer snakeskin, red and orange and yellow leaves—maple and beech and oak—meticulously gathered and pressed between dictionary pages. Gone were the pictures of her real father she had purposely left behind. Every scrap, every trace, every remnant of the angry, passionate, rebellious teenager who had lived there had been removed.

All had been replaced by gold carpeting, a tapestried bedspread with matching drapes. Walls a deep teal with white crown molding and window trim. Brass fixtures and lamps.

Tastefully done, but as sterile and impersonal and cold as a mausoleum—a window, perhaps, into her mother's life.

Gracie tossed her carry-on and purse onto the bed and kicked off her shoes.

Stocking feet silent on heavy carpet runner, whispering onto hardwood flooring, then back onto carpet, she walked down the hallway and looked into her half brother Harold's room, now filled with exercise equipment. Next to it, her half sister Lenora's old bedroom was being used for storage.

Well, Gracie sighed internally, at least she ranked a little higher than Morris's own children. Her old room still had a bed, used for something other than housing off-season holiday decorations and a set of old weights.

She padded down the massive winding staircase, veered off to the right into the den, and flipped on the light.

The specter of Morris rose from every facet of the room—enormous flat-screen television, plaques and pennants from the University of Michigan and every Detroit sports team, acrid overtones of cigars, glass-topped end and coffee tables, brown leather furniture, including her stepfather's favorite recliner, dented and worn from years of use. What there wasn't a sign of was the hole Gracie had blown in the wall with a double-barreled shotgun. That had been patched and painted over at least twice.

Gracie crossed the room to the built-in bookshelves where two spotless Waterford crystal tumblers sat on a silver tray next to a matching decanter, filled no doubt with Morris's drug of choice—Johnnie Walker Blue Label.

Gracie poured two fingers of the deep amber liquid and held it aloft. "To Morris," she said. "You son of a bitch. I will never forgive you for what you've done to me, to my mother, to everyone else. When you're gone, the world will be a better, brighter, sunnier place." She swallowed the drink in one gulp and spent the next three minutes hacking and coughing.

GRACIE merged the Ranger into the steady stream of traffic in the eastbound lanes of the 10 Freeway. She settled into the number three lane and set the cruise control for five miles an hour over the posted speed limit, ten miles an hour slower than the flow of traffic.

That morning she had returned to the hospital as promised, refusing to see Morris again, meeting her mother in the cafeteria instead. Evelyn, while dressed as immaculately as ever, looked even more haggard, more exhausted than the evening before. For ninety minutes, over a cinnamon roll and multiple cups of strong Colombian coffee, Gracie had listened to her mother chatter on, regaling her with stories about Morris and reminiscing about his accomplishments, fretting about who might and who might not come to the funeral and whether she should order gladiolas or lilies or roses for the casket and what color. When Evelyn had begged her daughter again to forgive Morris, Gracie had lied, telling her she would think about it.

Gracie glanced out the driver's window at Mount Baldy,

rising imposingly in the hazy blue sky, and back ahead to the Swift semi-truck she had been following, which blocked her entire view. She flipped on her turn signal, glanced in her rearview mirror, punched down the accelerator, slid passed the rig, then back into her lane in front of it.

The horizon opened up and Gracie did a double take. Up ahead, above the tops of the office buildings and trees, an enormous column of thick, dark smoke rose high into the late-afternoon sky.

"Holy shit," she whispered. Consumed as she had been with family during the past twenty-four hours, she had completely forgotten about the Shady Oak Fire burning at the base of the mountains.

She leaned over and snapped on the radio, scanning the frequencies until she found a station reporting on the fire. For the next twenty minutes, she listened about how multiple small brushfires, which officials believed had been set by a single arsonist, had spread quickly into surrounding residential neighborhoods and the national forest. Fanned by high winds and aided by high temperatures, low humidity, and heavy vegetation, suppressed for years into thick, sometimes impenetrable feasts for a fire, the small brushfires had grown, converging into two enormous demons of flame. Thousands of residents, schools, and businesses had been evacuated. Roads and neighborhoods had been closed. More than twenty thousand acres and seventeen structures, including seven homes, had been destroyed. One human life had been lost.

Gracie said a silent prayer for all those affected, but especially for those fighting the fire, both in the Command Post and in the field—brutal, scorching-hot, muscle-straining, backbreaking work.

A Skycrane helicopter roared overhead, dropping its enormous payload of red retardant slurry on the steep mountainside ahead, then soared away again.

As the Ranger traveled east, the plume of smoke grew larger, rising higher and higher into the air. "Holy shit,"

Gracie said again as it hit her for the first time that if either fire reached the Santa Anita Canyon—steep, heavily timbered, and running up the backside of the mountain range forming the southern boundary of the lovely valley in which she lived, the fire would roar, virtually unstoppable, all the way up to Timber Creek. If the winds shifted west, the southwestern end of the valley, including Camp Ponderosa, would be directly in its path; if winds shifted east, the fire would head for several small residential communities, including Gracie's.

Fear and dread kicked Gracie's anxiety level up several notches. The possibility of a fire coming into camp when it was chock-full of guests galvanized her into action. Abandoning her plan to drive up the longer, more scenic "back way" up to the valley, she took the first Timber Creek exit from the 10 Freeway and headed up the mountain "the front way," leading more directly and quickly up to camp.

Gracie spent more than two hours in the Gatehouse searching every file cabinet and bookshelf for a formal emergency evacuation plan or emergency procedures of any kind for the camp, turning up only a cursory, poorly written single photocopied sheet of generic bullet points. Appalled that she hadn't noticed the absence of any formal evacuation plan before, she spent the evening writing comprehensive risk management and emergency procedures plans, including a formal camp evacuation plan with maps of evacuation routes leading away from the property and out of the valley itself. She printed out multiple copies of the maps and posted them in every entrance of every building around camp.

With a quick phone call to Vivian Robinson to confirm they would be able to keep Minnie another night ("Oh, my, yes. Of course! Delighted!"), Gracie slept a fitful five hours in a sleeping bag thrown down on the carpeted floor of her office. At breakfast the next morning, she sat down with the leader of the church retreat group in camp for the next two days, talking at length with him about emergency policies and procedures, reassuring him that she would immediately notify the understandably skittish group at the first inkling of any real danger.

The remainder of the morning she spent doing paperwork and returning phone calls after which she helped Allen prepare and serve a lunch of chicken tacos to the church group. With the knowledge that the camp was in the head cook's capable hands, she headed back across the valley for a much-needed shower and to change out of what she called "city clothes."

Gracie zoomed the Ranger up the sweeping curves of Arcturus and turned into the driveway of her cabin. She gunned the engine to climb the steep hill and braked to a stop at the top.

She looked through the passenger's window and smiled. Acacia and Baxter sat together on a railroad tie lining the driveway, wide grins on their faces, like conspirators waiting for their prey. At their feet, Minnie sat at the very end of her leash, ears perked, entire rear end moving with her wagging tail.

As soon as the Ranger stopped, boy, girl, and dog jumped up and ran over. "Hi, guys!" Gracie said, climbing out of the truck.

"Hi, Gracie!" Acacia said.

"Yo ho ho, Gracie!" Baxter called.

Gracie grinned down at the boy. "I take it you're reading *Treasure Island*."

"Finished it," Baxter said, looking immensely pleased with himself.

"Already? Wow!" She leaned down to scratch Minnie's head. "Did you like it?"

"It was great!" His eyes were shining. "I had to look up a lot of words in my little dictionary, but that's okay."

Gracie straightened. Before she could ask, Baxter said, "Gran knows I'm around here somewhere. I have to be back to her house by four."

Acacia bounced up and down on her toes, pink-ribboned pigtails bobbing like corks. "We were waiting for you," she said. "Bax and I have already taken Minnie for two walks today. But can we take her for another one?"

Bax and I.

"Puleeeeeze," Baxter joined in.

For the first time since she had met Baxter, he looked relaxed, practically bursting at the seams with happiness. "Of course."

He handed Acacia Minnie's leash, explaining, "'Cacia takes her when we walk down the hill. I take her when we come up."

"Okay then . . ."

"Come on, Minnie," Acacia said.

"Be . . ."

"We'll be careful," Baxter said.

"And watch . . ."

"We'll watch out for cars," Acacia said.

They both giggled, skipping down the driveway and out of sight down the road.

IF THE SHADY Oak Fire entered the valley, Timber Creek Search and Rescue would be called in to assist with a swift, orderly evacuation of the more than twenty-five thousand permanent and part-time residents and however many tourists happened to be up in the valley at the time. Because Gracie needed to be packed and ready to go in advance of an evacuation notice, she spent the next two hours packing the Ranger. Acacia and Baxter returned with Minnie and spent the time lying on their stomachs on the living room floor, chins on hands, feet in the air, immersed in Monopoly.

Occasional peeks over the children's shoulders revealed to Gracie that Acacia played patiently, quietly, steadily building her stash of properties and pile of gold one-hundred-dollar bills. Baxter, on the other hand, was brash, reckless, all-in, all-out, whooping loudly enough to startle Minnie when his opponent landed on his property with a hotel.

Gracie hefted an extra-large duffel bag of clothes and
toiletries in behind the passenger's seat of the Ranger. Her
backpack carrying her laptop, power cords, and other elec-
tronic accoutrements she stowed on the passenger's side
floor atop a small Sentry safe containing her passport,
important papers, and several thousand dollars in cash saved
against a rainy day. Her SAR equipment, extra food and
water, survival equipment, and earthquake kit were already
stored in the bed truck. She plunked down the tailgate and
heaved all the way to the front a Rubbermaid storage bin
filled with photo albums, knickknacks, and other keepsakes
without which she simply couldn't live. On top of that she
hefted a second bin holding an extra twenty-pound bag of
dog food, treats, bowls, toys, and extra gallons of water for
Minnie. Several boxes of her most precious books were
shoved in beside the bins.

Only the few things she used every day—things she
could scoop up in a flash or leave behind altogether—
toothbrush, paste, and hairbrush, did she not pack.

At four o'clock on the nose, Gracie dropped Baxter at his
gran's in Pine Knot, then circled all the way around again,
driving west the entire length of the valley and back up to
camp to help Allen prepare, serve, and clean up after the
church group's evening meal. Foregoing the group's talent
show, something she always enjoyed, she drove home
instead. Much more enticing was a quiet evening on the
living room couch watching back-to-back coma-inducing
TV programs with Minnie.

WITH MINNIE ON heel, Gracie stepped past the line of giant
white boulders marking the end of the pavement at the top
of Arcturus and jogged up the steep road leading up to the
plateau. She ran, watching her feet to avoid slipping off the
smooth-packed dirt and onto the ragged gutter of talus running down the middle. Midway up the hill, she left the road,

veering off to the right onto a narrow trail running through
the woods.

As the passage of time diminished the feeling of vulnerability stemming from the crank phone call, Gracie relaxed,
realizing her fear of being attacked while running up on the
plateau stemmed mostly from the call itself. She made the
conscious decision to keeping running there, mostly because
it was conveniently close to home—any other jogging paths
a twenty minute or more drive away. Still, before she left the
cabin, she unearthed from a store of backpacking gear in the
attic a canister of pepper spray designed for repelling bears
in the wild, and clipped it to the strap of her water bottle sling.

It was quiet in the woods, the only sound that of Gracie's
own measured breathing and her and Minnie's footsteps.
Beneath the canopy of trees, the morning air was cold, a
herald of the approaching winter. But dressed as Gracie was
in Camp Ponderosa sweatshirt and pants, she welcomed it
as invigorating, and good for the firefighting crews of the
Shady Oak Fire. Shuffling through shed needles and last
year's fallen leaves sent up the sharp, fresh scent of partially
decomposed earthy matter.

Woman and dog climbed a final incline on the trail and
emerged out into sunlight on an old road that, in turn, led
to a maze of other old roads running through several square
miles of national forest—hilly, heavily wooded, and crisscrossed with rivulets and creeks.

Where the trail intersected the road, Gracie stopped and
took a swig from her water bottle, pouring a handful for
Minnie. Jogging again, she followed the road east up a short
hill, down the other side, veering right where the road turned
and ran along the bottom of the plateau.

Running up and down the gentle hills, into the shade,
then back out into the sun, Gracie's thoughts focused back
to Detroit, to her mother, to Morris and her inability—or
unwillingness—to forgive him. She thought about Ralph

and his apparent unwillingness to forgive her and the devastating emptiness that came with the loss of their friendship. She thought about Rob Christian and his engagement and the dawning realization that losing Rob brought an even deeper pain than losing Ralph, more pronounced, more devastating.

Gracie stumbled to an abrupt stop.

Twenty feet ahead of her in the middle of the road stood a boy, tall and beefy, his age, Gracie guessed, somewhere in the vicinity of fifteen. Next to him stood a girl, much smaller and younger.

Both children were dressed in woodland camouflage pants. The girl wore a hot pink top, the boy a black T-shirt with strange, indecipherable lettering on the front. There was something at the outer corner of the boy's right eye, possibly a tattoo of some kind.

Gracie might have thought they were ordinary children out for an ordinary morning stroll, except the boy held a black, semiautomatic assault rifle that was almost as big as he was and the girl had a pistol strapped to her waist.

Gracie didn't like guns. Had never owned one. Had never fired one, except for a shotgun one time, more than ten years before. She knew next to nothing about them except that they were really loud and could ruin lives.

She didn't like being in the vicinity of guns. Especially those carried by children.

Behind Gracie, Minnie growled.

"Shhh, Minnie," Gracie whispered. She unclipped the leash from around her waist and fastened it to the dog's collar, wrapping the other end several times around her hand to shorten its length and keep the dog close by her side. Then, surreptitiously, she unclipped the pepper spray from the sling and pushed it into the pocket of her sweatpants for easy access.

She looked back up to the two children who stood unmoving on the road ahead. "Hi," she said, lifting a hand.

Without warning, the boy commanded, "Whistle, Heather."

The girl grabbed up a pink whistle hanging from a lanyard around her neck and blew it.

Then with well-practiced ease, the boy dropped one knee to the ground. In one fluid move, he lifted the assault rifle, aimed it at Gracie, peered through the scope, and yelled, "Freeze or I'll shoot!"

CHAPTER

14

GRACIE froze, hand half-lifted, mouth agape. A warm breeze fluttered the ends of her hair. From somewhere above her head, a raven croaked.

Her heart boomed in her chest and her brain paddled furiously, like a duck's webbed feet below the surface of the water, trying to figure out how she was going to get out of this whole stupid mess without getting herself shot by a maniacal kid with a semiautomatic weapon.

The girl—Heather—was still blowing the whistle, shattering the silence with one long blast. Then a short blast. Then another long. Repeating the cycle. Over and over.

Minnie growled again. "Shhh, little girl," Gracie whispered without moving, suddenly terrified not only for herself, but for her dog.

As if by predetermined signal, Heather stopped blowing the whistle. She unclipped the keep on the holster attached to her belt, drew out the pistol, and aimed it at Gracie.

The girl looked all of seven.

What the hell ever happened to My Little Pony?

A rustling drew her eyes to the hill above the road where a cluster of children were emerging from the trees and into the open. One by one, they jumped down out onto the road and walked over to stand behind the lead boy. An even mixture of boys and girls, the group ranged in age from what couldn't have been more than five years old to as old as sixteen, maybe seventeen. Down to the smallest child, all were holding some type of weapon, all but one pointed straight at Gracie.

The one child who wasn't aiming his gun at Gracie was standing off to one side—a skinny boy with white-blond hair and thick-rimmed glasses.

Baxter.

He and Gracie stared wide-eyed at each other, neither giving any indication they recognized the other.

The barrel of Baxter's weapon was aimed at the ground. "I don't think we should be—" he began.

"Shut up, you goddamned mama's girl!" the lead boy yelled. "She's an enemy combatant. She's now our prisoner."

Baxter clapped his mouth shut, face blanching.

Gracie could see the lead boy's chest heaving, his breath coming in fast, short puffs. His being nervous wasn't doing a single thing to slow her own heart rate.

Seconds ticked by into years. Gracie's nerves stretched to piano-string taut, eyes flicking from one child to the next to the next. The hand clutching the pepper spray in her pocket was sweaty. Her arm, still raised, was growing tired. She could feel Minnie shivering against her leg.

She stared at the children and they stared back, as if waiting for something.

Finally Gracie inhaled and opened her mouth to say, "Enough is enough. I'm leaving," when a group of adults, men and women, crashed out of the trees on the hillside above the road and dropped down onto the dirt next to the children.

Neck, arm, and thigh muscles bulged. Some of the men were heavily tattooed. Every male head was bared and shaved.

Skinheads, Gracie's brain registered, eyes darting from face to face.

All were dressed head to foot in woodland camouflage. All wore face paint, some elaborate. All carried firearms—semiautomatic rifles and pistols, and shotguns.

In spite of the face paint, Gracie recognized one of the men as Lee, Baxter's father, the man who had tried to belt his son, instead striking his own mother so hard he had knocked her to the ground, the man onto whose back Gracie had jumped and who had elbowed her away with no more effort than swatting a horsefly.

Not looking good for the home team, Gracie thought and took a slow, careful step backward.

"Freeze!" the large boy yelled again.

Gracie froze again.

A lone man emerged from the trees and jumped down onto the road between Gracie and the rest of the group. At six foot five or six, he looked like a life-sized G.I. Joe action figure on steroids. Gracie recognized him as Baxter's uncle who had dragged Lee away from his son and mother, practically carrying him across the yard to their truck. The man appeared the size of a yeti, with arms and legs and trunk and everything four times larger than Gracie's.

Taking in the scene in a glance, the huge man barked in an incongruously high voice, "Lower your weapons!"

Everyone obeyed the order except the lead boy, who hadn't moved a muscle since training his sights on Gracie.

The huge man walked over to the boy and pressed the end of his semiautomatic weapon toward the ground with his hand. "Never point your weapon at anyone, Jordan," he said in a voice loud enough for Gracie to hear. "Until you're ready to fire. Until you're ready to kill."

Then he turned to face Gracie and said in a mild voice, "There's no reason to be afraid. No one's going to hurt you."

Gracie's fear drained away, laying bare the fury beneath.

"What the hell!" she yelled, shaking a clenched fist at the man. "They were pointing guns at me! What the *hell*?"

"We're conducting an enemy contact drill," the man answered as if that explained everything. "But if it makes you feel better . . ." He lifted the weapon from Jordan's hands, ejecting the large-capacity ammunition magazine, holding it out so Gracie could see it was empty, then snapping it back in place. "Their weapons aren't even loaded."

He said to the girl in the pink shirt, "Heather, may I have that, please?"

Beaming up at him, the girl strained to hold her heavy revolver up, holding it with both hands flat, as if it were an offering to the gods.

The man took the weapon as before, ejecting the clip and showing Gracie that it was empty. Slapping the clip back in place, he stuck the revolver in the waistband of his pants.

"We're in the national forest," Gracie said, her entire body shivering as if with cold. "I'm pretty damned sure kids aren't supposed to be out here carrying weapons, loaded or not, much less point them at people."

"We don't acknowledge the laws of the federal government," Lee said.

"We deny the rights of the federal government to exist," Jordan chimed in. "This is the people's land."

"Well, if it's the people's land," Gracie shot back, trying to keep her quivering voice from giving her away, "I'm one of the people, too, and you have no right . . . *no* right . . . to point a weapon at me."

"It's our right as Americans and patriots to bear arms," Jordan yelled. "As granted us by the Second Amendment of the United States Constitution. I'm willing to die to defend my Second Amendment rights. Are you willing to die trying to take them away from me?"

Gracie figured now was probably not the time to express the viewpoint that when the Founding Fathers constructed the Second Amendment to the Constitution to include "a well-regulated militia," they weren't talking about marauding gangs of children armed up the wazoo with AK-47s.

Her eyes moved back to the big man who was staring at her, head cocked, as if ciphering on something. "Don't I know you?" he asked.

"I think I would remember," Gracie growled.

"Why are you so hostile?

"Why? *Why?* How about going out for a peaceful run with my little dog on a fine morning and finding myself in the middle of the *Lord of the* Flippin' *Flies*? How about having a gun—multiple guns—pointed at me?"

"I showed you they weren't loaded," the man said in a mild voice. "You think we'd give loaded firearms to children?"

"How the hell do I know what you would and wouldn't do?" she snapped. She was so out of there she was already one of those little cartoon clouds with the whoosh marks off to the side. "Come on, Minnie." She backed up another step and turned to walk away.

"Grace Kinkaid."

Gracie stopped, mid-turn. "Wha . . . ?"

"Your name is Grace Kinkaid. You work up at that camp."

Gracie suddenly remembered exactly when and where she had met the big man before. Several months before. Up at camp. At the memorial service of a friend.

What was his name? An old-time cigarette brand. Pall Mall. Salem. Winston. That was it. Winston. Winston Ferguson. Baxter Edwards's Uncle Win.

Gracie remembered him, not only because he was larger than behemoth, but because he had introduced himself as her friend's fiancé when he had already been wearing a wedding band. And, she recalled, he had asked her, Gracie, if she was married.

Her eyes dropped to Winston's left hand, but he was wearing black tactical gloves.

"You were wearing a nice dress with a pretty paisley scarf," Winston continued, his tone conversational, as if they were shooting the breeze any old cloudy day. As if she weren't being stared down by a dozen pairs of eyes, most of which were looking like they wanted to have her as the main course at a wienie roast. "I remember because it's nice to see a beautiful woman wearing a nice dress."

"Uh . . ."

"What do you do there?"

"I'm . . ." Her voice cracked. She cleared her throat. ". . . the manager."

"That's a pretty big camp," Winston said. "What is it? Hundred acres? Hundred fifty?"

"Two hundred ten," Gracie answered automatically.

"Two-ten," Winston continued, standing casually on one leg, semiautomatic rifle cradled in his arms like an infant. "That's a lot of land. Anyway, I'm really sorry if we scared you. That wasn't our intent by any means. We're just playing around. That's why we come out pretty early in the day—try to avoid running into people. Don't want to scare anybody."

"I'm out of here," Gracie growled, spinning around and stalking away as quickly as she could with Minnie trotting at her heels.

"Nice to see you again, Grace," Winston said to her back.

BY THE TIME Gracie walked in through the front door of her cabin, the adrenaline had bled off, leaving her feeling as if she had been fed through the rollers of a wringer washer.

Except when she sat down on the couch in the living room, she stood up again. Sat down again. Jumped right back up and stormed back and forth across the wooden floor.

Minnie had given up trying to follow her around, hopping up onto her end of the couch and keeping an eye on Gracie from there.

"Those . . . those *Neanderthals*!" she raged. "How dare they point guns at me? Those . . . goon squad . . . wing nuts!"

Three times she picked up the telephone to call the Sheriff's

Department to report the incident. Three times she hung up the phone. The last time she had called to report someone's illegal behavior, that same someone had snuck onto her property and almost killed her dog. No way did she want to risk Minnie's life—or her own—again. "Forget about it, Kinkaid," she told herself. "Just don't jog out that way again."

But she couldn't just forget about it. In fact, she couldn't stop thinking about it, mentally gnawing on it over and over like a dog with a bone, the images of children with glaring eyes and semiautomatic weapons tumbling about in her head like ice cubes in a blender. The image of Baxter's face, pale, wide-eyed and afraid. He alone of the children hadn't pointed his weapon at her. Was he forced against his will to participate in these so-called trainings? Were these types of trainings one more reason for him to want to run away? She now, at least, had a better understanding of any antipathy Baxter harbored for the older boy, Jordan—he was a bully, mean and angry. *Whose son was he?* Gracie wondered. *Lee's?* No. Baxter had said the boy was a cousin. *So Winston's? Or someone else's?*

Was the group really only "playing around," as Winston put it, or were they up to no good? Was the group some kind of weird cult, or were they just normal run-of-the-mill American gun owners with nothing better to do on a Saturday morning? How serious would the fallout be if she made a report to the Sheriff's Department and it turned out to be nothing? Or if she didn't report it and it turned out to be something horrible?

"Ralphie, I wish I could talk to you. Ask your advice. You'd help me figure out what to do." She plopped down so hard onto the couch, she almost bounced Minnie right off. "Sorry, little girl," Gracie said, putting a hand out to soothe the dog. "No," she said, shaking her head. "Ralph wouldn't help me figure anything out. He would tell me not to jump to any conclusions. That I'm just being emotional. Not to let my imagination run away from me. Not to do anything impetuous. When the hell am I ever impetuous?"

Gracie put her feet up on the sea chest, dropping her head

back on the couch, trying to remember what she knew about Winston.

The winter before, her friend Jett had been dating Winston hot and heavy. Then, suddenly, she wasn't. With no real reason given except to say that he scared her.

Gracie sat up straight, plunking her feet onto the floor.

The journal!

She had forgotten all about it.

Jett had left Gracie a computer flash drive containing her journal, a sometimes excruciatingly detailed chronicle of her life, including at Camp Ponderosa where she worked as kitchen manager. After Jett's death, Gracie had handed the flash drive over to investigators. But not before copying the entire journal onto another flash drive of her own.

But where is it?

Deeming it too painful to read at the time, but vowing to retrieve it someday and read it all the way through, she had stashed it somewhere. But now she couldn't remember where.

She looked down at her watch. "Minnie!" she said, jumping to her feet and bounding up the stairs to the loft. "We're supposed to be at camp! Right now! Allen's gonna kill me!"

GRACIE LIFTED A large, square tray of chocolate sheet cake from a shelf in the walk-in refrigerator, backed out into the kitchen, and nudged the door closed with her hip. She set the tray on the butcher-block table, picked up a sharp knife, bit the upper corner of her lip, and began slicing the cake into long, narrow rows.

Allen stood at the huge stainless steel stove on Gracie's left, stirring a gigantic pot of spaghetti sauce. As always, he was dressed in a bright white T-shirt, blue jeans, and work boots. His long hair neatly braided and tucked up into the hairnet. His blue eyes were reflections of placidity, and even, Gracie decided, serenity.

"What?" Gracie said, without looking up.

"What do you mean, 'what'?" Allen asked.

"You're looking at me. I can feel your beady eyes on me."

"Can't I look at a beautiful woman with admiration and awe?"

Gracie shot him a look. "Baloney."

He chuckled. "Was wondering what's on your mind, sugar pea. You've been frowning ever since you got here. I'm concerned for the welfare of the cake."

Realizing he was right, Gracie tried to unfurrow her brow and concentrated on keeping her cuts parallel. "What do you think," she asked, "about people owning a lot of guns and spouting rhetoric about Second Amendment rights giving them the right to bear arms."

Allen stopped stirring and set the ladle down. He dipped into the pot with another spoon, took a sip of the sauce, then added a little pepper and garlic powder to the mix. "I think," he said finally, "that every Tom, Dick, and Jane owning a gun isn't really the problem. The problem is the few extrem ists who think it's their constitutionally guaranteed right to amass as many guns as they want without registering them. People have to register their cars. Have a license to drive. Hell, they have to have a license to pull a damn trout out of the lake. Why shouldn't they have to register or have a license to own a high-powered weapon?"

"What about people who don't think they have to obey the laws of the federal government?"

"These the same people who use the Constitution to avow their right to bear arms?"

Gracie looked up at Allen, who shrugged, picked up the ladle, and continued stirring. "Think about it, sweet pea. Can't have it both ways."

Gracie studied Allen for a moment, then asked, "You study to be a lawyer or something when you were in . . . ? When you were *in*."

"Nope. But I did find myself with quite a bit of time on my hands. Did a fair bit of reading."

Gracie finished her cut, turned the tray ninety degrees, and stopped again, knife poised to slice the cake in the other direction. Then she laid the knife down and walked over to a dry-erase board on the wall next to the dining room door. She picked up a red marker, and beneath a *To Buy* list with the single word *cinnamon* written beneath, drew a picture of the symbol she had seen carved into the tree stump, the diamond with legs with "88" beneath it. "Have you ever seen something like this?" she asked.

Setting the ladle down, Allen stepped over and stared at the picture, standing close enough that Gracie could smell his Old Spice aftershave. "Where did you see this?"

"Carved into a tree stump up the hill from my house. You know what it is?"

"Probably."

Seconds passed.

"Well?"

"I'm not exactly sure what the symbol is. But *H* is the eighth letter of the alphabet. Eighty-eight stands for HH."

"HH." Gracie stared at him, her face blank.

"The symbol is white supremacist," Allen said, his voice bland. "Neo-Nazi. HH stands for 'Heil Hitler.'"

CHAPTER

15

"IDIOTIC, high-powered-gun-toting, antigovernment whackos right in our nice little backyard, Minnie," Gracie complained to the dog, who lay on her bed next to her desk in the camp office. "Now neo-Nazis, too?" She rested her chin on her hand. "Or maybe they're all part of the same group. So much for living in paradise."

Gracie fired up the computer on her desk and did an Internet search for the diamond 88 symbol, starting with various combinations of *white supremacist*, *symbol*, and *diamond*. When nothing came up, she thought for a moment, started over and typed in *88 symbol hate*. One of the links listed was the Hate on Display page of the Anti-Defamation League's website. She clicked on the link and studied the page. On the right was a box for View Symbols by Category. She clicked on Neo-Nazi Symbols. The number 88 was at the top of the list. She scrolled down the list.

There it was: the diamond with legs.

The symbol was labeled the Othala Rune with a short explanation that, originally Norse, it had been adopted by

neo-Nazis and white supremacists to symbolize pride in
their Aryan heritage.

What were the odds that the Othala rune carved into the
tree stump was connected to Baxter's family? That not only
were they gun-toting extremists, but neo-Nazis as well?
"Better 'n two-to-one," Gracie whispered.

For the next half hour, Gracie sifted through the websites of
various groups—neo-Nazis, Aryan Brotherhood, skinheads—
all with one common theme: extreme rage and hatred.

Much to her consternation, she discovered a second anti–
federal government paramilitary group living in the Timber
Creek valley, south of the lake, not far from where Ralph
lived. And she learned that a chapter of the Ku Klux Klan
resided in one of the towns in the desert an hour's drive
down on the backside of the mountain. And multiple white
supremacist and neo-Nazi groups were spread out throughout the entire Inland Empire. A neo-Nazi rally was even
scheduled the following Friday in the desert community of
Desertview, a ninety-minute drive away.

Gracie sank back in the chair, feeling unsettled and on edge.

She had been living in blissful ignorance, with no idea
that, all around her, like a mythical leviathan lurking
beneath still, dark lake waters, groups of people existed for
no other reason than the annihilation of a particular group
of humanity. She had never imagined the extent or the sheer
variety of people and groups with so much hatred for and
the desire to kill others, based solely on race or religion or
sexual orientation or anything they believed was different
from themselves.

Fire required three components to burn: fuel, oxygen,
and heat. *Maybe that's what happens with some people*,
Gracie mused. Maybe the inferno that was hatred required
anger and fear in order to thrive. While some used logic and
knowledge and just plain goodness of heart to douse the
flames, others fed the blaze willingly, actively, enthusiasti-
cally, wanting to hate, wanting to hurt, wanting to kill.

Gracie simply couldn't fathom that level of hatred for anyone.

She sat up straight in her chair. "Yes, I can," she said aloud. "Morris."

If the blinding red mist of rage that obscured her vision whenever she thought about her stepfather wasn't hatred, it was the next closest thing to it.

"That's different," she snapped to the room, suddenly irritated and not quite sure why.

She tapped a fingertip on the desk for several seconds, then clicked on another website.

She scanned an article about a white supremacist who had murdered his sixteen-year-old babysitter by injecting her with heroin and methamphetamine. Pictures of the man showed him as frightening, glaring, with elaborate tattoos covering his entire body.

Gracie frowned.

The Edwards/Ferguson clan had tattoos. Lots of them.

Gracie started.

But so did Allen.

And Allen had known immediately what the symbol 88 meant.

Don't jump to conclusions, Kinkaid. She exited the site, leaned back in the chair, and rocked.

Lots of people had tattoos nowadays. It was way too much of a coincidence that Allen was a white supremacist working right there in camp. It might just mean Allen and the guy in the article had both spent time in prison. Or maybe they just both liked tattoos. And Allen might have seen the symbol in prison as well. Plus he seemed well-read, well-informed. Knowledge didn't equal guilt. Her labeling Allen a white supremacist simply because he and a white supremacist had multiple tattoos was like someone painting her a mass murderer because she and a mass murderer both liked to drink Coors Lite.

Allen a white supremacist was a ludicrous idea.

Wasn't it?

Gracie leaned forward once again, backed out of all the sites, and closed the browser altogether.

All this hatred was making her suspicious of someone she liked, darkening her mind, sapping her energy. "I need to do something else," she said, pushing away from the desk. "Something constructive. Something fun. Something outdoors."

BALANCING ON THE top step of an eight-foot ladder, Gracie rolled smooth lines of Nilla Vanilla paint along the front boards of the Gatehouse.

After the mad Labor Day rush, when camp had been bursting at the seams with families and church groups, the number of guests diminished to a less frantic, more manageable level and would remain so for the next six or so months of fall and winter. Now Gracie had time to catch her breath, actually learn the job for which she had been hired, and start on all the ideas and projects she had in mind for fixing up the camp, increasing its business, and improving its bottom line.

With the approaching winter, outdoor projects took precedence. Deciding the general air of seediness and neglect at the entrance to camp presented a poor welcome to incoming guests, Gracie had placed sprucing up the exterior of the Gatehouse at the top of the to-do list.

She mowed the small square of grass in front of the building with a push mower, relishing the strain on her muscles. Banging around in the maintenance shop, she had unearthed several cans of unopened paint. After pressure-washing the old and peeling yellow paint from the front of the building, she began painting the exterior walls the Nilla Vanilla, intending Calypso Blue on the trim and shutters.

There was something Zen-like in birds fluttering and chirping in nearby bushes and trees, the September air warm and soft, the afternoon sun on Gracie's shoulders and the backs of her bare legs. Physical work was the perfect antidote to thoughts of neo-Nazis and white supremacists and a fire raging down the hill. As Gracie painted, she hummed a little ditty to herself, aware of her mood lightening perceptibly.

The revving engine of a large vehicle engine climbing up to camp intruded on the peace. Gracie rolled the excess paint from her roller, then wrapped it in a plastic grocery bag to keep it from drying out.

She stepped off the ladder onto the grass just as a pickup truck roared up the final rise into view—a dark green Ford F-350.

Gracie went very still.

She had seen that same truck before, on the day Lee Edwards had tried to use his son as a punching bag.

She watched the pickup turn into a parking spot next to the Ranger and stop. The door opened and Winston Ferguson climbed out.

There was no time to hide, no time to pretend she wasn't there.

Winston had already seen her.

Gracie's eyes moved to where Minnie was lying in the shade, curled up on the mat before the front door At Winston's appearance, the dog had raised her head, tail swishing the sidewalk.

"Stay, Minnie," Gracie said, sidling over until she stood beside the dog, so that, if need be, she could grab her, jump inside the building, and lock the door.

Perhaps Gracie's trepidation revealed itself on her face or in her posture. Or perhaps Winston had a sixth sense for it. But, for whatever reason, the huge man stopped a non-threatening twenty feet away, and said in his characteristic high voice, "Hi, Grace."

Also nonthreatening was the pink Oxford, button down shirt he wore, perhaps, she thought cynically, for that very reason. The casual-day-at-the-office look was marred by steel-toed boots with red laces and a California Angels baseball cap. Winston's use of ball caps, sometimes incongruously, now made sense to Gracie. He used them to hide his shaved head in public.

She was reminded again how puny and weak and defenseless she felt in the face of such brawn. Being able to fend off any unwanted attack with a soggy paint roller didn't seem likely. Still, wanting to leave no mistake about exactly how she felt about seeing Winston again, Gracie lifted her chin, folded her arms in front of her, planted her feet apart another foot. Feeling like the boy shepherd in front of the giant Goliath, she asked, "What do you want?"

"Well, first, I want to apologize for barging in on your day unannounced. I don't suppose 'I was in the neighborhood and thought I would stop by' would fly." He smiled at her, showing surprisingly white, even teeth. The blue eyes with light, sloping eyebrows were soft, almost kind.

"Don't suppose it would," Gracie said.

"Well, to be honest, I wasn't in the neighborhood. I drove up here specifically to see if I could find you, talk to you."

"What do you want?" she asked again, having no trouble maintaining her stony glare.

"I wanted to say again how sorry I am for what happened this morning—for frightening you. I wanted to check on you. Make sure you're all right."

Don't get sucked in, Kinkaid. "I'm fine." She cocked her head. "You can go now."

Instead of being put off by her rudeness, Winston smiled again, this time wide and appealing, so disarming that Gracie almost shook her head in an attempt to retain her sanity and not succumb to the apparent remorse, the smile, the easy style, the kind eyes. This was, she reminded herself, the same man who might very possibly be a neo-Nazi, who most certainly allowed very small children to run around with semiautomatic weapons and point them at people, at her.

Winston's eyes slid over to Minnie "Is that your dog?"

"She's a trained killer," Gracie said.

Ears perked, Minnie wagged her tail as if begging to be noticed and petted.

Thanks, Minnie.

"She's cute." Winston glanced over at the ladder, the paint can, the half-painted front wall. "Sprucing things up a little? It looks nice. Makes a big difference. Good Christian people own this camp?"

"A church in L.A."

"Ah," he said, nodding his head. "Could you use a hand?" Without waiting for a reply, he rolled up his sleeves, crossed the lawn, picked up the hedge clippers lying on the grass, and began to trim back the shaggy yews in front of her office window.

Undecided, Gracie watched Winston. Then she shrugged. Why not?

Not wanting to work with her long, bare legs at Winston's eye level, Gracie moved the ladder to the other end of the building and started painting the Gatehouse wall from that end.

What would have taken Gracie an additional afternoon to complete took her and Winston three hours. With steady work, the big man's muscle, and minimal conversation—light and congenial for Winston's part, terse and clipped for Gracie's—they painted the rest of the front wall, as well as the window trim, gutters, and front door, installed a new front doorknob, trimmed the bushes, disposed of the clippings onto a new compost pile just outside the maintenance yard, pulled up the weeds in the sidewalk cracks, and returned the lawn mower and all the painting supplies to the shop.

Gracie stood at the far end of the front lawn, hands on hips, admiring how one afternoon's work had transformed the entrance of the camp from the dour grimace of Baba Yaga's hut into the cheerful welcoming smile of Snow White's little cottage in the woods.

She turned toward Winston, who was standing next to his truck. "Thanks for your help," she said, and almost stuck out her hand to shake his.

"You're welcome," Winston said with a nod. "I wondered . . ." He stopped, thrusting his hands deep into his pockets, scraping at little stones on the asphalt with his boot. "I wondered if you would honor me by having a cup of coffee with me sometime."

"Uhhh." Whatever she was expecting from Winston, it wasn't this. "Probably not a good idea."

"I didn't think so. But I figured there was no harm in asking." He smiled again. "In case I'm lucky enough for you to change your mind, here's my phone number." He reached through the driver's window of the F-350, grabbed up a piece of paper, tore off one corner and scribbled a phone number on it with a pen, walked over, and handed it to Gracie. "Call me anytime," he said, backing away again. "If you need help with something. Anything. I'm happy to come."

Winston climbed into the pickup and started the engine. He backed out of the space and, with a lift of his huge hand, drove out of camp.

As the cloud of dust drifted into the air and dissipated, Gracie ciphered on the walking conundrum that was Winston Edwards. Every time she had spoken with him, he had been polite, well mannered, almost deferential.

Yet, in spite of his kind eyes and easy smile, in spite of the good manners and benign temperament, there wasn't a doubt in her mind that she had just spent the afternoon tap-dancing with a Nile crocodile in a top hat.

Gracie had just turned off the computer in her office for the day when she heard another vehicle rumble up the dirt road and into camp. "Who's this now?" she wondered, pulling the front window curtain aside to peer outside. "I'm a busy woman. Got people to do. Things to see."

She watched as a red Jeep Wrangler convertible, the top

down, pulled into a parking space next to the Ranger, the same space Winston had vacated less than an hour before.

A man climbed down from the Jeep.

Gracie's mouth dropped open. A jolt of electricity traveled all the way down to her fingertips.

It was Rob.

CHAPTER
16

GRACIE sprinted up the hallway into the little bathroom. A glance in the mirror told her there was no hope. Fading bruises on her forehead and upper lip. Face devoid of makeup. Hair hastily caught up into a knot at the top of her head. She scraped tiny spots of Calypso Blue from her nose and chin with a stubby fingernail and did the old-fashioned thing by patting her cheeks to bring a little color into her face. She drew off the powder blue Camp Ponderosa sweatshirt she had turned inside out while painting, turned it right-side out, and hauled it back on. Not much she could do about the paint-spattered shorts.

Then with a sense of unreality, she walked through the outer reception area and out the front door.

Hands on his hips, Rob was standing next to the Jeep, looking around. Gracie noticed immediately that the hard "city" look had relaxed since the first time she had met him. Gone were the black pants and V-neck sweater. Gone were what she had dubbed butt-ugly roach-killer city shoes—black leather, over the ankle, alarmingly pointed. He was dressed now as any other stunningly gorgeous SoCal native going for an early autumn drive in the mountains—faded Levi's, blue, green, and white–striped rugby shirt, and sneakers. His hair shone like corn silk in the late afternoon sun. The only sign of extraordinary monetary wealth was the gold watch on his wrist.

Rob caught sight of Gracie walking down the front walkway and smiled, turning her legs into instant mashed potatoes.

He cut diagonally across the grass, put his hands on her upper arms, and kissed her on both cheeks, first the left, then the right. Nothing romantic. Nothing sexy. A kiss an acquaintance might give.

Or a brother.

Still, Rob's touch sent shock waves of electricity coursing through Gracie's body.

He smiled down at her with obvious affection and said, "Hi, twit. How are you?"

"Hi, dolt," she said, managing a tight smile in return. "Good. I'm good. What . . ." She swallowed, her mouth dry. "What . . . are you doing here?"

In an echo of the words Winston had spoken earlier that same afternoon, Rob said, "I was in the neighborhood."

Thumbs hooked in the back pockets of his jeans, Rob studied Gracie—her hair, her clothes, her face, the scrutiny making Gracie squirm. "Using the same makeup artist, I see," he said without smiling.

"I'm not . . . *what?*"

"The bruises on your face, love."

Love, Gracie thought, then reminded herself that Rob used the term of endearment frequently. It meant nothing, signified nothing. "And I see you're getting out of your cave once in a while." Ignoring Rob's look of consternation at her deliberate change of subject, she added, "The first time I saw you, you were the color of the down side of a right-side-up fish." She looked up into his face, trying to resurrect the smile. "Remember?"

He smiled then. "I remember."

"Your pants were soaked and Cashman gave you his pants to put on . . ." She knew she was chattering. "And you were hopping around on one foot . . ." She giggled at the memory. "Holy cow, were you white!"

He studied her face for a moment, brows merged into a line above the dark eyes. "Gracie, I—"

"Would you like . . ." she interrupted again. "I mean, can I . . . ?" She stopped. Everything she said sounded so stilted and formal. She cleared her throat and tried again. "Would you like to see around camp?"

"Love to," Rob said with a sigh. "I haven't given up, you know."

Pretending she didn't know what he meant, Gracie said, "The only group in camp is at dinner, so we shouldn't see anyone. Unless you need to eat. We could always . . ."

"No. I grabbed some take-away on the way up," he said. "Bloody awful. Tasted like cardboard."

"We have to walk," Gracie said. "That okay? No cars allowed past the main lodge."

"Of course. Lead on," Rob said with a dramatic sweep of his arm.

A brief introduction of Minnie to Rob resulted in instantaneous mutual adoration. With Rob holding Minnie's leash, they walked along the little road leading down from the Gatehouse, a modest two feet between them.

Like opposing magnets, Gracie thought.

In the cool shade of the cottonwoods, they strolled across the little creek.

"So, you're manager here now?" Rob asked.

"Interim manager, really."

"I know you're amazing and all, love, but wasn't that a fast ascendency?"

"It was. Good timing really. The previous manager . . ." She stopped, not wanting to relate the entire sordid tale of how she had acquired her job, then finished with, "left unexpectedly."

The two emerged back into the open between the Serrano Lodge parking lot and the rec field. They skipped a tour of the main lodge with the accompanying dinner crowd and continued in the dwindling daylight down the Main Road hill leading to the lower portion of camp, past two double-wide mobile homes, formerly employee lodging and now sitting empty.

As they walked, Gracie recovered from her initial shock of seeing Rob again. Her hands steadied. The horizon leveled. And the warm feeling in the pit of her stomach she felt whenever she was with Rob returned.

At the bottom of the Main Road hill, at the base of the driveway leading up to Mojave Lodge, Rob stopped, hands in pockets, studying an old wooden sign, painted brown, lettered in white. "What's this?"

"Names of movies filmed on the property."

His face lit up like a ray of sun emerging from behind storm clouds. "*The Trail of the Lonesome Pine* was filmed here?"

Gracie grinned at him. Once again, she had forgotten how Rob loved anything and everything to do with old American westerns.

"And *High Sierra*?"

Gracie studied the man examining the sign. The curling hair. The sparkling dark eyes. Heavy brows. Mouth curving up at the sides.

I'm in the right place when I'm with you, she thought. *On solid footing. At my best. Whole.*

This time there was no suffocating feeling of panic. No mental ping-pong game back and forth. No *What if this?* or *What if that?* No making excuses that it would never work. No dredging up of old hurts and rejections, telling herself she wasn't ready or that it was too soon.

I am all-in, she thought. *Full-body immersion. Heart and soul. In love with you.*

Then the champagne bubble of joy that had welled up inside burst as reality full-body-slammed into her.

He's engaged.

To someone else.

Gracie coughed to disguise an escaping sob.

Rob glanced over at her. "You okay, love?"

Gracie faked another cough, stepping back and turning away. "Yeah. Fine. Dust."

"I'll have to watch them all again," he said, eyes back on the sign. "Now that I've been here. Seen the camp."

"There are some rustic cabins up ahead there," Gracie said, gesturing farther down the road. "They were used for some segments of *Bonanza.*

"That's just brilliant!" he said. "I'm loving this!"

"They're used for storage. But I want to show you the team challenge course first. It's across here." Rob followed Gracie across a narrow wooden plank leading across a gully, rushing with water after a rain, but now dry and filled with fallen leaves and spent pine needles.

Standing among the tall pines on a soft, thick mat of shed needles, Gracie explained the purpose of each of the low-to-the-ground elements, designed for problem solving by teams of people, how each element was accomplished and its intended lesson.

Back out on the road, they walked past the three side-by-side single-wide trailers on the left, one occupied by twin sisters in housekeeping, one by Allen.

Gracie unlocked one of the rustic cabins, taking Minnie's leash, so that Rob could walk around inside, examine the thick logs and beams, and exclaim how it was "all-fired brilliant!"

Outside again, they stopped to drink out of the artesian well water by cupping their hands and catching the icy water as it gushed out of the ground. Then they continued alongside the lake and down the railroad tie steps to the high ropes course.

They stood on the mulch in the middle of the course, looking up to where thirty feet in the air cables stretched from tree to tree forming individual challenges. No need to mention that only a few months before, Gracie had almost been killed in a fall from the central belay cable fifty feet up. That sordid story could also wait for another time.

If, she reminded herself, *there is another time.* The full force of Rob's engagement hit her again and sadness almost overwhelmed her. She looked over at him standing next to an enormous ponderosa pine, head tipped back, scrutinizing the cables overhead.

The idea that she might never see Rob again hit her with a fresh shock that left her feeling chafed and raw. Never see those dark bright eyes. Never touch the soft hair. Never witness firsthand the brilliant smile. Or taste those soft lips. Or feel those hands—

Rob swung around toward Gracie, the golden smile at full wattage. "This is fantastic, Gracie." He walked up to where she stood in the middle of the mulch. "I got the numbers from The Sky's the Limit camp."

"Oh, yeah?" Suddenly anxious, she mentally hunched her shoulders, preparing for the bad news.

"Why are you getting all tense?"

Gracie had also forgotten how, as an actor, Rob was a student of mannerisms, inflection, body language. How he missed almost nothing.

"They were great, love," he said, bending to look into her face. "You did a fantastic job." He put his hands on her upper arms and kissed her cheek.

Again, very chaste. Very brotherly. Very irritating.

"Really," he said. "Fantastic. Thank you."

"You're welcome," Gracie said, turning away. No need for patting her cheeks to make them pink up. She could feel the hot flush travel up her neck and onto her face.

Gracie led Rob back up the railroad tie stairway, across the strip of sand that was the swim beach, and stood on the shore of Ponderosa Lake, the water a mirror, reflecting the opalescent sky, striped with long, dark tree shadows.

Minnie's ears perked as a pair of mallard ducks sailed in from the right, landed on the water with a faint splash, and paddled along the far shore, widening ripples in their wake.

"It's beautiful here," Rob said in a low voice, as if in reverence of the tranquility. "Stunning. I've been wanting to visit for months."

"You should have been here when the camp was full of kids. Your kids. It was awesome. They were awesome."

"Wish I could have," he said. "The summer was hellaciously busy. Seems like I haven't had a free afternoon for bloody months."

"I know the feeling," Gracie said. She studied his profile for a moment, aware that they were both stalling, both talking about anything and everything but . . . "Why are you here?"

Rob turned toward her. "Because . . ." He stopped.

Gracie closed her eyes, took in a breath and held it.

"I missed seeing you."

Gracie opened her eyes.

"Missed your down-to-earthness. Your sanity."

"I wouldn't go that far . . ."

"You ground me, Gracie. Keep me focused on what's really important in life."

"Okay, so if that's true . . ."

"Isn't that enough?"

"No. I . . . Yes. I mean . . ." She shook her head. "Never mind."

Rob took her hand. "Can we sit somewhere? Please?"

She gestured to a bench several feet away at the edge of the water. They walked over and sat down, Minnie lying in the sand at their feet.

Rob leaned forward with his elbows on his knees, hands clasped, looking out over the lake. "I wanted to see you," he said. "That's why I drove up today."

"Long drive."

"Awful, disgusting traffic."

"I might not have been here. Why didn't you let me know you were coming?"

He straightened. "I called."

"No, you didn't."

"Yes, I did. I left a message on your cell."

"Oh. Oops. Sorry. Forgot to check."

"When you didn't answer or return my call . . . as usual, I might add."

"Sorry. I've had . . . things . . . going on." The excuse faded away.

"I figured I'd drive up anyway. Take a chance. I wanted to . . . I . . . Before I . . ." He blew out a breath, running a hand through his hair and making it stick up in the back.

Gracie almost smiled. A global superstar tongue-tied. And vulnerable. One of the reasons she loved him.

"I wanted to see you," he said again. "Talk with you. Spend time with you. I haven't seen you since . . ." He sat up. "The last time I saw you, you bolted."

"I had to get back."

"You left without a bloody word, didn't you?"

"Yes. That I did do." And she was paying for it now. Bigtime.

Rob settled elbows on knees and looked over the water again. "I just wanted to sit and talk with you. For a little while." Then he reached out and took Gracie's hand. "If that's okay."

"I'd like that," Gracie said.

As the daylight waned, drawing in the exquisite mantle of stars and darkness along with an occasional mosquito, Gracie and Rob sat on the little bench overlooking Ponderosa Lake and talked. About what they had been doing over the past months, about the search for Baxter Edwards and Gracie's growing affection for the boy, about Rob's newest movie, a dark and brooding action-thriller taking place in the mean streets of Los Angeles.

Throughout, Gracie never mentioned the nightmare that was growing around her. And Rob never mentioned his impending marriage. Both, Gracie figured, holding on to the warmth and peace of the moment.

Finally, when Gracie shivered with cold, they had walked hand in hand back up to the Gatehouse. Rob had kissed her once, warm, soft, on the mouth, then climbed into the Jeep,

The internal warmth, the tingle of his lips on hers, and the swallowing hole of sadness that threatened to engulf her lasted all the way down Cedar Mill Road across town to her cabin.

WHEN GRACIE AND her dog walked through the front door of the cabin, the phone on the kitchen counter was ringing.

Gracie walked into the kitchen, set her pack on the chair, and checked the caller ID. *Timber Creek, CA.*

She stood with shoulders hunched and fists clenched on the counter, head bent, listening to her own succinct message asking callers to leave a name and number and she would return the call as soon as possible.

The beep.

The shriek of a whistle pierced the kitchen.

Even though she was prepared, the sound sent an icicle of adrenaline right down to Gracie's feet.

But instead of slapping the machine off, she stepped back, clapping her hands over her ears.

For two minutes, the whistle blasted, interrupted only by short silences when, Gracie assumed, the caller ran out of breath and stopped blowing the whistle to take in another.

Another beep.

The cabin was plunged into silence.

Gracie's hands were shaking. Her heart was pounding a timpani in her chest.

The first call hadn't been a prank, placed at random. A second call had obliterated that possibility. She was being targeted, deliberately, maliciously.

The first call had been a man's voice. The second a whistle.

Could it be someone from the Edwards clan? The little girl Heather had blown a whistle. But whistles were as easy to come by as five minutes at the local Kmart. There were plenty of men in the Edwards family. But, she recalled, thinking back, the first call had come before she was really involved with them.

Were the calls a warning of some kind? Or was someone simply trying to scare her?

If that was the case, it was working.

Gracie shot around the kitchen, letting down the window blinds, drawing the curtains closed. She stepped into the mudroom, pulled down the window shade on the door, locked the knob and dead bolt. Locked the front doorknob and dead bolt. Jogged into the living room, letting down blinds, closing curtains. Locked the sliding glass door in the living room. Laid a trekking pole inside along the bottom, so it couldn't be opened from the outside. Let down the blinds.

Then, with a second trekking pole clenched in her hand, she turned off the living room light, climbed up the stairs to the loft, and stretched down on her bed, fully clothed, pole on the floor beside her.

She lay in the darkness, listening to the sounds of the night. Every creak of the old cabin was a man stepping up onto the porch outside, every squeak of a tree branch fingernails scraping down glass.

CHAPTER

17

GRACIE'S eyes flared open in the darkness. She glanced over at the clock on the little table next to the bed. Giant red numbers read 1:17 a.m.

Two hours after lying down, she had finally fallen asleep. *So why am I awake?*

She reached out and felt for Minnie. But instead of being curled up into a black Jelly Belly on her bed next to Gracie's, the dog was sitting up at full alert.

Her hand slid off the side of the bed. Fingers closed around the cool metal of the trekking pole.

She listened, straining to hear again whatever it was that might have awakened her.

Nothing.

Her eyes moved across the ceiling to the little west-facing window.

Gracie kicked free of the sheets and hurtled from the bed. She fell to her knees in front of the window and looked outside.

Through the tree branches on the hillside below, an orange light shifted.

Fire!

Fear flared down her body to her feet.

Her worst nightmare—a fire downhill from her cabin.

Lunging to her feet, Gracie grabbed up the phone from the bedside table and dialed 911. She waited for what seemed like an infinity for a dispatcher to answer, rattled off her name and address, and reported what looked like a structure fire down the hill from her.

She depressed the receiver. Let it up. Dialed the number of her neighbor across the street. Counted off the rings. Eight. Nine. She hung up.

With Minnie right behind, she clumped down the stairs to the first floor, stuffed her laptop into her backpack, and slung it over a shoulder. Hauling SAR shirt and pants off the hanger in the mudroom, she grabbed up a fleece jacket from a hook next to the door and ran outside to the truck.

She flung the passenger's door open. "Minnie! Inside!" The dog sailed in. Gracie dumped her armload on the seat, slammed the door, ran around the front of the truck, threw herself into the driver's seat, and screeched back down the highway. As she raced past, she double-checked her neighbor's house for telltale signs of life. The house was dark.

The truck rocketed down the curving street. At the bottom, Gracie stood on the brakes and squealed to a stop.

In the middle of the block, a house was burning, flames illuminating the front window like a single demon's eye.

Oh, God!

The burning house was John and Vivian's.

The Robinsons' blue Subaru was parked in the carport. The family was still inside.

ONLY WHEN GRACIE erupted from the truck did she see Acacia, standing alone in the middle of the street, fingertips to her mouth, eyes saucer wide and focused on the flames, tears streaming down her cheeks.

Gracie ran up to the girl. "Acacia! Are you hurt? Are you burned anywhere?"

A shake of the head.

In the distance, sirens and air horns blasted.

"Where's Nana and Oompah?"

Acacia pointed toward the house.

Without another word, Gracie swept the girl, light as a feather, up into her arms. She half ran back to the Ranger and set her on the passenger's seat. Then she dove back behind the wheel, jammed the truck into Reverse, floored the accelerator, screeched backward fifteen feet, slammed it into Drive, and careened around the corner onto the adjoining street, out of the way of fire trucks, away from the smoke, and, if need be, ready for a fast getaway. She slammed to a stop and jammed it into Park, leaving the engine running.

"Acacia, you stay here with Minnie." Gracie pulled a blanket from behind the seat, shook it out, and tucked it around the girl. "You keep each other warm."

From a stuff sack in the truck bed, Gracie pulled fire-retardant Nomex pants and jacket, stiff, leather gloves stuffed in the pockets. Standing in the street, oblivious to the curious stares of neighbors drawn from their houses by the commotion, she hauled the oversized pants on over her shorts, taking ten precious seconds to lace up her boots. The Nomex jacket she threw on over her sweatshirt. She clipped her climbing helmet on her head and hauled on the leather gloves as she ran back up the street and rounded the corner onto Arcturus.

Flames inside the bungalow bathed the front yard in hell's red glow. Smoke, thick and gray, billowed up into the night sky. The tops of surrounding pines swayed and flickered with reflected light.

Gracie dropped down into the yard and ran along the side of the house, through the gate in the fence, and around back, dark and untouched by the fire.

Drawing off a glove, she tested the knob of the back door

with a bare hand. Cool, but locked. She pounded on the door with her fist. "John! Vivian!"

No sound. No movement. No sign of life from inside the house. Adrenaline banged a bass drum in Gracie's ears.

Drawing the glove back on, she turned and aimed an elbow at the door window. Hesitated. Introducing more oxygen into the house would feed the flames. But there was no other way. She banged an elbow against the glass.

It didn't break. But it did hurt like hell. "Dammit!"

She stepped back, grabbed on to the porch railing, and kicked the door window with her boot. The glass spiderwebbed. She kicked again. The window shattered. She thrust her hand through the hole, unlocked the door, and burst into the kitchen.

At the far end of the hallway, the living room was a brilliant furnace. Heavy smoke, acrid, suffocating, curled and writhed around the ceiling like a living being.

Gracie dropped to a crouch and yelled, "Vivian! John!" No response.

Drawing a cotton handkerchief from a jacket pocket, she tied it bandit-style over her mouth and nose. "Vivian! John!"

Then she heard it. Faint. Muffled. "Help!"

"John!" Crunching on broken glass, Gracie dropped onto hands and knees and crawled across the kitchen vinyl, up the hallway, and into the first room on the left.

Vivian was lying in a heap on the floor next to the bed. On his knees beside her, John was trying to lift his unconscious wife into her wheelchair.

Gracie flew across the floor. "Forget the wheelchair!" she yelled. "No time! We have to get her out of here!" She hauled the quilt off the bed and laid it out on the floor next to Vivian. "Straighten her legs!" Together they straightened the woman's body, then, with Gracie pulling and John pushing, rolled her onto the quilt, throwing the corners around her.

The smoke was descending from the ceiling, thicker,

more lethal. Gracie's eyes teared. She could barely see. Throat and lungs burned, feeling as if hands were squeezing them closed. She coughed, barely able to draw in a breath.

John's breath was coming in ragged gasps.

The wail of a fire engine's siren wound down on the street in front of the house.

Grabbing the quilt in her fists, Gracie thrust herself backward, the heavy tread of her boots gripping the floor. Quilt and Nomex pants slid along the slick hardwood. She lost her grip. Fell back. Elbowed her way up off the floor. Regained a handhold. Feet flat, she pushed off again.

John wormed along the floor after, shoving his wife's inert form with his shoulder, pushing off with bare feet from the bedside table, the wall, the doorjamb.

Together, Gracie and John hauled the unconscious woman out of the room, down the short hallway, through the kitchen to the back door.

There they lifted the blanket and carried Vivian out of the door into fresh air. Between hoarse, painful coughs, Gracie gasped in huge inhalations of sweet air as she backed down the steps and out onto the yard.

Laying her end of Vivian's unconscious body carefully on the ground, she stumbled around the corner of the house. Through the open gate, she saw a firefighter running alongside the house toward the back, dressed head to toe in firefighting gear, yellow helmet, an axe over a shoulder. "We need an ambulance!" she croaked, her scorched throat raw. "Notify Flight for Life!"

WITH HAIR STILL wet from a shower to rid her body of the nauseating smell of smoke, Gracie lay on her bed, one hand resting lightly on the soft fur of Minnie's back. A blacksmith's hammer pounded an anvil inside her head. Her eyes stung. Her throat and lungs burned.

Chaotic memories wheeling in her mind's eye were

keeping sleep at bay. Sirens wailing, air horns blasting, the choking smell of smoke mixed with diesel, tangerine flames crackling against the night sky, emergency lights throbbing blue, red, and white, the chug of idling fire trucks, the shouts of firefighters, muted voices over radios, glass breaking, the whoosh of spraying water.

The single unforgettable mental snapshot of John holding his granddaughter's hand, a bent, frail figure, ashen, watching the paramedics lift his wife's stretcher into the back of the ambulance.

And the final enormous crash of the bungalow's roof caving in, blasting curls of smoke and sparks into the darkness overhead.

Gracie closed her eyes. Opened them again. Looked at the clock. Twenty-four minutes after two. Closed her eyes. Opened them again. Looked at the clock. Two minutes after three.

Three fifteen.

Three forty-one.

Four oh two.

At five thirteen, certain she hadn't slept a single second, she pushed back the covers and dragged on jeans and a sweatshirt. Eyes propped open by the panda mug of Folgers Instant, she drove down to the bottom of the Arcturus hill.

A pink ribbon along the eastern horizon heralded the dawn. One by one, birds hidden among the tree branches began their morning conversations.

Standing on the road uphill from the blackened exoskeleton of cinder block—all that remained of the Robinsons' delightful home—Gracie watched bleary-eyed firefighters roll up huge fire hoses and pick through the still-smoking rubble, her mind dark with thoughts of anger, hatred, and prejudice, and the torching of the house of an elderly black couple.

CHAPTER

18

THE knife sliced through the latex glove and deep into Gracie's index finger. Brain barely registering the pain, she stared with detached fascination at the bright red drops of blood oozing through the slit in the blue latex and splatting onto the butcher-block table in the camp kitchen.

"What the hell?" Allen yelled, jumping over and grabbing her finger with a wadded-up paper towel. He led her over to the sink and held her hand under an icy stream of water.

Gracie stood mute, passive, as Allen hauled off the glove, daubed antibiotic cream on the cut, and wrapped the finger tightly with gauze and white medical tape. Then he handed her another glove and three heads of iceberg lettuce with instructions to tear it up with her hands and make the lunch salad. Anything requiring sharp implements he would handle.

Eyebrows merged into a frown, Gracie sat on the three-legged stool, ripping the lettuce apart with nine fingers and dropping the shredded portions into a giant stainless steel bowl. Throwing to the wind her suspicions of Allen as a white supremacist, she said, "Allen, can I ask you something?"

The head cook was arranging mini-boxes of breakfast cereal onto a giant tray. "Fire away, sweet cheeks," he said.

"Where does racial prejudice come from? I'm not talking the casual, fleeting, surface kind. I'm talking the deep-seated hatred with a capital *H* kind. Where do you think that comes from?"

"A bright, cheerful topic."

"People aren't born that way," Gracie pressed. "It's learned. Taught. But how does such deep-seated hatred begin? And how does it get so bad that you're willing to kill for it? "

"Well, I—"

"Way back when, when I lived in Detroit, I used to work in advertising . . ."

"Back in the Stone Age?"

"I worked with all kinds of people. It didn't matter what their politics or religious beliefs were. What mattered was whether they were good at their jobs, if they were competent. Mostly what mattered was whether they were good people or not."

"Hold that thought," Allen said. He picked up the tray of cereal and backed through the swinging door leading out to the dining hall. Reappearing seconds later, he walked over to the stove, picked up a ladle, and stirred a giant steaming pot of oatmeal.

Shredding the lettuce again, Gracie picked up her thread of thought. "I've witnessed racial discrimination and hatred directed at others. Studied about religious persecution. Watched it on TV and movies. But, since living in Timber Creek, for the most part, except for the male chauvinist jerk wienies in the Sheriff's Department, I've had the luxury of living my life as if that type of hatred doesn't exist, certainly without it directed at me or affecting me personally."

"Until now?" Allen asked.

"I'm not sure," she answered. "People seem to fear and hate entire races, religions, or classes of people they've never even met, or know anything about." She looked down at the lettuce lying limply in her hands and began shredding again and dropping the pieces into the bowl. "I don't get that."

She sighed and looked up.

Allen was standing on the opposite side of the butcher-block table watching her.

"That's all," she said with a shrug. "I've just never thought about it before." For some reason, she felt compelled to say, "Thanks."

"Glad I could be of help, gumdrop," Allen said and winked.

WITH A JERK, Gracie awoke from a deep, dreamless sleep and stared up at a flat ceiling of pine wood. *Where the hell am I?* She turned her head and looked at a bare white wall. Three feet up from the floor was the hem of a heavy green and gold curtain. She looked back over her head at a beige metal desk.

"Oh, yeah," she said. "Now I remember." She was in her office, lying on her sleeping bag.

While helping Allen serve breakfast to the church group, Gracie had dropped a full container of newly washed forks with a splendid crash. A minute later, she dropped an entire jar of salsa, the glass smashing into a million pieces, diced tomato and green pepper splattering the prep table, stainless steel serving counter, and Allen's bright white T-shirt, after which he had growled, "Get out of my kitchen. Go catch some z's somewhere. Forward the damn phones down here."

Gracie had stumbled down the back hallway right past where Minnie lay on her bed in the back closet, Allen calling after her, "And don't worry about Minnie." As she pushed through the back screen door, she might have heard him grumble, "She's safer here with me anyway."

Still groggy from a three-hour coma-like sleep and a pillow crease in her cheek the depth of the Grand Canyon, Gracie staggered to her feet and padded barefoot up the carpeted hallway to the kitchen.

She filled a camp mug with cold coffee and stuck it in the microwave for a minute.

Brushing her hair back from her face with a wrist, she leaned on the counter and looked out the window above the sink.

A misty shroud hung over the tops of the trees.

Not mist.

Smoke.

In an instant, Gracie was wide-awake.

She ran to the front door, threw it open, stepped outside, and pulled in a deep breath.

The smell of wood smoke filled her nostrils.

Had the Shady Oak Fire raced up Santa Anita Canyon and entered the valley while she was sleeping? Or was it simply a shift in the wind, pushing the smoke up and over the mountain?

She yanked her pager off her waistband and peered at the minuscule screen. No page.

Back inside the Gatehouse, she jogged from room to room, closing and sealing every window by locking it. Her throat and lungs still hurt from the night before. She didn't need to be breathing in any more smoke.

She grabbed up the telephone in her office and punched in the three-digit extension for the kitchen.

It had barely finished its first ring before Allen answered. "What the hell have you been doing?" he hissed. "I've been calling you every other minute. All I got was a busy signal." It was the first time Gracie had heard the man sounding anything remotely akin to rattled.

"I've been sleeping," she answered. "I forwarded calls down to the kitchen. As you so ordered. When you called, you were basically calling yourself. That's why you got a busy signal."

A pause. "Oh. Well, Mr. Jackson from the Baptist church has been here in the dining hall for the last hour, all in a fussbudgetyflibbertigibbetytizzy. He's bordering on panic about the smoke, making noise about pulling the whole group out."

"Have you heard anything?" Gracie asked. "Is the smoke from down the hill or is the fire in the valley?"

"That's why I keep the radio tuned to the local station, insipid music as it plays. It's a wind shift. Still no imminent danger to the valley."

"Okay, good" Gracie said, blowing out the breath she hadn't realized she had been holding. "Give Mr. Jackson a cup of coffee and a piece of cake and tell him I'll be there in a few minutes to talk to him." She started to hang up, stopped, and said, "Tell him to have everyone close every window in their rooms. Keep out the smoke. It might get worse before it gets better."

"Already done," Allen said and disconnected.

Gracie hung up the phone, leaned back in the chair, and blew out another long breath of relief. Just a bad wind day. *Hopefully*, she thought, *this is as bad as it gets.*

GRACIE SNAPPED ON the light in the kitchen of her cabin, opened the refrigerator, and examined its meager contents. "Shopping list," she said to herself. "Buy everything." She lifted the last can of Coors Light from the shelf and let the door swing closed. She was popping the can open when a knock on the front door made her jump.

Minnie barked and hopped up from her little bed next to the door.

Gracie set the beer down on the counter and waited.

Another knock.

Minnie barked again.

"Shhh, Minnie," she whispered as she grabbed up one of her trekking poles leaning in the corner.

The dog sat down and stared intently at the bottom of the door.

Gracie leaned over and glanced out the side window.

Then, replacing the trekking pole and blocking Minnie's way with her leg, she pulled the door open a dozen inches and slid outside.

Baxter stood on the deck, a picture of pain and dejection. Arms hung limply at his sides, a book Gracie had loaned him in each hand. Shoulders hunched. Tears glistened on his cheeks. "'Cacia's house is gone," he said, voice wavering.

"I know," Gracie said.

"It . . . it burned down."

"I know."

"What . . . what happened?"

"You don't know what happened?"

He shook his head. "No."

Gracie studied the boy's face, hating the suspicion, the anger. Hating that she didn't really believe him.

"Is 'Cacia okay?" he asked.

"Yes. Well, at least physically she is. Her gran's not doing well. She was hurt. Smoke inhalation. They took her away in an ambulance. Probably flew her in a helicopter to the hospital down the hill."

"Do you know where 'Cacia is?"

"No, I don't."

"I feel really bad," Baxter said, bottom lip quivering.

"So do I."

"I liked their little house. It was nice and clean inside. You could see things." He looked down at his feet, then back up at Gracie. "Can I come inside, Gracie?"

"I don't think that's a good idea," she answered slowly. "In fact, I think it's best if you don't come here anymore."

Baxter looked as utterly stricken as if she had slapped him across the face. "But . . . why?"

"I don't like the idea of children with guns. I especially don't like the idea of children . . . or anyone for that matter . . . pointing guns at me."

Fresh tears filled his eyes and slid unheeded down his face. "I'm sorry, Gracie," he said with a sob. He hugged the books to his chest. "I'm sorry. I don't want to do it. I hate doing it. But they make me."

Gracie's steely will was crumbling. "Who makes you, Bax?"

"My dad. My grandpop. My uncle Win." He hung his head. "I'm so sorry, Gracie. Don't . . . make me go away. Please don't make me go away." He hiccoughed in a breath. "You're my only friend."

"What about your gran?"

"She's okay, but she . . . hugs me too much. And worries all the time. She's always crying. She's not like you."

Gracie looked at him several more seconds, then said in a quiet voice, "Okay, Bax." She crouched down and put her arms around him. "You can stay. I'm still your friend." He clung to her like a limpet, sobbing as if he was carrying the world's cares and sorrows on his thin shoulders, which, Gracie realized, in many ways he was.

CHAPTER

19

GRACIE and Baxter sat in chairs on the west-facing deck of the cabin. While the tang of smoke still clung to the air, a late-afternoon shift in the wind had blown the smoke from the Shady Oak Fire directly south, clearing the valley of most of the haze, revealing the mountains and a cloudless sky.

In companionable silence, they watched the sun drop to the horizon, a brilliant ball of orange fire against a pink sky.

"It looks so red because of the residual smoke in the air," Gracie said.

The sun shrank to half an orb, a dot of flame, then winked out.

"That was cool, Gracie," Baxter said. "We can't see the sun set from—"

Beep! Beep! Beep!

"Uh-oh," Gracie said, sliding her pager off the waistband of her sweatpants.

"What's that?" Baxter asked.

"Search and Rescue pager." Gracie read the minuscule screen.

"What does it say?"

"The Sheriff's Department has issued a non-mandatory evacuation."

"What does that mean?"

"It means they're advising people to leave the valley because of the Shady Oak Fire."

"It's coming up here?" Gracie could hear the fear in his voice.

"No. This is a just-in-case. It means people should leave if they want to. And everyone else should get ready to evacuate. Pack up their stuff and be ready to leave at a moment's notice. They've put Search and Rescue on standby. That means we get ready in case the evacuation order becomes mandatory. We help with that. Try to get things organized a little bit so there's not mass chaos as people are leaving." She clipped the pager back onto the waistband of her pants. "I have to go to a meeting first thing in the morning about it."

"I heard my dad and Uncle Win talking . . ." Baxter said.

"That seems to happen a lot."

"I like to know what's going on. They never pay attention to me."

"Useful sometimes."

"We're not leaving."

"What?"

"If there's a fire. We're not going to leave."

"That's your . . . or your parents' prerogative," Gracie said, while at the same time thinking, *That's stupid. Asinine. Irresponsible.* Adults could make those decisions for themselves, but not evacuating children needlessly put innocent lives at risk, not to mention the lives of rescuers.

"Grandpop Martin says there's no fire. It's a government 'spiracy to get us to leave the property so they can take it over. He says anyone sets foot on our land, anyone tries to make us leave, they're going to shoot 'em. I know there's really a fire, but we'll be safe. If the fire comes, we'll go to the bunker."

"You have a bunker?"

"Uh-huh." The brown eyes had regained their sparkle. "It's really cool. There are beds and a bathroom and a kitchen with food and everything. Under the ground."

"Really? I thought it was solid rock there."

"They built it on the side of the hill. Then they covered it up with dirt."

"Must have taken a long time."

"They're always building on it. For as long as I can remember."

Not that it was remotely her business, but Gracie asked, "That must take a lot of money. How can they afford all that?"

"Oh, my grandpop gets his disability check every month."

"Why's he on disability?"

"He got shot in Vietnam. He only has one leg. He's in a wheelchair."

Before Gracie could adequately process that information, Baxter added, "All the parents work. But don't worry. The older kids take care of the younger kids when they're gone."

"Where do they work?"

"Um, my dad and Uncle Win work construction. Mom Brianna works part-time at the grocery store. Mom Michelle works at a bank. Mom Angela works in an office. She's a secretary or something like that."

"You call all of them *Mom*?"

"Mom Brianna is my real mom. The others aren't my real moms. They're just married to my dad. We just call 'em Mom Brianna, Mom Angela, like that, to keep 'em straight."

"So your dad . . . uh . . . so . . ." Gracie cleared her throat. "How many wives does he have?"

"Three."

"Three. And your uncle Win? How many wives does he have?"

"Two."

"And those are what? Your aunts?"

"Yup. Auntie Jennifer. Auntie Kimberly. Auntie Kimberly's my dad's sister."

"And what about your grandpop? How many wives does he have?"

"Just one besides Gran Sharon."

"I see. And what does your gran Sharon think about that?"

"She left Grandpop."

"I don't blame her. How many kids live there . . . in the compound?"

"Um . . ." Baxter thought, tapping his chin with a finger. "Maybe twelve. Thirteen. Something like that."

"So Jordan is your cousin?"

"Yeah."

Gracie thought for a moment, then said, "At the training the other day, there were other people there—other men. Do they live at the compound, too?

"Some of them do. But not all of them. They just come with us when there's a training."

"And what are they training for?"

"I don't know," he said, raising a shoulder. "We just train."

"Are they planning something?"

"I don't know."

"Oh, come on, Bax. This is your family."

He threw his hands out, palms up. "I don't know anything. I haven't been initiated yet."

"Initiated. What does that mean?"

"When the boys turn fifteen, we're initiated. That's when I'll find out all kinds of stuff."

"And what's involved in this initiation? What will you have to do?"

"I don't know that I have to *do* anything. I get a badge of honor though."

"Badge of honor. What's that?"

"A tattoo."

"What kind of a tattoo?"

"A tear. Right here." He pointed to the outer corner of his left eye.

"That boy, that young man, Jordan," Gracie said. "He

had something at the corner of his eye. I couldn't see it because I was too far away. Was it a teardrop tattoo? Was that his badge of honor?"

He nodded. "His birthday was in May, but he only got the tattoo a few weeks ago. I dunno why."

"What does the teardrop signify?"

"I dunno. There're some other ones, too. There's this one . . ." He scrunched up his face. "I can't really describe it."

"Can you draw a picture?"

"Okay."

"Come on. Let's go inside."

In the kitchen, Baxter sat down at the table. Gracie grabbed a piece of paper and pencil from next to the telephone, slid them in front of the boy, and sat down in the chair opposite.

Tongue showing at the corner of his mouth, Baxter carefully drew a picture, then he turned the paper around and pushed it across the table in front of Gracie.

She looked down, her breath catching. The symbol was one she had seen on the Anti-Defamation League's Hate on Display page. "It looks like part of a peace sign," she said. "Upside down. Without the circle."

"What's a peace sign?"

Gracie picked up the pencil and drew the peace symbol.

"Yeah," Baxter agreed. "It does look kinda like that."

"But you don't know what it means?"

Baxter shook his head, then said, "There's another one."

Gracie slid the paper back in front of him.

Baxter started drawing. "Wait." He scribbled it out. He tried again, but scribbled that out, too. "I can't get it. It looks like a spider web. They get that on their elbow."

Gracie took the pencil from his hand and drew the diamond with legs with the 88 beneath. "Have you ever seen one that looks like this?"

Baxter slid the picture so that it was in front of him. He stared down at the picture, unmoving.

"Bax? Do you recognize it?"

"Yeah. I have that one."

"You do?"

He stood up and, with both hands, grabbed the bottom of his black T-shirt and lifted it completely off his head.

Then he turned away from Gracie, pointing over his shoulder to his back. "See? Right there."

Between the boy's shoulder blades was a small tattoo of the diamond with legs with the numbers 88 below. But instead of fixing on the symbol, Gracie's eyes were locked on black and yellow splotches covering Baxter's back and ribs—a mass of fading bruises. "Bax," she breathed. "What happened to you?"

"It's just a tattoo."

"No. Those are bruises."

"Oh," Baxter said, turning around again and donning his T-shirt. "That was Jordan. He got mad and hit me."

He slid back onto his chair, hands in his lap, eyes lowered.

Gracie sank down into the chair opposite, staring at the bent head. She reached out to smooth the blond hair, but stopped and withdrew her hand. "Bax?"

"Yeah?"

"Have you told anyone about this, shown anyone this . . . what he did?"

The slightest shake of the blond head.

"Not even Grandma Sharon?"

Another shake of the head.

"Baxter, I have to report this," she said in a gentle voice. "I have to call Child and Family Services."

The boy's head snapped up, his eyes as round as full moons behind the heavy-rimmed glasses. "No!" he yelled. He jumped to his feet, shoving the chair back so hard it tipped backward, banged against the wall, and stayed there. "You can't tell! He'll do things! He'll hurt her!"

Gracie managed to find her voice. "Who will he hurt?"

"Swear you won't tell anybody! You have to swear!"

"Sit down, Bax."

The boy stayed where he was, fists clenched, body trembling. "Swear!"

"Okay. Okay, I swear I won't tell anybody. For now at least. Sit down, Bax."

The boy righted his chair and sat back down, hands hanging on either side of the chair, head bent.

"Why don't you want me to tell anyone?"

"Jordan said he'll hurt Grandma Sharon." His eyes flicked up to hers, then back down again. "He likes to burn things. He said he would burn her house down." He stopped, motionless in his chair. Then he looked up at Gracie and said, "I think he might have burned down 'Cacia's house."

CHAPTER

20

"He likes to burn things," Baxter had said about his fifteen-year-old cousin.

Gracie sat in one of the ladder-backed chairs, elbows on the kitchen table, head in her hands, stomach roiling like a witch's brew.

It was late, almost eleven o'clock. She should be in bed and asleep. Not only did she need to be at the SO at eight o'clock the next morning, she needed to be something resembling coherent.

But she knew she wouldn't be able to fall asleep.

At least not yet.

She pushed herself to her feet, poured herself a tumbler of skim milk, stirred in a tablespoon of baking soda, downed the concoction in three gulps, set the glass in the sink, and sat back down at the table to think about the boy/man with the angry eyes who, with the cool aplomb of a trained killer, had pointed a semiautomatic weapon at her.

Who had beaten his younger cousin black-and-blue.

Who had threatened to burn down his own grandmother's house.

What else was Jordan capable of?

Burning down the Robinsons' home?

Somehow—*somehow*—she had to find out.

First though, infinitely more important, she needed to facilitate the removal of Baxter from his abusive family.

Calling the county's Child and Family Services was the most obvious solution to that problem.

But she had sworn to Baxter, for the time being at least, that she wouldn't tell anyone.

Plus, the last time she had contacted the social services agency, she had almost lost her beloved dog.

She looked over to where Minnie was curled up and sleeping peacefully on her little round bed in the corner of the kitchen.

Was she willing to risk Minnie's life again? Or Sharon's? Possibly even Baxter's?

She couldn't *not* risk it. She wouldn't . . . couldn't . . . honor her promise to the boy. She had a moral obligation to report the physical abuse of a child.

No, she decided. Instead of calling social services, she would tell Sharon Edwards. Let her handle it. The woman was the boy's grandmother. Gracie was no one in particular to Baxter. She was just . . . Gracie.

That decision made, she closed her eyes and mentally sifted back through the events of that horrific day in June. The day all hell had broken loose at camp, the day she had almost lost her life, until she remembered exactly what she had done with the little flash drive containing the journal her friend Jett had left for her.

She stood up again, walked into the living room to where her day pack lay on the couch, unzipped a tiny outside pocket, and fished out the flash drive with two fingers.

Back at the table in the kitchen, she inserted the flash drive into the port on her laptop.

There was only one file—*Camp*.

Gracie clicked on it.

Her friend's diary began almost three years earlier. There were over six hundred files, one folder for every month, one file for each entry.

Months later, the pain of her friend's death was still so keen, Gracie avoided the portions of the journal describing what had been happening at camp and the events that had led slowly and inexorably to her death, instead doing a search for Winston and concentrating solely on those portions pertaining to Jett's relationship with him.

The story read like a bad bodice ripper, but without the happily ever after.

Jett had met Winston in the frozen pizza section at Stater Bros. and believed the man was the answer to her prayers. She had never been with a man who treated her as well—the perfect gentlemen, sweet, attentive, picking up the dinner tab, holding doors open for her, asking for permission to kiss her. She believed that she was in love with him and that he loved her back. He had resisted having sex with her until their fifth date, a first for Jett. And apparently what fabulous sex it was. Gracie skipped over long, graphic descriptions of contortions in various venues, face flushed with embarrassment at the intrusion into her late friend's sex life.

With the sensation of stepping off already shaky ground into a quagmire, Gracie read about Winston's increasing insistence for Jett to go off the pill, to have a baby with him. Then, several weeks into the relationship came the single jaw-dropping pronouncement: "He's married!" Jett's words screamed off the page in forty-eight-point typeface. "He admitted it!" she raged. "To my face! He said he loves me. Wants to marry me! Wants my baby! For his army! WTF? I'm outa there!!!"

"Hell's bells, Jett," Gracie whispered. "No wonder you dropped him like a cast-iron skillet." The journal went on to describe how, when Jett had tried to break up with the man,

Dr. Winston Jekyll had become Mr. Winston Hyde. He had grabbed her, squeezing her jaw with his fingers, pressing the tip of a knife blade to the inner corner of her eye, whispering in her ear that he would cut it out if she left him, until finally she relented and promised to keep seeing him. For the months following, Jett had hidden out at camp like a frightened rabbit from a hunter, thankful for the camp's remoteness and inaccessibility by telephone. Winston had written letters, at first enraged, threatening, then remorseful and pleading. Finally, they had trickled away to nothing.

Gracie thought back to the reception following Jett's memorial service at camp, where she had met Winston for the first time. Within the first minute, he had told her that he loved Jett, that he was her fiancé, and he had asked Gracie if she was married. What made the event stick in her mind was that he had been wearing a wedding band. Eventually Gracie had shrugged off her suspicions, choosing the less creepy, more logical explanations. *Winston's a widower and still carrying a torch for his dead wife.* Or *He's divorced and still carrying a torch for his ex.* Or *He was asking for a lonely single friend.*

Gracie shivered. The answer had been none of the above. Her initial inclination that there was something not right with the man had been spot-on. Winston had been on the prowl for yet another wife with whom to have another baby for his so-called army.

"Yeeesh," Gracie whispered. She exited the journal altogether and leaned back in her chair.

There was nothing in what Jett had written to suggest that Winston was a white supremacist or to connect anyone from the Edwards/Ferguson clan, including Jordan, to the burning of Vivian and John's home. Nothing to even suggest the fire was anything but an accident due to faulty wiring or an overturned candle.

She couldn't go to the Sheriff's Department with what amounted to three fistfuls of mountain air, a bunch of tiny dots of information, none of which connected together in any coherent sense, much less amounting to anything criminal at all. Gardner would just use it as another notch in his anti-Gracie campaign belt.

Gracie returned the flash drive to her day pack, zipping it into the same outer pocket. Then she reopened the Anti-Defamation League's website and did a general search for *teardrop tattoo*. Nothing came up. She searched under General Hate Symbols, then more specifically Neo-Nazi and Hate Group Symbols. Still nothing. Frustrated and impatient, she exited the site altogether and did a general Internet search for *teardrop tattoo meaning*.

Pages of listings came up.

She clicked on the first site, Wikipedia, and read that the tattoo could have several meanings, including that the wearer had killed someone.

That the wearer has killed someone.

Gracie felt herself being sucked further into the mire.

Was it possible that the boy's tattoo, his "badge of honor," indicated that he, in some way, had participated in a killing? Was he a murderer?

Gracie exited Wikipedia and clicked on the next site on the list. There she read that a teardrop tattoo completely colored in by ink, as Jordan's was, represented a murder committed by the wearer. A third and fourth website turned up similar results.

Gracie wiped her hands down her face.

She looked down at her watch. Eleven twenty-seven.

"So much for sleeping tonight," she said. "I'm wide awake."

"WHERE IS IT?" Gracie leaned over the back of the driver's seat of her truck, throwing aside blankets, digging past storage bins and gear all the way down to the floor. "Where the hell's my ID?"

The lanyard holding her Sheriff's Department picture ID was always draped around the hanger from which her Search and Rescue uniform shirt and field pants hung behind the driver's seat of the Ranger, ready for a callout.

Now, suddenly, her ID wasn't there.

She had already scoured every inch of ground between the cabin and the truck. Had it fallen out somehow at camp? There was no time now to drive all the way up there to look. The pre-evacuation briefing was slated to begin in twenty minutes, barely enough time to drive from her cabin to the SO.

"It's supposed to be *right here*!"

But it wasn't. She sat back on her heels and tipped her head back, closing her eyes. "Oh, God! Gardner!"

"YOU'VE PUT THE lives of every law enforcement officer on the Department at risk," Sergeant Gardner said in a voice much louder than necessary in the tiny office.

Hands clasped behind her, Gracie shifted her weight from one long leg to the other, then back again.

During the drive from her cabin to the SO, she had called Allen on her cell phone, asking him to double-check the Serrano Lodge and Gatehouse parking lots for her ID. A return call twenty minutes later had reported negative results.

Gracie slipped into the Sheriff's Office building along with Jon and Lenny. Sitting among the field of orange shirts, she could barely stand to look at Gardner standing pompously at the front of the room, giving the pre-evacuation briefing in a condescending tone, issuing instructions, explaining maps and procedures. She craned her neck, looking for Ralph's familiar silver crew cut, but he wasn't there. Surreptitiously she texted him: WHERE ARE YOU? AT SO FOR FIRE MEETING. But she received no response. Throughout the briefing she sat on pins and needles, expecting someone to tap her on the shoulder and ask to see her Sheriff's ID.

Without an ID, she couldn't work the mandatory evacuation if it was issued, couldn't respond to any searches, couldn't participate in anything SAR-related. As the meeting broke up, deciding to just get it over with, she walked down the hallway of the SO to the Watch Commander's office, feeling as if she were riding in a tumbrel to the guillotine.

"Get down to the HQ," Gardner ordered. "Get another ID. Today. Capiche?"

"Yes." Resisting the inane impulse to follow up with a thank-you, Gracie turned to leave.

"I got a report that you were brawling in public."

Gracie turned back. "What?"

"In uniform."

"Ah," she said. Her altercation with Mrs. Lucas in the Stater Bros. parking lot. "I wasn't brawling. I—"

"Those are Department patches on your shirt."

"I know. She—"

"As part of this department, you're an official representative of the Sheriff himself."

Gracie had reached her Sergeant Gardner daily tolerance quota. "I'm aware of that," she said, her voice sharp. "I wasn't brawling. I was attacked. Blindsided. Head-butted. I was defending myself. I can't really afford to replace all my front teeth."

She hadn't thought it was possible for the man to narrow his eyes even further and still be able to see. "You think this is a joke?" he growled.

She snorted. "No. I don't think this is a joke."

"You're a loose cannon, Kinkaid."

Gracie opened her mouth to protest, but didn't get the chance.

"You're unpredictable and unreliable and that makes you unprofessional."

"Now wait a—"

"Your judgment is questionable."

Gracie shut her mouth, realizing suddenly that Gardner was lashing out with everything he could think of, valid and invalid, true and untrue, baiting her into a reaction he might be able to use against her. She took in a breath and made a

conscious effort to remain calm, unemotional, and to let the
accusations slide off her armor of indifference. But Gardner's verbal darts found the chinks in the steel, penetrated,
stung, humiliated, diminished.

"You're an embarrassment to the Department," the Sergeant continued. "That makes you a liability and a
problem—the Sheriff's problem. And *that* makes you *my*
problem." She heard him mumble what sounded like, "Goddam volunteers," under his breath. Then, as if it had just
occurred to him, he said, "I'm writing you up."

Gracie found her voice again. "*What?* Why? On what . . . ?"

"You're lucky I'm not booting you off the team, Kinkaid.
But, with this fire thing, all incompetence aside, I need every
man I can get. I'm writing up an official reprimand. It'll go into
your personnel file. Consider this your final warning. You won't
get another chance. You screw up again, you're off the team."

Gardner had scored a direct hit. The threat to kick her
off the team hit Gracie like a sucker punch to the gut. Without Search and Rescue, she had her job, but not much else.
The team was her life, the guys on the team her family.
Without them, except for Minnie, and maybe Allen, she had
no one. A yawning emptiness opened up at her feet.

Gracie spun on her heel and left the room. To her retreat-
ing back she heard the sergeant say, "ID. Today. Otherwise
don't bother."

GRACIE stepped out of the elevator and let the doors glide closed behind her.

For the second time in less than a week, she was inside a hospital. She didn't like hospitals. She especially didn't like elevators in hospitals. Within their slick, steel walls, she felt she already had two feet in the coffin.

Having her picture retaken for her Sheriff's Department ID had required that, after her face-to-face with Gardner, she race up to camp to help Allen prepare and serve lunch, then, once again, feeling guilt-stricken for leaving Minnie behind, drive all the way down the mountain.

Pulling away from the Sheriff's Headquarters, newly minted Search and Rescue ID in the front pocket of her uniform shirt, she realized that the regional medical center with the burn center was only a few miles away. She had driven over, not really expecting to see Vivian, but wanting to try to check on her nonetheless, and maybe Acacia and John.

Standing in front of the elevator, Gracie looked in both

directions. Zeroing in on what looked like a nurse's station down the hall on her right, she turned in that direction.

Before she had taken two steps, John rounded the corner up ahead. Looking years older, like a man beaten, he shuffled down the corridor toward her, head bowed, back bent, leaning on a cane.

Gracie stepped toward him. "John," she said in a soft voice.

The man looked up at her with red-rimmed eyes. "What are you doing here?" he snapped.

Gracie stopped, stunned. "I—I came to see how Vivian was doing. How you were doing. And Acacia."

"They've got my wife stuck full of needles. Tubes running in and out." His voice was gruff, sharp, bitter. He stopped to cough, the sound wet and deep in his lungs. His whole body shuddered.

Gracie put a hand on his arm, but he slapped it away.

"She can't breathe but for a tube down her throat. She's got machines everywhere keeping track of whether she's alive or dead. How do you think she's doing?"

"I'm so sorry. But her prognosis is good? She'll recover?"

"No telling." With sneering bitterness, he said, "'Sup to the Almighty in his infinite wisdom and mercy."

"I'm sorry," Gracie said again, feeling the words inadequate. "Have you learned anything about the fire? Have the police learned anything about how it started?"

The old man leaned in toward Gracie until his face was only inches from her own. "Arson."

"Arson. How . . . ?"

"Firebomb through the front window. That give you what you lookin' for?"

"I . . ." Gracie stopped. Swallowed. Tried again. "Is there anything I can do for you? For Acacia?"

John glowered down at her. "Whatchoo doin' here?"

"I . . . It's . . . I was concerned about Vivian. About Acacia."

"Acacia's back with her mother," he spat. "Get away from me. From us. We don't need no help from you. You got nothin' we need."

Openmouthed, Gracie watched John shuffle away from her down the hallway.

DISTURBED AND DISTRACTED by John Robinson's bitter outburst and the possibility that Baxter's cousin Jordan might have burned down the bungalow at the bottom of Arcturus hill, Gracie drove out of the medical center parking lot on autopilot. Barely aware of what she was doing, she merged the Ranger into the stream of eastbound traffic on the I-10.

A mile down the highway, a mishmash of signs came into view. Gracie's eyes flicked to one announcing the 215 Highway exit north to Barstow.

What day is it today?

She counted back through the days of the previous week, then forward again until she was confident that it was, in fact, Friday.

Confirming by the dashboard clock that she had enough time for a long detour before heading back up the mountain to Timber Creek, Gracie cut across two lanes of traffic onto the long, sweeping exit ramp curving over the I-10 and heading north.

The curving four-lane Mojave Freeway climbed up into the mountains. Gracie zoomed past semi-trucks laboring up the long incline, their side panels blaring UPS, MAYFLOWER, and TARGET, past cars and motorcycles, climbing slowly up to the Cajon Pass. She slid down the long, gentle descent on the other side, all way to the desert floor and along the pin-straight highway decorated with billboards, signs, and power lines. An hour after leaving the regional medical center, the Ranger glided past the sign announcing DESERTVIEW CITY LIMITS; POPULATION: 119,206; ELEVATION: 2,863.

Following signs for the Civic Center, Gracie exited the

highway and drove along flat, traffic-clogged streets, through a commercial section of strip malls landscaped with white gravel and pink oleander and palm trees, finally turning onto a street that led into downtown.

As she neared the center of town, signs of organized activity increased—barricaded streets, vehicles jamming curbs, people walking singly or in groups of two or three, purposefully, in the same direction, some carrying signs, some cameras.

Gracie parked the truck in a King Soopers parking lot. Opting out of acting as a walking advertisement for the Sheriff's Department, she shed her orange SAR uniform shirt. Pushing up the sleeves of her white turtleneck top and wishing she were wearing shorts and Tevas rather than pea green uniform jeans and hiking boots, she emerged from the cool, air-conditioned interior of the Ranger and into the open desert air. It was like stepping into an oven set on Broil.

In the relative coolness of the building shadows, Gracie walked the several blocks to the central square of the city. Up ahead, a crowd of protesters had gathered across the intersection, holding signs and banners, shouting, taunting, blowing whistles and noisemakers to drown out the chants of marchers as yet unseen. A woman wearing a multicolored clown outfit and an electric-blue wig was playing an upbeat polka on an accordion.

Visible over the heads of the crowd, a Confederate flag flowed by along with several handheld signs. A slight breeze caught another flag, unfurling it for an instant, displaying in the center a spiderlike, and instantly recognizable symbol—a swastika.

Melting into the throng of people, Gracie edged around the corner, mashing herself between bodies and the building, and headed down the block to where the crowd thinned enough for her to shoulder her way through to the front. She stopped at a barrier and looked up the street.

Protesters lined both sides of the streets, held in place by

yellow police tape and steel barriers. Men and women.
Young and old. Latinos, whites, blacks. Some held signs
reading NAZI GO HOME and PEACE! and I DISLIKE YOUR
HATE. And a long, white banner with red lettering: RISE
ABOVE RACISM. Others were obviously simply looky-loos,
snapping pictures of the spectacle.

A phalanx of law enforcement from different agencies—
city police, Sheriff's Department, state patrol, even what
looked like National Guard, some in riot gear, some on
bicycles—were stretched along the street between the
marchers and the protesters.

There were thirty or so marchers, both men and women.
Some wore black long-sleeved shirts and black cargo pants
tucked into black army boots. Some wore white T-shirts, red
suspenders holding up blue jeans, steel-toed work boots with
red laces. Others wore what appeared to be derivations of the
black uniforms of the Nazi Gestapo. A few wore black caps,
but most heads were bare, closely shaven with a scalp tattoo
here and there.

Rage emanating in palpable waves, the group marched down
the street at a fast, determined pace, quickly reaching the point
where Gracie stood. As they passed, a man toward the front
shouted into a bullhorn. Fists pumping the air with the strong-
arm salute of the Third Reich, the marchers responded to his
call, the rhythmic chants clashing with the cacophony of protester yells and whistles and noisemakers.

Gracie scanned the faces of the marchers, looking for
someone she recognized. Certainly Winston wasn't there.
He would have stood a head taller than almost everyone
around him.

About two-thirds of the way back in the parade, she spotted Lee Edwards, Baxter's father. Eyes focused straight ahead,
mouth set in a grim line, light brown eyebrows furrowed,
head shaven. That he was wearing a white T-shirt and holding
one of the red, white, blue, and black flags with the swastika
in the middle was all that Gracie could see of the man.

On the near side of Lee was another man she recognized from the training—small framed, a couple of inches shorter. White T-shirt displaying sinewy forearms with multiple elaborate tattoos. Shaved head with a neatly trimmed black goatee. Thin, straight nose. Gold hoop in one ear.

As Gracie watched, the man's eyes, the startling blue of glacier ice, slid over to meet hers, lingered for a moment, then slid away.

Gracie backed into the anonymity of the crowd, suddenly wary and uncomfortable that the man had seen her there, possibly recognizing her.

Several feet up from where Gracie stood, a young white man clambered over the steel barrier and screamed at the marchers, "Shut up! Shut up!"

Two Sheriff's deputies muscled him back behind the barrier and onto the sidewalk.

The noise of the crowd swelled, growing more agitated, angrier, jeering, and taunting. Some leaned far out over the barriers, shaking their fists at the marchers and yelling, "Go home! Go home!"

Across the street another man, a young Latino, hopped the barrier. He ran into the street, scooped up a rock, held it aloft, and yelled something unintelligible.

Two of the neo-Nazis fell out of line. Police descended, pushing the marchers back in line and tussling with the young man, strong-arming him back behind the barricade.

The crowd yelled louder.

Gracie glanced around her, suddenly aware of heightening emotions, the volatility of a situation that could turn very ugly and lethal very fast.

I'm outta here.

Dropping back out of the crowd, she rounded the corner and escaped up the street, relieved as the crowds and clamor receded.

Halfway up the block, she stopped, backed up, and stood staring at a white pickup truck parked along the street.

Toyota Tacoma. No shell. Brown racing stripes. A couple of rust spots and a dent here and there. Empty gun rack in the back window. Tiny Confederate flag decal in the bottom-right corner.

A memory swam to the forefront of her brain. A similar truck had driven past the Robinson bungalow the night she and Vivian had sat outside on the front deck, counting the cars driving up and down Arcturus, remarking how wonderful, how peaceful it was that there was so little traffic on their road. Tinted windows had prevented her from seeing the driver of the pickup as it coasted back down past the house again.

Was it the same truck? Gracie couldn't be sure. Small white pickups were ubiquitous in Southern California. *And so what if it was the same one?* she asked herself. There was no way to tell whether the owner was a marcher, a protester, or someone totally uninvolved in the tumult half a block away.

She kept walking.

CHAPTER

22

THE Ranger zigzagged up the back side of the mountain, slowing almost to a stop for a hairpin turn, then accelerating for the short straightaway, slowing once again for a tight turn, speeding up for yet another straightaway. In twenty minutes, the truck gained almost thirty-five hundred feet in elevation. The flat khaki-colored desert dotted with mesquite and Joshua trees gradually surrendered to giant mounds of California granite and piñon and juniper. Halfway up the precipitous incline, Gracie turned off the air-conditioning and opened her window, draping her arm on the sill and reveling in the dropping temperature.

Normally, Gracie took particular delight in the lightning-quick transition from desert to mountain. But, this time, as she braked, rounded a sharp curve, sped up, braked again, and rounded another curve, she realized that, once again, she felt as if someone had tied a knot in her stomach—the aftereffects of the neo-Nazi parade. Leaving the steep incline with its Mojave vistas in the rearview mirror, Gracie sped up for another long straightaway, slowing once again for the curving stretch that led up and over the final rise, then down into the far eastern end of the valley.

Relieved to be back on her own turf—cool, quiet, and peaceful—Gracie circled the Ranger around the north shore of what remained of Greene's Lake, mostly empty from the long summer, white patches of alkali showing on the exposed lake bottom.

Suddenly remembering her decision to call Sharon Edwards about her two grandsons, Gracie pulled into a turnout, yellow-page-searched for the woman's number on her phone and made the call. Twenty minutes later, obligation fulfilled, she edged the Ranger back out onto the highway and continued toward home.

Gracie flipped on her left-hand turn signal and slowed the truck for the turn onto the road leading to the southern end of the valley. At the last minute, she flipped the signal off, swooped back into the main lane, and continued straight ahead, along the winding northern shoreline of Timber Lake and into the little village of Buckskin.

With a hand resting on the warm hood of the Ranger, Gracie stood on the gravel shoulder of the road, staring unbelieving at a red, white, and blue RE/MAX FOR SALE sign pushed into the rocky hillside in front of Ralph's log cabin.

At the top of the cement driveway, the door of the narrow fieldstone garage stood open. As Gracie watched, Ralph emerged from the cabin, a box in his arms, and walked across the driveway into the garage.

She climbed up the driveway. "When were you going to tell me?" she asked as she neared the top.

Ralph set the box on top of a wide stack of boxes and turned around to face her. He wore a torn, heather-gray T-shirt with ARMY in black lettering on the front, faded Levi's, and paint-spattered work boots. His short-cropped silver hair gleamed in the late afternoon sun. Still pale, Gracie observed, but his pallor was shades better than the dried mud of the previous week.

Winded from the short, but steep climb, Gracie stopped ten feet away and sucked air into her lungs through her nose. "Or was the plan to not tell me?"

"I left you a message." Ralph's voice was neutral, a stranger's.

"When?"

"Yesterday."

"Where?"

"On your machine at home."

Shit. "So . . . you . . . you're leaving me?" she asked, unable to keep from making the question personal.

"This isn't directed at you or meant to hurt you."

"Well, it is hurting me," she said. "A lot."

"Believe what you like." Ralph turned away, lifted a box from the floor, and set it atop the pile.

"Why are you acting like this?"

"I'm not acting any way."

"Yes, you are. You're cold. You're distant. You act like . . ." She almost said, *like you don't love me anymore*, but the words stuck to the roof of her mouth like peanut butter.

Without turning around, Ralph said, "I had a heart attack."

Gracie actually took a step backward. "What? When?"

"Five . . . six weeks ago."

"You worked the Edwards search. Last week."

"'Bout did me in."

"But you're so . . . young."

"It happens."

"Why didn't you tell me?"

"It was mild."

"So that makes it not important enough to tell me? Saying a heart attack is mild is like saying . . ." She stopped, unable to think of a good analogy. "Why didn't you tell me?" she asked again.

"I told Gardner. I thought he would tell the team."

"Well, he didn't," Gracie said. *The bastard.* "Ralphie. Why didn't you tell *me*?"

"I . . . Because . . ." He stopped.

"What? Because you didn't want me hassling you? Bothering you?"

"No." He shook his head. "No."

"Then *why*?"

"There was nothing you could have done—"

"I could have been there . . . here."

"I didn't want you here."

It felt as if Ralph had reached inside her chest and wrenched out her heart.

Seeing the pain registered on her face, Ralph closed his gray-blue eyes for a moment, inhaled, then opened his eyes again, his face softening. "I didn't want you to see me that way, Gracie girl," he said.

It hit her then. Ralph was used to being the strong one in their relationship, at work, in everything, the man in charge, in control. He hadn't wanted Gracie to see him weak, vulnerable.

"I didn't want your . . ." he continued.

"Pity? Again, you mean?"

Ralph looked out across the neighbors' yard and slowly nodded.

Gracie cleared her throat to dislodge the lump that had risen and stuck her hands in the back pockets of her pants. "Where are you moving to?"

He turned, picked up the same box from the pile, then set it down again. "Tucson."

"You hate the desert."

"Sometimes one has to do what one has to do. Sounds like a line from a goddam movie."

"What's in Tucson?"

"Not what. Who. My daughter."

"I didn't . . ." Gracie stopped. She tried to swallow, but her throat was parched. "I didn't know you had a daughter."

Ralph looked directly at her and said, "You never asked."

The truth slammed into Gracie like a two-by-twelve to

the side of the head. "I haven't been a very good friend to you, have I?" she said, her voice wobbling. "I'm sorry, Ralphie. I'm sorry you had a heart attack and you didn't think I was capable of being there to help. I'm sorry I let you down. Sorry I hurt you." She swiped a hand across her cheek and looked down at her fingertips. They were wet. She hadn't even been aware she was crying.

Ralph walked over to Gracie and put his arms around her. "You didn't let me down, Gracie girl," he said, his voice gentle, warm, quiet. The old Ralphie's voice.

Gracie wrapped her arms around his neck and mumbled into his warm shoulder, "You're all I have."

"No, I'm not."

"Yes, you are. You're my best friend. I love you. Don't get mad at me, but would you stay if I said I'd marry you?"

She felt him chuckle. "No. That was a . . ." She felt him shaking his head. "I'm not the right man for you."

"You're the most important man in my life."

"No, I'm not. You and I both know it." He pulled away and kissed her hair. "I'll be back to visit."

But Gracie knew he never would.

23

GRACIE steered the Ranger around a slow-moving delivery truck and back onto the westbound highway lane leading into town. Behind her, the morning sun, still low in the sky, shone down the length of the valley, illuminating the sentinel pines lining the road.

Minnie's chin rested on her shoulder. She reached back and stroked the silky head.

Despite feeling as if she hadn't slept in weeks, Gracie spent the night of her disastrous day kicking off blankets, pulling them back up, staring into the darkness, sitting up, turning on the light, turning it off, lying back down, and turning the light on again. Once again, she was unable to stop the pinwheels of thoughts and images spinning around in her brain. Children carrying high-powered weapons. Baxter's tearstained face and bruised body. Angry men marching and chanting angry, hateful words. Ralph's heart attack. Vivian and John's house burning. Ralph moving away. John's angry face leaning in toward hers. Tattoos. Swastikas.

At four thirty in the morning she finally fell asleep only

to slap the buzzing alarm clock off ninety minutes later. She sleepwalked through the day at camp. Practically comatose, she helped serve the breakfast, waved good-bye to the church group, spent several hours in the middle of the day supposedly catching up on paperwork, trying not to lay her head down on the desk lest she never pick it up again. In the late afternoon, she greeted the arriving group of a dozen corporate executives. Finally, after a steak dinner grilled outdoors next to the lake, she drove home and collapsed onto her bed, unconscious almost immediately, sleeping straight through until her alarm went off the following morning.

The new group in camp was small enough for Allen to handle preparing and serving the breakfast alone. Promising the head cook the afternoon off—he hadn't had time off in over a week—Gracie set her alarm for eighty thirty, allowing herself an additional three hours of sleep.

But thirteen hours of sleep and two panda mugs of Folgers Instant hadn't been enough. Her eyelids still felt as if tiny gnomes were perched there, pressing them closed. "Time for the big guns," she mumbled and turned into the Safeway parking lot.

After parking, she told Minnie, "Be right back," and walked into the store. Ten minutes later she reemerged, Venti Double Chocolaty Chip Frappuccino in hand.

She stopped just outside the double front doors and took a sip. "Ahhh." She looked around, then glanced behind her at the newspaper and magazine stands lined up against the outer wall of the grocery store, wondering if she had read the most recent issue of the *Grizzly*, the local newspaper. She walked over, recognized the headlines concerning the Shady Oak Fire, dug in her pack for change, thumbed three quarters into the machine, opened the door, and pulled out a copy.

Coffee in hand, newspaper under an arm, she headed back to the truck.

Three vehicles down the row, she stopped at a white Toyota Tacoma pickup. No shell. Brown racing stripes.

Dents. Rust spots. Gun rack in the back window. Confederate flag decal.

This time there was no doubt it was the same truck she had seen parked along the street two days earlier in Desertview.

Setting her coffee and the newspaper on the ground, Gracie dug her cell phone out of the top pouch of her day pack and snapped pictures of the truck, the gun rack, the flag decal, and the license plate. What she was going to do with the pictures, she had no idea, except to positively identify the truck if she ever saw it again. She had no convenient contact in the California Department of Motor Vehicles to tell her who owned it.

"Looking to buy?" asked a male voice right next to her.

Gracie straightened with a yelp.

Glacier-blue eyes. Black goatee. Gold earring. Shaved head. Two feet away stood the same man she had seen marching in the neo-Nazi parade, the man she had recognized from the paramilitary training the previous Saturday.

"Is this your truck?" Gracie asked, face burning with the guilt of someone caught snooping.

"And if it is?"

"Nothing. I've seen it before. A couple of days ago in Desertview. And on my—" She stopped herself in time.

The man cocked his head, staring at her as if by looking long and hard enough, he could see into her head as to what she was going to say.

"I've seen you before, too," she said. "In Desertview. And at the training in the woods. *Lord of the Flies*."

The man nodded, icy eyes crinkling into the hint of a smile. "That would be correct." Then he said, "Things aren't always as they seem."

Gracie narrowed her eyes at him, trying to appear more stalwart, more menacing in order to hide the fact that she was shaking like an aspen leaf in a breeze. "And some things are exactly as they seem."

"Your name's Grace, right?"

"Perhaps."

The man smiled and reached out a hand. "Name's Boojum."

"Boojum."

"That's right."

The hand was still outstretched.

Gracie reached out slowly and took it, hard, callused, but warm.

She tried to let go, but Boojum held on. Alarmed, she looked into his face, even with hers.

The ice-blue eyes were surprisingly feminine with long lashes, thick and black. And they were filled with a profound sadness.

Boojum put his other hand on top of Gracie's and leaned forward so that his mouth was only inches from hers, a surprising, but nonthreatening invasion of space, so close she could see the whisker stubble on his upper lip. "You don't want to be a part of this, Grace," he said, his voice gentle. "Any of it."

Trying to pull away was like trying to remove her hand from a vise grip. "What are you . . . talking about?"

"I don't know what you think you're doing, but do not get involved in what's going on here. Any of it."

"These aren't the droids I'm looking for?"

He chuckled. "Something like that."

He leaned even closer and put his mouth next to her ear, his breath tickling her ear. "Do not . . . get involved here." he said again. "Do you hear what I'm telling you?"

"I don't—"

"Do you hear what I'm telling you?"

She looked back at him. "I hear what you're telling me."

"Good." Boojum let go of her hand, stepped back, spun around, and disappeared among the parked cars.

HUNCHED ON THE three-legged stool in the camp kitchen, Gracie sat with her elbows on the butcher-block table, chin on her hands, staring into space and puzzling over the man named

Boojum. He didn't seem to fit with the rest of the Edwards clan. He was different. He seemed nice. But then, crappy judge of character that she was turning out to be, so had Winston.

As soon as Boojum disappeared among the cars in the parking lot, Gracie regretted she didn't have enough time to play private investigator, hanging around, skulking in the shadows, to see if he eventually returned to the truck, climbed inside, and drove away.

She would have known then whether the truck had a hole in the muffler, which would point even more convincingly to it being the same truck she had seen on Arcturus a couple of days before the Robinsons' house had been firebombed. And it would confirm that the truck belonged to a man who was affiliated with a white supremacist group. Everything tied up in a neat little package.

But she hadn't had the time.

Boojum had given her a very specific warning to not get involved in any of it. But what exactly was *it*? The Edwards/Ferguson clan? White supremacists in general? And why? Was he trying to keep her from learning more about what the group was involved in, what nefarious plots they might be hatching? Or was he trying to keep her from tying the family in general or him specifically with the firebombing of an elderly black couple's home? There was no way of knowing.

Gracie sighed, slid off the stool, and picked up the newspaper from on top of her day pack propped up against the table leg. She sat back down again and studied the four-color map comprising the entire front page, depicting which areas the Shady Oak Fire had already burned, which areas had been contained, the neighborhoods that had already been evacuated, and those designated for pre-evacuation.

She sighed again and flipped through the rest of the paper, scanning the pages. Her eye caught on a headline at the bottom of page four, an article so small she almost missed it. She read how the human remains discovered weeks before in the desert along the I-15 corridor near

Barstow had been identified as belonging to two people, a man and a woman. Names were being held pending notification of the families.

Gracie stared down at the article and thought again about the hands they had found in the plastic bag, about the tattoo on the inside of one of the wrists.

Tattoos again, she noted, mentally filing the information away for later. She was tired of thinking. Tired of feeling. Tired, in fact, of everything.

She paged through the rest of the paper, past real estate ads and articles about valley schools reopening for the year, and so-and-so running for reelection for city council.

She closed the paper. Headlines at the top of the back page read: NEW RESIDENT DIES IN LOCAL HOUSE FIRE.

"Oh, my *God*!"

Gracie's eyes flew down the article, reading how Vivian Robinson, sixty-four, a new resident to the valley, had died Friday night of smoke inhalation sustained in a house fire. Her husband, John, had sustained minor injuries. A granddaughter, aged nine, was unhurt. The cause of the blaze was still under investigation.

Gracie covered her face with her hands. "She's dead!" Tears seeped out between her fingers. With a stabbing pain of emptiness, she wept for the loss of an innocent life, a gentle spirit, a wise mind, a compassionate heart, for a rosebud of a friendship cut short, and for lives blasted to shrapnel by a single despicable act.

Whoever had firebombed Vivian and John's house had moved up in the world. Whereas before, guilty of only arson, that person was now also guilty of murder.

The final scene from *West Side Story* stepped to center stage in her brain. Maria standing in the harsh spotlight of the playground, gun in hand, new husband Tony lying dead at her feet, shot and killed by a rival gang member. In grief and anger, Maria points the gun at first to one man, then another, and another, screaming that they were all guilty of murdering Tony and his friend Riff, and her own brother, Nardo, because of their hatred for each other, and that now she can kill, too.

"'Because now,'" Gracie whispered the quote. "'I have hate.'"

She dropped her hands and stared straight ahead, eyes cold, half-closed. Thinking. Considering.

She climbed down from the stool, walked down the back hallway, past Minnie on her bed in the closet, and pushed out through the screen door, letting it slap closed behind her. She pulled open the passenger door of the Ranger, flipped open the glove compartment, and pulled out a scrap of paper lying inside.

She walked back into the kitchen, lifted the receiver from the telephone on the wall, and dialed the number scribbled on the paper in blue ink.

She listened to the telephone ringing on the other end of the line.

A voice answered.

"Winston? It's Grace Kinkaid. I wondered if your offer to have coffee still stands."

24

GRACIE took a sip of her iced tea and resisted the urge to pick at the sandal strap digging into her left heel.

For the second time in almost a decade, she was wearing a dress, the same simple black shift she had worn to Jett's memorial service the first time she had met Winston, the same one he had noticed enough to remember and remark on several months later.

Jumping late into the shower had left her without enough time to let her thick, shoulder-length hair air-dry. For the first time in years, she had blown it dry, whipping it into a voluminous auburn cloud. "I look like the Flying Nun," she squawked to her reflection in the mirror. "One good gust of wind and I'll be in Barstow." She gathered her hair up and clipped it in a heap at the top of her head.

The first thing Winston said as he walked up the sidewalk outside the Ancient Mariner restaurant was, "You look beautiful, Gracie. You have your hair up. And you're wearing that dress I like."

The man, almost a full foot taller than Gracie, wore a

white short-sleeved dress shirt, red-and-blue-striped tie, the ever-present red suspenders holding up gray dress slacks, and steel-toed boots with red laces. For the first time, his cleanly shaved head remained uncovered.

In true gentlemanly fashion, Winston held the front door open for her. She fought the temptation to shrug off his hand on her lower back as he escorted her inside the nautical-themed restaurant dominated by navy blue and white, polished wood, and walls adorned with sea lanterns and signal flags in bright primaries: yellow, red, and blue.

At a table looking out over Timber Lake, Winston pulled back Gracie's chair. As she took her seat, she glanced down at his left hand. No wedding ring.

Over an uninspired dinner of dry sea scallops with sides of overcooked broccoli and bland rice, Gracie engaged in conversation with the man who most definitely was a polygamist, who might or might not be a white supremacist and the instigator of hatred, bigotry, and violence in children, possibly complicit in the firebombing of a house with its owners sleeping inside.

Three minutes into the meal, Gracie realized Winston was information gathering, asking Gracie so many questions about herself she began to feel like she was sitting in an interview for potential wifehood, which, she figured, she was. She wouldn't have been surprised if he had pulled out a pencil and checklist from his shirt pocket. Where did you grow up? In and around Detroit, Michigan. Check. What were your favorite subjects in grade school? Reading and geography. Check. Are you fertile? Presumably. Check.

On a fishing expedition of her own, Gracie countered with, Where did you grow up? Canon City, Colorado. How far did you get in school? Graduated high school. What was your favorite subject? Phys ed. Oh, and shop, too. He liked the band saw. When she tried to steer the dialogue toward what he did for a living, Winston adroitly flipped the conversation back in her direction by asking her about Search and Rescue, specifically if she had any survival training, to which she replied with her most winning smile, "But of course."

Over tasteless peach cobbler, Winston got down to the nitty-gritty, remarking, "I seem to remember that you're not married."

"I wouldn't be out with you if I were," Gracie shot back, and decided if this was going to work, she would need to work harder at suppressing her animosity. She gave him what she hoped was another dazzling smile and softened her tone. "No. I'm not married. I'm hoping that you aren't either," she said, ending on the up note of a question.

Winston grunted noncommittally and said, "I do have two kids. You met . . . er, well, those were my kids you met the other day. Out in the woods. The girl and boy."

"Jordan and Heather."

"Good memory! I like that in a woman."

Unable to stop herself, she said, "I tend to remember the names of people who point guns at me."

Rather than take offense, Winston chuckled. "Yeah, I still feel really bad about that. It'll never happen again. We learned our lesson there. From now on, every group has at least one adult."

As he launched into a discourse on the brilliant potential of his children, Gracie studied the man's face. No part in and of itself was noteworthy, rendering the whole unremarkable: fleshy cheeks, sharp nose, flaring nostrils, thin lips.

She remembered thinking the first time she had met him that the soft, blue eyes were kind. But now she noticed that when he smiled, the sparkle never reached his eyes. She couldn't help comparing him to Boojum, where, she felt, if one burrowed beneath the tough exterior, one would find a soul. If one burrowed beneath to Winston Ferguson's core, Gracie suspected one would strike stone.

When Winston had reached the end of his soliloquy, Gracie took in a deep breath and asked, "Did you hear about that house fire? The one that killed that woman?"

Winston's eyes moved up to meet hers, then down again to his peach cobbler, revealing nothing. "Read about it," he said.

"It's a tragedy, don't you think?"

Winston made another noncommittal sound, not looking up.

"They say it's arson."

No response.

"Who would do such a thing?" Gracie crossed her arms on the table in front of her. "Who would set fire to someone's house? While they were sleeping? I know the family. Vivian was a good woman. Smart. Articulate. She used to teach English. High school. She was full of wisdom and compassion. An old soul, you know what I mean?"

Winston scraped his dessert bowl with his spoon. "No."

"I heard someone firebombed the house."

The blue eyes met hers again, then dropped back to the bowl.

"Vivian was an asset to her community, her world, her universe. And now she's gone. Poof!" Words poured out of Gracie's mouth. "Why? Because of the willful hatred of some sick Neanderthal lacking the most basic brainpower? Because of vile, twisted, perverted minds of people who hate others simply because their skin is a different color?"

Winston had stopped moving.

"They're the types who drive around in those *biiig* daddy mambo trucks with *biiig* daddy mambo tires and *loud* engines. They're the types who have to overcompensate for their piss-poor self-images by hating somebody because they don't look like they do or act like they do."

Heads in the restaurant turned in Gracie's direction.

"How do people end up that way?" It was as if someone else were controlling her brain, as if once the floodgates were opened, it was impossible to stanch the flow of words. "They're sick, that's what they are. They're demented and bigoted, with shit for brains. Don't you think so, Winston?" Gracie leaned forward. "Don't you?"

Winston had dropped his hand to the table, fork in his

fist, tines up. He sat unmoving except for the muscle working in his jaw and the blue vein pulsing visibly on his temple. Shoulders hunched, nostrils flared, he looked as if, at any second, he would lunge forward across the table and plunge the fork into the side of Gracie's neck.

He looked up with eyes as dead as a shark's and said in a flat voice that sent a jolt of adrenaline sizzling right down to Gracie's toes, "No, *Grace Louise*. I don't think so."

Then he stood up so fast and hard, the heavy wooden chair fell backward with a crash, making everyone in the restaurant, including Gracie, jump.

With the dead eyes fixed on Gracie, Winston slid his wallet out of his back pocket, pulled out a hundred-dollar bill, and dropped it on the table. Then he turned and walked away.

Before reaching the outer door, he grabbed up another heavy chair, lifted it high over his head, and smashed it down on the glass display case. Glass flew everywhere. Diners screamed.

Winston pulled a sheaf of bills from his wallet and threw them up into the air. Hundred-dollar bills floated down to the floor like autumn leaves. With blood oozing from cuts on his forehead and cheeks, Winston shot one last searing look back at Gracie and pushed through the door out of the restaurant.

Gracie plopped back in her chair. "Wow," she said. "Guess my having his babies is o-u-t."

CHAPTER

25

ARMS filled with several days' worth of mail, backpack slung over one shoulder, and Minnie trotting along behind, Gracie slunk up the side of her cabin, eyes darting behind her, from bush to tree, then back behind her again, certain someone was hiding in the near darkness, waiting to leap out at her.

The previous night and all day at camp she had flinched at every loud noise, twitched at every sudden voice, so hair-trigger jumpy that by the end of the afternoon she was irritating herself and had pushed Allen's patience beyond the boiling point.

Exactly what she was expecting, she didn't know, but she simply couldn't believe she had opened Pandora's can of worms with Winston and wasn't going to pay for it *somehow*.

She stepped up onto the front porch of her cabin. Grabbing up a flyer that had been stuck into the crack of the front door, she inserted her key in the lock, pushed the door open, snapped on the light as Minnie ran past her inside, then nudged the door closed with her foot, locking and dead-bolting it behind her.

In the kitchen, she dumped the mail onto the table and scooped a cupful of dog food into Minnie's dish. Then picking a Coors Light out of the refrigerator, she popped it open and padded back into the living room, laptop under one arm. In the darkened room, the only light coming from the last gasp of daylight showing through the front window, she sank down onto the couch, put her feet up on the sea chest, and took a swig of beer.

"I'm lucky I'm alive," Gracie said to the empty room, still stunned by what had poured out of her mouth at the restaurant the evening before.

Her intent had been to have a nice, harmless chat with Winston, to get to know him better, maybe prod him a little to see if he would rise to the bait, give himself away, reveal, in some small way, his true nature.

But she had lost control, allowing her anger and grief over Vivian's death to take over.

As a result, what Gracie had gotten wasn't disclosure of anything to connect Winston or any of the Edwards clan to the Robinson house fire or anything remotely extremist. No hate-filled rhetoric. No strong-arm salute. What Gracie had gotten was the same simmering below-the-surface rage, the same penchant for violence as Baxter's father's. What Gracie had gotten was the transformation of a seemingly harmless garden snake into a full-blown basilisk.

Finished with her dinner, Minnie trotted into the room, jumped up onto a blanket folded up at the opposite end of the couch, curled up in a black ball, and went to sleep.

Gracie slumped back against the couch, worrying an already-bleeding cuticle with a canine.

The fact that Winston had called her "Grace Louise," her mother's pet name for her, nagged at her. That he had managed to tap her home phone or read her mother's letters somehow seemed over-the-top. *Then how did he know?* Maybe it was a mere coincidence that Winston had called her by the name used by only one other person on earth.

Maybe it was as easily explained as he had done a search online because he was interested in her as the third mother of his children and had discovered her middle name.

She sat up again, opened her laptop, then an Internet browser, and typed in *Gracie Kinkaid.*

The first several listings were paid advertisements, the first one a site called People Low-k8r. She clicked on the link.

A page opened with the heading: "We Found Gracie Kinkaid!" Beneath it were the words: "Current Address, Phone, and Age. Find Gracie Kinkaid, anywhere."

With a growing sense of unease, she clicked on the link.

A new page opened displaying multiple boxes and an announcement: "3 people named Gracie Kinkaid in the United States Found!"

She clicked on the link.

Three Gracie Kinkaids were listed. She was the third. Beneath the heading were variations of her name: Grace L. Kinkaid. Grace Louise Kinkaid. Gracie L. Kinkaid.

"Distressingly easy as Sunday morning," she moaned.

Farther down the page, her age was listed.

"Fifty-one!" Gracie yelled. "What the hell!"

Minnie's head came up.

"Sorry, Minnie," she muttered.

A third column, Has Lived In, listed Timber Creek, CA, Ann Arbor, Michigan, along with Southfield and Grosse Pointe Farms. Added into the mix was an inexplicable, inaccurate stint in New Port Richey, Florida. Beneath Possible Relations were Evelyn Kinkaid, Michael Kinkaid, Harold Rodgers, and Lenora Rodgers Vander Kamp.

Gracie clicked the box beneath Phone Number, Address, and Other Details. Several boxes appeared giving her the opportunity to purchase varying degrees of background information.

She exited the site altogether, feeling eerily exposed and not a little paranoid that someone willing to spend upward of $19.99 could ostensibly gather her address, property records, and, if she had had them, judgments and liens, and a criminal history.

Gracie leaned back, took another sip of beer, and remembered the article about the identification being made of the owners of the body parts in the desert and the tattoo on the inside of one of the wrists.

She looked up at the ceiling, trying again to remember exactly what the tattoo looked like. She remembered a skull and crossbones with some illegible script across the top. "'Anti-' something," Gracie said. Along the bottom were three uppercase letters. "Not *NRA*. But something like it. *ANA* or *ARA* . . ."

She sat up again and typed *skull and crossbones tattoo* into the Search box on her laptop. Thousands of results came up. She started paging through them, but stopped after only two pages, feeling even more dark and unsettled, and wondering, *What's the fascination?*

She typed in *ANA* plus *skull and crossbones*. Again, thousands of results.

Substituting *ARA* for *ANA* produced a similarly daunting number of listings.

She typed in only the letters *ARA*, hit Enter, and read down the list that appeared.

"A constellation. A state in northeast India. A baby's name. Used in a Japanese phrase." Somehow she didn't think any of those were it. She kept reading and stopped at Definition by Acronym. Clicked on it. Read down the list. "American Rental Association. Australian Retailers Association. Automotive Recyclers Association. Alliance for Retired Americans. Anti-Racist Action."

Anti-Racist Action.

She clicked on the link and began reading.

"The Anti-Racist Action Network is a decentralized network of anti-fascists . . ."

Antifascist. Could that have been the word at the top of the tattoo?

". . . and anti-racists in North America. ARA activists organize actions to disrupt neo-Nazi and white supremacist groups, and help organize activities against fascist and racist ideologies."

Gracie read faster.

"ARA groups also oppose sexism, homophobia, hetero-sexism, anti-Semitism, and the anti-abortion movement. ARA originated from the skinhead and punk cultures."

"Has to be it," Gracie whispered.

In the Search box, she typed in *Anti-racist Action.* The window that opened displayed a headline with a symbol of a girl with black hair and a black bandanna over the bottom half of her face, holding a cocked slingshot. On the left side of the page was a square with a skull and crossbones, the word *Anti-fascista* across the top, *ARA 2013* on the bottom.

"That's it!" Gracie exclaimed. "That's the tattoo." She looked more closely and realized that the crossbones were, in fact, baseball bats.

She read about the organization, about its philosophy, its goals, its tactics, all the time wondering whether it was possible the dead people had crossed the Edwards/Ferguson clan in some way and been murdered for it.

"Okay," Gracie said, closing her laptop, sliding it off her legs and onto the sea chest. "That's all of this light, breezy crap I can stand." She pushed herself to her feet and padded into the kitchen for a cup of chamomile tea in hopes of staving off another night of tossing and turning and staring at the ceiling.

As the panda mug of water heated in the microwave, Gracie flipped through the pile of mail on the table—electric bill, *Backpacker* magazine, *Outside* magazine, and a large envelope. "Jury duty? Again?" At the bottom of the pile was the flyer she had pulled out of the crack in her front door.

She picked it up and turned it over. Her mouth dropped open.

The flyer was a handmade wanted poster with a glued-on paper target. Staring back at her from the bull's-eye—taken from her high school yearbook—was a picture of Gracie. Beneath it, in giant cutout letters: WANTED: DEAD OR ALIVE! The words *or alive* had been x-ed out with a Magic Marker. In smaller letters below that: CASH REWORD.

The microwave dinged.

Gracie sank down into a kitchen chair.

Gracie Kinkaid. Wanted: Dead!

Whoever it was that wanted her dead knew where she lived. But that could be anyone nowadays. She had just witnessed how easy it was to find out all kinds of personal information.

Would Winston have done this? Somehow it didn't seem like his style. If he really wanted her dead, he wouldn't threaten her; he'd just splatter her all over the sidewalk like a beetle.

Boojum? Why would he want her dead? Or was this a heavy-handed method of warning her off again.

Gracie studied the poster, amateurish and crudely made with so many misspellings as to have been made by a child.

Could one of the Edwards children have made it? she wondered. *Maybe even Jordan?*

But again, why? What was the message?

How seriously should she take the threat? If copies had been made and distributed, pretty damn seriously, she decided. Whether the intent was to scare her or to put a genuine price on her head, anyone reading the poster might see it as an opportunity for a little quick cash.

So what the hell am I going to do about it?

Even though this was a personal matter, if she contacted anyone in the Sheriff's Department, it should be her direct supervisor on Search and Rescue, and that was Sergeant Gardner. But if she went to Gardner, he would probably laugh in her face, tell her she was overreacting, being overemotional again, maybe even using it as an excuse to boot her off the team. If she bypassed Gardner altogether, contacting someone higher up the Department food chain or another law enforcement agency altogether, there would be hell to pay with the sergeant, once again, giving him an excuse to boot her off the team.

She stared down at the poster. Like the phone calls, if the poster's sole purpose was to scare her, it had worked.

Gracie jumped up from the table, ran into the living room, and took the steps up to her bedroom two at a time.

Most of the clothes she wore on a regular basis were already packed and stored in the truck until the fire danger was over. Hauling out the drawers of her dresser, she emptied the remaining tops, bottoms, socks, and underwear into a plastic trash bag. With one arm she scraped everything off the bedside table on top of the clothes—clock radio, five library books, multiple pens and pencils, and a pad of lined paper.

Ten minutes and three trips to the truck later, Minnie on her bed behind the front seats, the dog bed and food, backpack with laptop and several books, and the trash bag were stowed on the front passenger's seat. Gracie screeched backward down her steep driveway and roared down Arcturus.

Sparse traffic on a September night rendered the drive across town smooth and uneventful. Twenty minutes later the Ranger rolled beneath the arched entranceway of camp, down the little hill and across the bridge at the bottom, past the Serrano Lodge parking lot and the carved sign-holding bear, and down the Main Road hill.

Set back in the trees, three single-wide trailers were visible from the road only as peaked roofs above the tops of the scrub oak. Gracie parked the truck on the road and, in the absolute darkness of nighttime in the mountains, shuffled through the thick carpet of duff and last year's fallen leaves and stepped up onto the little porch.

Muffled sounds emanated from the television inside. A dim flickering light showed through the curtains hanging in the fly-specked window.

She lifted her fist to the door and hesitated. She didn't like knocking on doors in what was, for all intents and purposes, the middle of the night, but her need to see Allen was greater than the need not to disturb him.

She knocked.

A split second later, the window curtain parted, fell back in place, and the door was pulled open.

Barefoot, dressed in black sweatpants and the perennial white T-shirt, Allen looked out at her, frowning. Then he pushed the screen door open and stepped back.

She brushed past him into the room.

The tiny living room was sparsely furnished with cheap thrift shop furniture, but it was neat and clean and surprisingly homey.

"What's up, toots?" Allen asked, leaning forward to look into her face, his own cautious, but interested.

"Someone left me a wanted poster," Gracie said. "With my own picture in the bull's-eye of a target. Wanted: dead. I'm moving up to camp for a while. I'll sleep in the Gatehouse."

"Sounds like a good plan," Allen said. "Any idea of who would do such a thing?"

"A couple of possibilities, but no one person positively."

"So what can I do to help you?"

Gracie stood, arms crossed, head bowed. Then she looked up at Allen and, like one neighbor asking another for a cup of sugar, asked, "Do you have a gun I could borrow?"

GRACIE gripped the butt of the five-round Taurus .38 revolver, left hand cupping the right, and sighted down the barrel to the paper silhouette of a man fastened to a hay bale thirty feet away. The weapon felt heavy, the steel cold, alien, and unpleasant.

Even though it was still early morning and she was wearing a floppy hat, she could feel the heat of the desert sun beating down on her head and arms. Beneath red earmuffs, her heart whooshed in her ears.

In the state of California it was illegal for Allen, a convicted felon, to own a gun. Not surprisingly, that didn't stop him from possessing one. At her request the night before, he had left Gracie standing in the middle of the living room, reappearing moments later with the revolver and two boxes of .38 ammunition in his hands. "Have you ever fired a weapon?"

"A shotgun. My stepfather broke my mother's arm, so I shot off his toupee. Kind of a long story."

Allen's eyes crinkled. "Love to hear it."

"I'll buy ya a beer sometime."

"Okay, sugar pea," Allen said. "Here's the deal. Tomorrow morning, first thing, you drive down the hill to the shooting range in Lucerne and learn how to use this. Agreed?"

"But—"

"No buts. No excuses. Agreed?"

"Agreed."

With a long look, Allen placed the revolver and ammunition in Gracie's hands.

"Don't pull the trigger. Squeeze it," the instructor standing next to Gracie said, loudly enough so she could hear him through the earmuffs. Standing four inches shorter than Gracie's five-eight and wearing a Green Bay Packers T-shirt and ball cap, he had introduced himself with an Upper Midwest twang and an expectant gleam in his eye as "Jim, but most people call me . . . Jim."

When Gracie shot him a smile, he winked at her.

She liked Jim from the start, feeling comfortable enough to tell him, "I hate guns. They scare me."

"You don't need to be scared. But it is good to respect the weapon and what it can do. If ya ask me, people don't treat 'em with enough respect. Collect 'em like them stupid plates my wife has."

"People in other countries think everyone in America owns a gun," Gracie said. "That we all walk around with 'em. Like gunslingers. I've never even been in the vicinity of a gun firing." *Liar, liar, pants on fire.*

"Don't be scared. Go ahead and squeeze the trigger."

"Is that right? Gun firing? Not shooting." She knew she was chattering, stalling before pulling the trigger. "Or discharging?" Her arms were getting tired. "Except for a shotgun, I've never really even seen a gun up close before. Except maybe a Revolutionary War musket or something like that. In a museum."

"Squeeze the trigger."

"Is that what they used back then, muskets? Blunder-busses? I love that word. It—"

Twenty feet away, a big-bore rifle boomed, so loud it practically lifted Gracie up off the ground.

"Holy shit!" Gracie said, pulling off her ear protection and looking over. "That was loud! What the hell was that? A friggin' cannon?"

"Concentrate," Jim said. "Get back in position."

"Why am I doing this?" she muttered. "There's no way I'm ever going to be able to shoot anyone anyway, so why . . ."

"You carry a weapon so hopefully you'll never have to shoot someone."

"Whatever that means," Gracie said and lifted the revolver again. She inhaled, took aim, and squeezed the trigger.

POW!

The weapon bucked in her hands and she barely managed to hold on to it. "Holy cow, that was loud! My ears are ring-ing. Even with these ear thingies on." She squinted down at the target. "Did I hit it?"

"No. Do it again. This time try keeping your eyes open."

"I hate this," she grumbled. "There's nothing fun about this."

"It's not a toy."

"Yeah, well, the way some people act, you wouldn't know it."

"Try it again."

"I don't get the attraction of these stupid things. Never will."

"Let's give it another try."

Gracie lifted the revolver. "I guess maybe it gives people the semblance of power. Or maybe not the semblance." She looked down the barrel. "Maybe it just gives them power they don't feel they have otherwise. Some sense of control. This is harder than it looks." She closed her eyes and squeezed the trigger.

POW!

"Did I hit it this time?

"No." Jim took off his hat, scratched his head, then replaced the cap. "Okay, Annie Oakley, let's try somethin' else. I want you to try shootin' from the hip. Don't aim or anythin'. Just pull the trigger. Three times. Bang, bang, bang."

"Okay."

"Try to keep your eyes open and actually look at what you're shootin' at."

Gracie shook out her hands, relaxed her shoulders, and let the revolver hang loosely at her side. "I feel like a gun-fighter at the O.K. Corral or something. Who was that? Matt Dillon? Jesse James?" A bead of sweat trickled down her temple.

"Whenever you're ready, just shoot.

"No, Wyatt Earp. Somebody else was there, but I can't remember who."

"Just fire the weapon. See what you hit."

Gracie looked down at the target.

Lifted the revolver.

Pow, pow, pow!

"Did I miss again?" She squinted at the target.

Beside her, Jim coughed a laugh. "Nice grouping."

There was a single large hole in the target right in the middle of the silhouette man's crotch.

GRACIE SWOOPED UP the long highway switchbacks lead-ing up the backside of the mountain from the desert. She sped up for the straightaway, braked for the sharp hairpin curve, sped up again.

Her ears still rang and her hands were tired from gripping the heavy revolver. "And that gun is teeny," she said out loud.

In the end, when she had taken aim and actually hit the target, nicking the silhouette man's pinky finger, she had sighed with relief and called it good, saying thanks and good-bye to Jim and that she would see him again the fol-lowing week. He had looked less than thrilled.

Beep! Beep! Beep!

Gracie unclipped her SAR pager from the waistband of her shorts and looked at the screen.

"Mandatory evacuation issued for entire valley. All SAR report to SO."

"Oh, shit! This is it," she said and floored the accelerator.

As Gracie wove back and forth on the switchbacks, she was preoccupied with her deadeye with a gun. Once she received the evacuation page, she noticed what hadn't registered before—pickups and cars filled with boxes and furniture, larger trucks pulling fifth wheel RVs and animal trailers, all leaving the valley, a harbinger of the bumper-to-bumper traffic nightmare to come.

The Ranger soared over the final rise leading down onto the eastern portion of the valley. Gracie gasped, hauled on the steering wheel, slammed on the brakes, and slid to a stop on the gravel at the side of the highway.

The Timber Creek valley lay nestled between long parallel mountain ranges, a medley of evergreens dabbed with earth and granite. Timber Lake announced its presence as a strip of cobalt blue in the distance. Overshadowing all else, billowing high into the cloudless morning sky from a point on the southern mountains, was a tower of thick, gray smoke.

"Oh, my God," Gracie whispered. Gripping the steering wheel with both hands, leaning forward to stare out through the windshield, she allowed herself several moments of sheer awe at the terrifying power of nature. Then turning off the choking fear like a water faucet, she swung the Ranger back out onto the pavement and raced down the highway into the valley.

Gaining reception as soon as she topped the rise, Gracie grabbed up her cell phone from the passenger's seat and speed-dialed the camp kitchen. Allen answered after only one ring.

"Allen. Gracie. The Sheriff's Department has issued a mandatory evacuation for the entire valley. We need to evacuate camp. I'm way out by Greene's Lake. Twenty-five, maybe thirty minutes out depending on how backed up traffic is already. Will you go find Mr. Mowry and start the evacuation process? I'll be there as soon as I can."

"On it," Allen said, his voice calm, unruffled. If Gracie had been standing next to him, she would have kissed him. "Can't see any smoke up here for the trees," he continued. "But you can smell it."

"I don't know anything about the fire yet—where it is exactly and how much time we have. But I'm assuming worst-case scenario. As quickly as possible, you need to get the hell out of there, too."

Gracie and Allen had worked out in advance that, in the event of an evacuation, Allen would drive down to West Covina to stay with his mother. And he knew that Gracie would remain up in Timber Creek, working the evacuation.

Even though Gracie also knew Allen would take her dog with him to his mother's, she double-checked, "You'll take Minnie?"

"Don't give the little girl another thought. She'll be safe and sound with me."

"Thank you," Gracie said, tears blurring her eyes "Gotta go. See ya in twenty-five or so."

"Later."

Steering with her left hand, Gracie guided the Ranger around the north side of Greene's Lake. Phone in her other hand, she disconnected from camp and speed-dialed the Sheriff's Office. To the deputy who answered, she said, "Gracie Kinkaid, Search and Rescue. ETA is I hope not more than two hours." Even though she knew the deputy was swamped with incoming calls, she couldn't help asking, "Is the fire in the Santa Anita Canyon?"

"Affirmative," the deputy answered. "As of about thirty minutes ago."

"Okay, thanks," Gracie said and disconnected.

Her third and last call was to the office of the church that

owned Camp Ponderosa. In the previous week, she had spent
several hours on the telephone with church officers and their
insurance company discussing priorities and policies and
procedures, working out in advance every detail of a camp
evacuation. Now that the evacuation notice had been issued,
the call proved quick and painless.

Gracie disconnected, tossed the phone onto the seat beside
her, and punched the accelerator all the way down to the floor.

CHAPTER

27

GRACIE turned the Ranger into the parking lot of the Sheriff's Office.

It had taken her less than two hours to drive across town and up to camp, wave good-bye to the corporate executives as well as Allen and Minnie, load into her truck a single small box of irreplaceables, flash drives, and the safe from the office, change into her SAR uniform, and drive back down winding Cedar Mill Road from camp. All the way through town, slowed by the burgeoning traffic, she trailed a caravan of green National Forest Service vehicles and a single bright red box truck announcing in bold, white lettering ARAPAHO HOT SHOTS.

Gracie pulled into a space in the SO parking lot and trotted inside the substation building. Ten minutes later, trailing behind Carrie Matthews, she walked out again with an HT wedged into a pouch on her radio chest pack.

Carrie split off to grab her gear from the trunk of her car. She heaved it into the bed of the Ranger and climbed into the passenger's seat as Gracie started the engine.

The Ranger made a left turn out of the parking lot. "What's your call sign?" Gracie asked.

"Ten Rescue Fifty-one."

Gracie thumbed the microphone on the radio. "Control, Ten Rescue Twenty-two."

"Ten Rescue Twenty-two," replied a male dispatcher.

"Departing the SO with Ten Rescue Fifty-one on board."

"At eleven oh six."

The women drove two miles east to the only venue large enough for a large-incident Command Post—the valley's Convention Center, a wide, one-story brick building with a low-angle green metal roof and ringed by tall ponderosa pines. In the wide, undulating field behind, domed firefighter tents had already sprouted like green and orange and blue mushrooms.

In the parking lot, Gracie threaded the truck in and out of the rows of cars, trucks, and other vehicles identified by insignias and emblems as belonging to agencies from multiple jurisdictions: local, county, and state fire, National Forest Service, Sheriff's Department, Search and Rescue, California Highway Patrol. Finally locating an open space at the far corner of the lot, she left Carrie behind and wound her way back through the sea of vehicles, waving across to two men from a neighboring SAR team whose faces she remembered, but whose names she didn't.

Taped to the front of one of two reinforced steel entry doors were hand-printed signs, one reading MEDIA with an arrow pointing to the right, another announcing in huge block letters, ALL INCOMING PERSONNEL MUST CHECK IN HERE!

Gracie walked in through a propped-open door and was immersed in the organized chaos that was a large-incident Command Post in the Initial Attack stage.

Every light blazed. The cavernous main room bristled with activity—men and women wearing white, gray, or orange uniform shirts, or yellow Nomex. Several people sat eating their lunches at the long rows of conference tables and steel folding chairs that had been set up in the middle of the room. Affixed to easels and cream-colored cement-block walls along the right side of the room were three enormous briefing maps along with laminated boards displaying Incident Objectives, Organization Assignments, Safety Reminders, and other critical incident information. Doors along the far wall opened up to rooms bursting with desks, laptops, copy machines, boxes of paper, telephones, currently or soon to be occupied by, Gracie figured, the incident mucketymucks—Incident Commander and Section Chiefs for Planning, Logistics, and Finance.

Somewhere out in the field was the Operations Section Chief, tasked with the monumental job of directing all firefighting personnel and equipment—strike teams and task forces, bulldozers, water tenders, helicopters, and fixed-wing aircraft.

The enormity and complexity of fighting a large-scale wildfire was mind-boggling, the expenditure in terms of manpower and dollars staggering.

To the left of the door where Gracie entered was a long table to which a sign written in the same large block letters had been taped: ALL PERSONNEL CHECK IN HERE! Behind the table, a woman, already looking as frazzled as her bushy silver hair, stood separating rumpled sign-in sheets into piles and muttering something about herding cats. Orange Sheriff's Department patches on her white uniform shirt identified her as a Citizen Volunteer. The orange name tape above the breast pocket read: K. PARKER.

Gracie walked up to the check-in table. "Gracie Kinkaid," she said. "Checking in two members of Timber Creek SAR."

K. Parker handed Gracie a clipboard. "Need both names and info on the 211. Vehicle info on the 218."

According to the ICS Form 211, Lenny, Warren, Jon, and

four other Timber Creek SAR members had arrived ninety
minutes earlier and were presumably already out in the field
working their assignments.

As Gracie filled in the forms, K. Parker asked, "Did you
check in with SAR Staging?"

She shook her head. "Didn't see anyone around."

"They're scrambling. Always hard playing catch-up.
When you're outside, let 'em know you're here."

"Got it."

"They'll give you an assignment and paperwork."

Gracie indulged herself a half minute to study four USGS
topographical maps taped together to create one large map
of the Timber Creek valley and the southern mountains,
depicting the perimeter of the Shady Oak Fire and evacuation zones as of six o'clock that morning.

She stepped sideways to a laminated chart displaying the
most current updates on the fire, zeroing in on Weather at the
bottom of the page. Relative Humidity: 14 percent. She bypassed
Haines Index and focused on the day's forecast: Sunny. Temps
low to mid-80s. Sustained winds SE. 10–12 mph. Gusting to 25.

Anxiety gave the knot in Gracie's stomach an extra twist.
An afternoon of high, hot, dry winds from the southeast,
and Camp Ponderosa could explode like a blowtorch.

"SAR GROUP, GROUND Four," Gracie said into the radio
microphone as she steered the Ranger off to the side of the
road. Carrie was out of her seat before the truck came to a stop.

"Go ahead, Ground Four," a male voice answered over
the radio.

"Beginning assignment at corner of State Route 38 and
Peter Pan."

"At twelve fifty-two."

Cutting the engine, Gracie climbed out of the truck and
circled around back where Carrie was already threading
arms through the straps of her backpack.

Ground Four's evacuation assignment was a neighborhood north of Timber Lake, an eclectic mix of ramshackle and higher-priced houses and cabins, already frenetic with activity—families and young people and seniors cramming everything they reasonably and not so reasonably could into whatever vehicles they possessed: cars, pickups, trailers, campers, RVs.

"Kinda like a really jumpy block party," Gracie said, hauling on her own backpack.

A California Department of Forestry helicopter, looking like a behemoth prehistoric insect, its water bucket dangling beneath, cut a wide swath over their heads, then dropped out of sight behind the tall pines at the end of the block.

Gracie gathered up assignment maps and information flyers, handing Carrie half. "Wanna take the right side of the street?" she asked. "I'll take the left?"

"Sure."

"Work our way down to the end, left on Tinker Bell, left on Tiger Lily, right on Nana, that way."

"Got it."

"Got flagging tape?"

Carrie held up a roll of the neon orange plastic ribbon. "When we contact someone personally, right?"

"Yeah. Somewhere visible. Mailbox. Porch railing."

"Got it."

"Pen and paper?"

Carrie patted the side pocket of her pants.

"Okay," Gracie said. "Let's go."

The Ground Four team walked quickly from street to street, stopping at every house within the assignment area, talking with every person they saw, handing out flyers, imparting information about the fire itself, evacuation routes, emergency shelters down the hill.

A jittery tension sparked the air. Some people were relaxed, friendly, even laughing, exhibiting an amped-up energy as if they were embarking on a grand adventure. Others were fraught with worry, afraid, anxious to leave the valley and be out of harm's way. Some had lived through an evacuation before. For some it was a new nightmare.

Thirty minutes into their assignment, Gracie turned onto Michael Street and kicked something with the toe of her hiking boot. She looked down. In the duff of pine needles lay a jackknife. "Hey!" She bent to pick it up. Brushing off the grit, she opened it. Two blades, pliers, screwdriver, corkscrew, wire cutter. "Look what I just found." She held up the knife so Carrie could see from across the street. "Almost new!"

"Jealous!" Carrie called back.

Gracie slipped the knife into the side pocket of her pants as she climbed the front steps of the house on the corner. "Sheriff's Department Search and Rescue," she called, knocking on the rusty screen door. "This is a mandatory evacuation."

Seconds passed. No one answered the door. But someone was home—a beat-up old pickup truck was parked in the overgrown driveway along the side of the house.

Gracie knocked again. "Search and Rescue. The valley's under a mandatory evacuation order."

The front door was yanked open. A man, unshaven, graying hair askew, holes in a dirty white T-shirt, glared out at her through the screen and barked, "Get the hell off my porch!"

"I'm with the Sheriff's Department Search and Rescue. There's—"

"I ain't leavin'!"

"For your own safety," Gracie said, "Fire officials and the Sheriff's Department are strongly urging everyone to leave the valley. If you choose to remain, you're doing so at your—"

"Take my chances. Get the hell off my porch!"

"Thank you. Have a good day." Gracie walked back out to the road, making a note of the address on a sheet of paper on a clipboard. Then she tied a streamer of orange flagging tape to the mailbox, its paint chipped and the pole tilted south.

The next couple of houses were clearly unoccupied, no vehicles in the driveway, no answer to a knock or ring of the doorbell, window shades pulled down, curtains drawn.

Walking past a vacant lot filled with sage and rabbitbrush, Gracie lifted her nose to the air and inhaled. Nothing at first, then she caught it, as if floating in on a high breeze, the faintest hint of smoke. She craned her neck, trying to catch a glimpse of the smoke, but the neighborhood pines were too tall and close together.

She stepped up onto the porch of the next house, past plastic pots with fake pink geraniums, and pressed the doorbell.

She waited.

No one came to the door.

Someone was definitely home. She could hear stealthy movements inside the house.

Hopefully not another old sourpuss. Or worse. She took a step back, wondering if the business end of a shotgun was going to emerge from a window.

Finally someone fiddled with the front lock for what seemed like a full minute, then the door slowly opened. What emerged was not a shotgun, but the quintessential little old lady. Frail. Arms as thin as twigs. The backs of her hands covered with quarter-sized bruises.

Through the open door, Gracie could see the interior of the house was a throwback to the 1950s with an entire wall filled with framed black-and-white pictures and tidy lace doilies pinned to the backs of twin raspberry-colored armchairs. Bing Crosby crooned up from somewhere inside.

The woman looked up at Gracie with blue eyes, milky with cataracts. "Can I help you?" she asked in a voice so faint Gracie had to lean down to catch her words. "Are you lost?"

Gracie smiled down at her. "No, ma'am. I'm with—"

A reedy male voice floated out over the woman's shoulder. "Who is it, Frieda?"

"I'm with the Sheriff's Department," Gracie said. "Search and Rescue."

From inside the house, louder this time. "Gosh dang it, Frieda! Who is it?"

The woman turned away from the door, hand gripping the frame as if it was the only thing keeping her upright. "Did you say something?"

"I'm askin' who's at the gosh dang door!"

The woman turned back toward Gracie. "Who are you again?"

"Search and Rescue."

"It's Search and Rescue."

"Ma'am, there's a fire—"

A man with a cane tottered into view, his face a scowling mass of wrinkles, suspenders holding pants up to his chest. "What do they want?"

"What do you want, dearie?"

"Ma'am, did you know there's a wildfire heading into the valley?"

"A what?"

The man pulled the door open wider. "A fire, you say?"

"Oh, my, no," the woman said. "We didn't know there was a wildfire. Did we, Daddy?"

"How'd you expect us to know there was a gosh dang fire? We got no TV."

"Used to have, dearie," his wife said. "It broke. Last year."

"In gosh dang 1999," the man yelled.

"You don't have a radio?" Gracie asked.

"Oh, my, yes. But Daddy likes to listen to his records on the Victrola."

Gracie smiled again. "Ma'am, sir, there's a mandatory evacuation."

"Land sakes!"

"What in tarnation does that mean?"

"It's not safe here," Gracie said. "I'm afraid you need to leave your home."

"We look like we can leave here by ourselves? Look like a coupla Jack LaLannes, do we?"

"You don't have family or friends who can help you leave?"

"Oh, no," the woman said. "Our boy, Billy, he died, why, just last year, I think."

"Twenty-four years ago, gosh dang it!"

Lordy Lord, Gracie thought.

THE Ranger, with Gracie and Carrie inside, sat at a dead standstill on the highway leading down the back side of the mountain to the desert. Even with the windows rolled up and the air-conditioning recirculating the air, smoke had wheedled its way inside the truck.

Ahead of them, bumper-to-bumper traffic snaked along the two-lane highway, eventually disappearing into the smoky gloom.

As Carrie continued on with their search assignment, Gracie had waited the forty minutes for a Citizen Patrol unit to arrive and drive the delightful old couple away to safety, absorbed by thoughts of what would have happened to them if they had still been sitting in their nice armchairs in their nice home listening to Bing Crosby on the Victrola when the fire roared through the valley.

Fifteen minutes later, the Ground Four team had completed its assignment and been issued another over the radio—a long, narrow neighborhood skirting the west and south shores of Greene's Lake at the east end of the valley.

As the afternoon progressed, the wind direction shifted from southeast to southwest. Over the course of two hours, a creeping veil of smoke had obscured the surrounding mountains, blotted out the sun, and filled the entire valley. Two in the afternoon looked like twilight.

What was good news for Camp Ponderosa boded poorly for Gracie's own neighborhood. She had no idea exactly where the fire was now and where it was headed, how many acres and what structures, if any, had been consumed. Even now her little cabin on Arcturus might be engulfed in flames.

"Gawd," Carrie said, startling Gracie out of her morose thoughts. "I knew traffic was going to be bad, but I didn't know it was going to be this bad."

Gracie ripped open the Velcro on her radio chest pack and hauled out a piece of grape bubble gum, passing one to her partner. "We'll turn off onto a side street up ahead there," Gracie said, pointing to the gravel road branching off from the highway. "Leave this mess behind."

Immediately in front of the Ranger sat a red F-150 pickup. At first, it hit Gracie with a sickening jolt that the truck was Ralph's, until she noticed through the back window what appeared to be a small woman behind the wheel with a child in the passenger's seat and an infant in a car seat between them.

The Ranger's headlights lit up the pickup's open bed overflowing with boxes and multiple suitcases with two enormous Rottweilers, the size of small bears, chained at the front.

"Those dogs look like they weigh more than me," Carrie said.

"Für Elise" played from the cell phone in the front pocket of Gracie's shirt. "They look like they weigh more than *me*," she said, pulling the phone out and peering at the caller ID. "It's my mom. I know we're on duty, but . . ."

"Answer it," Carrie said. "It's not like we're doing anything really important at the moment."

Gracie pressed Answer. "Hi, Mom. How are you? How's

Morris?" She let up on the brake. The truck drifted forward several more feet. Gracie turned toward Carrie and silently mouthed, *shit*.

What? Carrie mouthed back.

"I'm so sorry," Gracie said into the phone. "I know you love him very much . . . Okay . . . Try not to worry about that now." She listened. "You know I'd be there if I could." Her voice broke in spite of herself. "I'm at work right now. You know, my boring life." She shot another look at Carrie. "I'll try to call you later, okay? Maybe not tonight, but tomorrow. Okay. Bye." She hung up the phone and dropped it back into her pocket.

Carrie was watching her. "Bad news?"

"My stepfather just died."

"Ooooh. Sorry."

"Thanks." Gracie sighed. "I feel bad for my mom. She's all alone now. She said something once about selling her house and moving out here to live with me. She doesn't have any idea. She'll take one look at my cabin and hightail it down to my sister's McMansion in Laguna. Much more her style." She glanced over at Carrie again. "Sorry. Didn't mean to air my dirty laundry."

"At least you talk to your family. When's the funeral?"

"Saturday. In Detroit."

Gracie stared at the two massive black heads looking back at her from the F-150 ahead. *So Morris finally kicked the bucket.* She couldn't quite put her finger on what she was feeling. Sadness for her mother. Maybe for Harold and Lenora, Morris's two children from a previous marriage. She doubted they would be heartbroken by their father's passing. More likely they'd be chomping at the bit for his will to be read and his substantial estate to be distributed. Gracie knew she didn't have anything to worry about on that score. Morris had cut her out of his will a long time ago.

But the news of her stepfather's death left her feeling strangely empty, untethered, as if something against which she had been leaning had been yanked away.

A gap opened up in front of the Ranger. Gracie let up on the brake. The truck rolled forward and stopped again.

"Wow. Ten whole feet," Carrie said.

"Für Elise" played again from her shirt pocket. "What is this, Gracie Central Station?" She lifted out the phone and looked at the number. Her breath caught. It was a Los Angeles exchange. "It's Rob," Gracie said. "I don't know if I want to answer it."

"Rob Christian?" Carrie asked, turning in her seat. "Are you batshit *insane*? Answer it!"

"Crap, my hands are shaking."

"Answer the damn phone before he hangs up!"

Gracie pressed Answer. "Hello?"

"Gracie love, are you all right? It's Rob."

As if that voice, as rich as warm molasses, wasn't instantly recognizable. "Hi," Gracie said, eyes flicking across to Carrie, whose entire face was lit up with a smile. "How are you? Where are you?"

"Who gives a bloody damn about me? We're here . . . We're . . . *I'm* here in L.A. Where are you? I just heard it on the news. They're evacuating your valley. Come and stay with us . . . me."

"But . . . what about . . . ?"

"There's plenty of room. I want you here with me. I want you safe."

"But . . . I'm working," Gracie said. "Search and Rescue helps—"

Carrie screamed, staring out the windshield, a horrified look on her face.

One of the Rottweilers had jumped over the side of the F-150. Caught by the chain attached to its collar, it was hanging by the neck, strangling, legs kicking several inches off the ground.

"Shit!" Gracie yelled.

As they watched, the woman driver scrambled out of the F-150, ran back, and threw her arms around the flailing dog

"Gotta go!" Gracie yelled into the phone and tossed it aside. Slamming the truck into Park, she jumped out of the Ranger.

Acrid smoke stung eyes and nose and lungs. With Carrie right behind, Gracie ran up to where the tiny woman was trying to lift the dog up and over the side panel of the truck bed.

They threw their arms around the huge animal.

Claws raked Carrie's arm and Gracie's stomach.

"Take the collar off!" Gracie panted. "We'll lift!" She fell to her knees on the uneven pavement, put her shoulder beneath the dog's haunches, and shoved upward with all her strength. Muscles strained. She gulped in smoky air.

The woman picked frantically at the dog's collar. "I can't get it!"

The dog scrabbled against the side of the truck, strength failing. Then it went limp.

"Champ!" the woman screamed.

Urine dripped onto the pavement.

"He's dying!"

Gracie shoved her hand into her pants pocket. Fingers closed around the jackknife. She pulled it out, opened the blade, inserted it beneath the dog's collar, and sawed away at the heavy leather.

The Rottweiler hung without moving.

Gracie sawed.

The leather broke.

The dog dropped to the ground and lay unmoving on its side.

Gracie fell backward onto the pavement.

The woman fell sobbing to her knees beside the animal. "He's dead!"

"Just stunned," Carrie said, out of breath and kneeling on the ground, a hand on the dog's rib cage. "Heart's beating."

The dog opened its eyes.

"Oh, Champ!" The woman laid her head on its shoulder.

Chest heaving with the effort, Gracie sat on the pavement, staring down at the jackknife in her open palm.

* * *

ASH FLOATED DOWN from the sky like snow, cloaking the eastern end of the Timber Creek valley in a fawn-brown haze.

Gracie sat behind the wheel of Timber Creek SAR's Suburban. Before its headlights, the smoke was so thick she could barely see the road ten feet ahead. Her breath condensed behind her air filter, making it slippery with sweat. Her eyes and throat burned. Her lungs hurt.

The world was eerie, silent, devoid of life. The Suburban crept through the empty streets, houses looming up like specters, then sliding back into the brown gloom.

For the most part, evacuation of the valley residents had been completed the night before. SAR teams now patrolled the empty streets and neighborhoods, keeping an eye out for looters or suspicious circumstances. Road Patrol Twelve consisted of Gracie and two men from a neighboring team whom she had met for the first time that morning.

Ken was riding shotgun. With gray brushing his temples, the man was thin with a sallow complexion. Breath, warm and moist, from behind his mask was fogging up his glasses so that every four or five minutes, he removed them, wiping them clean on a shirttail

Staring sullenly out the window from the backseat directly behind Ken was Bryan. Topping six foot five, knees practically up to his chin, everything about the man seemed square: glasses, head, jaw, shoulders, hands.

In the three hours they had been in the field that day, Bryan had spoken barely a dozen words. Gracie had no way of knowing if it was because he was a man of few words or if he was pouting because, as a local who knew the streets and neighborhoods, she had been assigned to drive and he had been relegated to the backseat. Or if he simply couldn't get a word in edgewise because, for the past three hours, his teammate Ken hadn't stopped talking. As if volume equaled veracity, he regaled Gracie in a loud voice with stories of his heroic exploits during the eight months he had been on Search and Rescue, expounding upon his vast knowledge as a tracker and winter mountaineering expert, how many searches he had been on, how many times he had saved the day. Gracie listened, with half an ear, considering Ken to be a harmless attention seeker, until the man launched into a story about how, on a search for a missing woman, as he was clinging to the side of a steep and rocky incline in the mist, he realized the women's husband, several feet away from him, had probably killed her.

Gracie glanced over at Ken, who was staring straight ahead. She recognized the story. She had been on that search and Ken hadn't been there. In fact, the incident occurred several years before he was even on Search and Rescue.

Gracie steered the Suburban around the corner and wondered how much else of what Ken had been saying was pure bluster. *Most of it*, she thought, and tuned the man out altogether.

The night before, Gracie's shift had ended at ten o'clock. She had set up her one-person bivy tent among the other tents in the field behind the Convention Center and crawled inside. Sitting in the doorway, she tugged off her hiking boots and heavy cotton outer socks by the light of her headlamp. Rather than leave the boots outside in the little vestibule, she zipped them inside the bivy, not wanting to discover in the morning that creepy crawlies or even a snake had found them a cozy place for a nap. Stretching out her legs, she wriggled out of her shirt and pants, folding them neatly and pushing them down with her feet to the bottom of the sleeping bag. In T-shirt and panties, she set the alarm on her watch for five thirty, slipped inside the bag, and closed her eyes with a sigh.

"Rob!" Gracie's eyes flew open and she sat up. She had hung up on him when the Rottweiler had jumped out of the truck, and she'd never called him back. Unable to wait until morning, she pulled her pants back on, climbed outside the tent, and clumped in unlaced hiking boots back into the

Command Post, where she had left her cell phone charging behind a pile of boxes of Gatorade.

Even in the middle of the night, the Command Post was brightly lit and humming with activity. But it was quieter, voices softer, conversation more muted. The deep breath before the morning plunge.

Hidden by the Gatorade, Gracie slid down the wall to a crouch as she dialed Rob's number.

He answered almost immediately.

"Hi," Gracie said in a low voice. "It's me. Sorry . . ."

"Where the bloody hell are you? I've been worried sick . . ."

"I thought I . . . I'm still up in the valley. Search and Rescue helps with evacuations."

"You're still up there? Where's the fire then? Are you in danger?"

"I'm in the Command Post right now." She looked around. "This is about as safe a place as anywhere in the valley."

She heard him mutter, "Bloody hell." Then he said, "I don't suppose I could convince you to abandon your post, light a shuck out of there, come down to L.A. and stay here with me until it's over."

"But . . . what about *her*? Your fiancée?" Unable to keep the snarkiness out of her voice, she said, "You're getting married, remember?" She added under her breath, "Pretty damn fast if you ask me." She closed her eyes, rubbing her forehead with her fingers, waiting for the executioner's blade.

Silence on the other end of the line, then, "I called it off."

Gracie's eyes flew open. *"What?"*

"I couldn't go through with it. It hurt her. A lot. She cried. Bugger it all."

Gracie's heart began a slow steady throb in her temple.

"I thought it was the right thing and all that," Rob said, "The right time. The right girl. But when I get married again, it has to be the last time I get married. And, effing bloody friggin' hell, I found I couldn't stop thinking about *you*. It wasn't fair to her."

Gracie couldn't think of a single thing to say.

"Will you come down to L.A.?" Rob asked. "I really want you here."

"I can't. I'm working."

"No. After the fire."

"You mean to visit?"

"To live."

"In *L.A.*? I *hate* cities. And I love the mountains."

"They have mountains in L.A."

"Barely."

"A visit then. You can stay as long as you want. A week. A month."

"I have a job. I can't just take off—"

"You can find something else," he said, a hint of exasperation in his voice.

Gracie felt the hackles rising. "I don't want to find something else."

"You can have your own room."

"I have my own *cabin*."

"Your own wing then. You can have anything you want. You wouldn't have to worry about anything."

"I don't want to be a kept woman."

"You wouldn't be a bloody kept woman!"

"Quit pushing me!"

"I'm not pushing you! I—" Rob stopped and cursed under his breath. Then he chuckled. "You're right. You have your job. Your cabin. Your own life. I understand that. I'm sorry."

The air cleared. The hackles vanished. Gracie blew out a breath. "I'm sorry. I'm tired, I guess. I shouldn't have gotten . . . I get all . . ."

"Look, love," Rob said. "I hate not being able to reach you. To hear your voice. To talk to you." A sigh. "I just want you near . . . nearer."

"I . . . uh . . ."

"Will you at least think about it?"

Gracie opened her mouth. Closed it. Opened it again. "Yes," she said finally. "I'll think about it."

In a voice that smiled down the line, Rob said, "God knows why, but I've really missed you."

Gracie spread her fingers wide and stared unseeing at her dirt-rimmed fingernails. "God knows why, but I've missed you, too."

Less than six hours later, only marginally awake, Gracie dragged on the clothes she had worn the day before and crawled out of her bivy tent. She washed her face and brushed her teeth at one of a row of outdoor sinks set up behind the Convention Center, poured herself a Styrofoam cup of coffee strong and black enough to turn her hair new-penny copper, and grabbed a piping-hot scrambled-egg burrito from an enormous stainless steel chow wagon set up in the parking lot.

Taking bites of burrito between sips of coffee, Gracie stood at the back of a predominantly testosterone-filled ocean of yellow Nomex shirts, enjoying the rear view of hunky wildland firefighters waiting for the 6 a.m. briefing to begin.

The Planning Section Chief, a short, squat, gray-haired man whose crinkling eyes made him appear as if he were smiling even when he wasn't, walked up to the front of the crowd and stood next to an easel holding a giant map of the fire. As the man thanked everyone present for their hard work and dedication, Gracie glanced around at the mostly men and a few tough women with admiration and respect. Fighting wildland fires was the most physically taxing, most difficult job she knew—hazardous in the extreme, backbreaking, often literally scorching work.

Her eyes wandered over to her left, spotting Sergeant Gardner standing with another man she recognized, after a moment, as her ultimate Search and Rescue boss, the Sheriff himself.

Gracie studied the man. Good-looking with a cleanly shaven square jaw, dark eyes, and straight nose, he was what could almost be characterized as a pretty boy. He was slightly taller than the sergeant, with broader shoulders and less of a paunch, formidable in his neatly starched putty-gray uniform shirt and black Department ball cap. *He looks more like a politician than law enforcement*, Gracie mused. Curious that she had been a volunteer on the man's busiest Search and Rescue team for ten years, logging the most hours on the team for the past three, and she had never met him. In fact, she had seen him only three or four times in the entire time she had been on the team. *A sad reflection on someone*, she thought. But whether on her or the Sheriff, she wasn't sure.

Gracie's head snapped forward. She had heard the word, *camp*. Craning her neck to see over the tops of taller heads and yellow helmets, she could see the man at the front of the crowd indicating an area of cross-hatching on the fire map.

Tossing her burrito and coffee into a nearby trash can, Gracie pushed her way through the crowd and up to the front.

The cross-hatching on the map indicated the area that had burned the day before.

Gracie's heart sank to the ground.

The fire had blasted right through the middle of Camp Ponderosa.

"How much of Camp Ponderosa burned?" she blurted, not caring if she was interrupting, not caring if a hundred firefighters, Command personnel, and the Sheriff himself were waiting. She needed to know.

Face sun-weathered, eyes bagging, with graying hair and a giant handlebar mustache, the man who Gracie assumed was the Operations Section Chief stopped mid-sentence and looked over at her.

"I manage the camp," Gracie said.

In a booming voice, the man continued with his evaluation of the fire's progress, giving Gracie her answer.

The Timber Creek arm of the Shady Oak Fire had claimed 726 acres the previous twenty-four hours. That included 48 of Camp Ponderosa's 210 acres, fingers of flame spreading out through the developed portion, burning some buildings and cabins, leaving others unscathed. Exactly which had burned and which remained, there was no way to tell.

Lodges and cabins could be rebuilt. *But all those beautiful trees destroyed! All those animals killed!* Gracie fought back the tears, not wanting anyone to see her cry, not wanting to appear weak or soft in front of men and women who were heading out for the day to work at a job that might easily cost them their lives. A single tear snuck through to creep down her cheek. She slapped it away with her palm. *Get a grip, Kinkaid. There's nothing you can do right now, except your job.*

She shuddered in a breath, dragged a barely there tissue from her pants pocket, and blew her nose.

She heard only snippets of the rest of the briefing, gleaning only peripherally that shifting winds were expected later in the morning, with a cold front, possibly even rain, moving in later that afternoon.

Gracie returned to the present, braking the Suburban to a stop at the intersection of two streets.

She rolled down her window and stuck her arm outside. The air felt cooler than before. And the wind had indeed shifted from southeast to north-northeast.

A north wind would blow the fire back on itself, away from the residential areas, away from her own cabin. Good news all around for firefighters and everyone else. Rain would be better still.

Ken was still talking, this time about a mistake someone on his team had made at some time. In the backseat, Bryan remained sullenly silent.

"Für Elise" played from Gracie's shirt pocket. Pulling out her phone, she looked at the number, not recognizing it.

Figuring anything was better than listening to Ken, she answered it. "Hello?" she said, voice sounding as if she were talking in a cave. She pulled up her air filter and said again, "Hello?"

"Gracie?" a tremulous female voice asked.

"Yah."

"Baxter's gone!" Sharon Edwards wailed into her ear.

BAXTER'S grandmother's words tumbled out so fast and garbled, Gracie couldn't make heads or tails of what she was saying.

She swerved the Suburban to the side of the road and stopped.

"What are we doing?" Ken asked in a loud voice.

"Sharon," Gracie said. "Slow down. I can't understand what you're saying. Start over."

She and Baxter had agreed in advance, the woman told her, that if an evacuation order for the valley was issued, they would meet at the end of the compound driveway and she would bring him with her down the hill. "But he was acting so strange when I picked him up," she said.

"Strange how?"

Leaning forward and staring at her, Ken asked, more loudly, "Why are we stopped?"

Gracie held up a finger to indicate "just a second," then used it to plug her ear.

"Keyed up," Sharon was saying. "Like he was scared. He kept babbling on and on about how something was going down and he needed to call you."

Oh. Shit. "Where is he now?" Gracie asked.

"I don't know! We were driving down the hill the back way. I slowed down because all the cars were backed up and he jumped right out of the truck and ran into the woods. I couldn't follow him! I didn't know what to do! The Sheriff's Department's not going to do anything. They're so busy with the fire and everything. The fire! Oh, God! I just didn't know who else to call!"

"I'll go look for him. I'll call you when I know something." Gracie disconnected and let up on the brake.

"Finally," she heard Ken mutter.

She swung the Suburban around in the middle of the intersection and drove back out of the development.

"Where are we going now?" Ken asked.

"Back to the ICP," Gracie said. "I have a family emergency."

"But this isn't our team's vehicle. What are we going to ride around in?"

Unable to stop herself, Gracie said, "With all your experience, I'm sure you'll figure something out."

GRACIE SWEPT BACK the branches of the hideout and shined the beam of her flashlight into the murky interior. "Bax?"

"Gracie?" Baxter's dirt- and tear-smeared face rose up out of the depths of the shelter, then he threw his arms around her. "I knew you would come."

Gracie could feel the boy's thin body shaking. "You're shivering."

"It got cold."

"That's a good thing. Maybe it'll actually rain and help put the fire out. Let's get you out of here and warmed up. My truck's at the bottom of the hill."

With Baxter following, Gracie backed out of the shelter.

As hoped for, a cold front had moved into the valley. The entire plateau lay in heavy cloud, the moisture in the air palpable.

Gracie and Baxter walked down the more stable, brush- and grass-matted incline paralleling the gravel road leading down to the top of Arcturus. "What are you doing here?" Gracie asked as she stood on a mound of grass waiting for the boy to negotiate his way down to her. "Even though the smoke's almost gone, it's very dangerous up here."

"I was waiting for you to find me," he said as he landed on the grassy mound next to her.

Gracie continued on down the incline. "How'd you get all the way back up here? Gran Sharon told me you jumped out of her car halfway down the hill."

"You told her what Jordan did to me."

"I know. I'm sorry I broke my promise to you. But let's talk about that later. How did you get all the way back up the hill?"

"I hitchhiked."

"Someone actually gave you a ride *up* the mountain?"

He nodded.

Moron. "What's going on, Bax? Your gran said you told her something was going down."

"I had to see you, to talk to you and I didn't know any other way to get ahold of you."

Gracie stopped and turned back to face the boy. "So now you got me. What's up? What's going down?"

Baxter slid to a stop beside Gracie, looking up at her, eyes huge, reflecting back fear. "I heard my grandpop Martin talking with my dad and Uncle Win. It's going to go down soon. Tomorrow morning."

"What's about to go down? What are they planning?"

"I don't know . . ."

Gracie inhaled to protest.

"But I saw a bomb."

Gracie's heart kicked up a notch. "A *bomb*?"

"I think it was a bomb. A metal tube thing with lots of wires sticking out of it. I could show you."

"I wouldn't know a bomb from a friggin' engine piston," Gracie said. "Where'd you see this bomb . . . thing?"

"The Inner Sanctum."

"What the heck is the Inner Sanctum?"

"At the compound. Down in the bunker."

Gracie stared at the boy. "We are *not* going to the compound. Are you out of your mind *crazy*?"

"If it's dark, nobody would see us."

"N-o, Bax." She turned and continued the descent.

"We can wait until everyone's in bed. You have to help me, Gracie. You just have to."

"What I just *have* to do is go to the police, the authorities, someone," Gracie said, reaching the bottom of the steep incline and stepping between two of the giant boulders marking the beginning of the pavement. "*They* can go in and stop them."

"You think they're going to listen to us?" Baxter asked, following her to where the Ranger was parked at the top of the road.

"Probably not," Gracie said, unlocking the passenger's seat door of the truck and pulling it open. "Get in."

Climbing into the driver's seat and shutting the door, Gracie pulled out her cell phone. "I'm not calling 911," she said. "They have their hands so full already. If this turns out to be nothing . . . The last thing I need on top of everything else is to be labeled one of those crackpots who calls 911 when they can't get through on the Butterball turkey hotline."

"What's a Butterball turkey?"

She looked sidelong at Baxter. "Never mind." She looked down at her phone. "No reception here. We'll have to go to my cabin. Use the landline there."

The air inside Gracie's cabin was stuffy and warm, but free of smoke. Gracie grabbed up the phone on the kitchen counter, dialed the non-emergency number for the Sheriff's Department from memory, listened to it ring on the other end, then to a recording saying the Timber Creek valley was under a mandatory evacuation order and where emergency shelters down the hill were located. She hung up. "What's your gran's cell number again?"

Gracie dialed the number Baxter provided, telling Gran Sharon that she had found Baxter. "He's safe with me," she told the woman, who was weeping with relief. She winked at Baxter, who was sitting sideways in a chair at the table, elbows on knees, chin on hands. "Right now, we're at my cabin. I'll keep him with me for right now. I won't let him out of my sight. I promise."

Gracie hung up and stood looking down at the phone in her hand.

Then she punched in 911.

"THANK YOU, DETECTIVE," Gracie said and placed the receiver back in its cradle.

"Are they going to do something?" Baxter asked.

"I'm not sure," Gracie said, sitting down at the table opposite the boy. "It all depends on if they consider it a credible threat. And if they think you and I are credible sources or not."

"What if they don't believe you?"

"I don't know."

"We have to go anyway."

"No."

"We *have* to do it."

"No, we don't."

"It's the right thing to do."

"I'm beginning to regret giving you all those books to read."

"If you won't help me, I'll run anyway again."

"That's blackmail."

"You promised Gran you wouldn't let me out of your sight. A promise is an oath. Your word of honor. A sacred bond."

Gracie shot him a look. "Like I said about those books . . ."

"You already broke one promise," Baxter said carefully.

"That's not fair and you know it. I had to tell your gran—"

He threw out his hands. "Come on, Gracie. You have to help me. You just *have* to." He stood up, pushed his arms through the straps of his backpack, and walked to the front door, his hand on the knob. As if reading her mind, he said, "I'm scared, too, Gracie. And I don't want to get caught either. But what if that detective didn't believe you? What if they don't come? I have to do what I can to stop them. I have to try."

Gracie looked over at the boy who was turning into a man in front of her eyes, willing to take an enormous risk to do what he felt was the right thing.

Baxter pulled the door open. "I'm leaving now. Are you coming with me or not?"

GRACIE TURNED THE Ranger off the highway onto Maple and drove up the long incline to the little community of Pine Knot. At the fire station, she made a left turn, then another immediate left into the parking lot of the local park. She backed into a spot so she could keep an eye on the road and shifted into Park.

As the afternoon had faded, Gracie and Baxter waited, the boy sitting cross-legged on the living room couch, engrossed in *The Absolutely True Diary of a Part-time Indian*, Gracie, gnawing on the same reluctant cuticle while standing at the front window watching rain splatting against the glass, mood equally somber, thinking of how the fortuitous shift in weather had come a day too late to save the camp she loved.

While eating two MREs Gracie had dug from her

emergency stash in the bed of the Ranger, she and Baxter talked about books, about families and fathers and being strong within oneself in spite of what people who are supposed to love you say or do.

"How'd you turn out so well?" Gracie asked.

The boy shrugged. "Grandma Sharon, I guess."

"You're really lucky to have her."

Baxter looked at her. "She says I'm better than all of them put together in a blender."

"She's right about that," Gracie said. "She's right about a lot of things."

Before they left the cabin, Gracie had shown Baxter the flyer with her face pasted in the bull's-eye. "Have you seen this before?"

He shook his head, staring at the flyer.

"Know who would have made it? Sent it to me?"

"No."

"Could Jordan have made this?"

Baxter frowned. "It could be Jordan," he said. "He's a sucky speller."

At full dark, they had left the cabin and driven up to Pine Knot to wait for nine o'clock, the family's usual bedtime.

Baxter had nodded off and Gracie had given him the extra minutes of sleep, giving herself the extra minutes to fortify her nonexistent courage.

As the boy slept, rain drenched the surrounding ground and trees, rivulets of water running down the gutters on either side of the road. Gracie stared at the fogged-up windshield, wringing the steering wheel, fretting, fidgeting, knowing she was being foolhardy, boneheaded, and every other adjective she could think of, that she should just drive Baxter down the hill and let law enforcement do whatever they were going to do, knowing that if she did, the moment she slowed the Ranger, Baxter would hop out of the truck and disappear into the woods. Short of hog-tying him to the fender, there wasn't much she could do.

Gracie checked the glowing dial of her watch, leaned over, and patted the boy on the leg. "Baxter. Time to wake up."

At Baxter's direction, Gracie wound the Ranger through the streets of Pine Knot, up this hill, around that corner, until eventually he pointed to a driveway up ahead and said, "Turn in there."

Gracie turned into the driveway of a house, stopped, and turned off the engine. "Whose house is this?"

"I dunno. But everybody's gone, remember?" he said, shouldering open the passenger's door. "We're not very far from the compound."

The rain had stopped, but everything was sodden, dripping. Clouds hovered low on the tops of the trees and their breath showed in bursts of white vapor.

Gracie reached behind the seat for her Search and Rescue fleece jacket, then thought better of it. Bright orange probably wasn't the ideal color for cat burgling. Instead, she grabbed up her black North Face rain jacket and threw it on, zipping it up to her chin.

Deciding her pack would be too cumbersome, she opted for carrying only her water bottle sling, clipping it on over her jacket.

Then she leaned back inside the truck again, slid her hand beneath the driver's seat, and withdrew Allen's revolver.

Weighing the heavy weapon in her hand, she pondered the wisdom of bringing it along with her, the odds of her being able to shoot her way out of anything or perhaps getting shot herself because of her inexperience.

Deciding that having it if she needed it was better than not having it if she needed it, she pulled her webbed belt free of her pants loops, threaded the belt through the holster, then back through the loops again, and clipped it closed, pulling the back of her jacket down low over the weapon.

She eased the door of the truck closed and showed Baxter where she was putting the keys atop the front right tire in case he should return to the truck before her. Then she followed the boy down the driveway and off into the woods on the right.

For several minutes they walked through the trees, intermittently using the light from Gracie's LED flashlight, the only sounds the drip-drip-dripping from tree branches and the scrunching of boots on soggy pine needles.

For no reason that Gracie could discern, Baxter stopped and said, "It's electric, so don't touch it."

Gracie aimed her flashlight at the ground and turned it on. Two feet in front of her, a wire fence stretched from tree to tree to tree. She switched the flashlight off. "Wouldn't dream of touching it."

They walked parallel to the fence until they reached the green metal gate barring the entrance of the compound driveway. They crunched onto the gravel and stopped. Baxter pointed to two tall pines on either side of the gate. "Motion detectors," he said in a low voice. "With spotlights. They'll turn on if you try to walk around the gate. And there are cameras all over the place."

"Terrific," Gracie said, keeping her own voice low.

"Stay close to me," he said. "We can go a lot of the way on the driveway. Then we have to go through the woods so they can't see us from the house."

"Terrific," she said again.

The boy punched a five-digit code into the keypad. With a faint squeak, the wheeled gate slid open. Gracie and Baxter walked through. With another push of a button, the gate slid closed.

The two walked up the long driveway. Where it made a sharp right-hand bend, Baxter stopped, whispering, "We go through the woods here. But we can't use the flashlight very much because we're getting close."

"Okay."

"But don't worry, Gracie. I know the way. Want me to hold your hand?"

She smiled in the darkness. "My eyes will adjust. Thanks anyway."

Baxter left the driveway, cutting into the woods with Gracie right behind.

"Where are all these so-called booby traps?" she whispered.

"The first one's right up there."

"I can't see anything."

"There's a wire between those two trees. A little way off the ground."

"What would happen if I tripped over it?"

Baxter made the sound of an explosion.

"Got it."

Baxter walked up to the wire, invisible to Gracie, and blithely stepped over it.

Gracie walked up and stopped. Spreading her fingers over the end of the flashlight, she turned it on and focused the diminished light on a wire three inches off the ground, trying not to imagine what would happen to her body if she touched it. She turned the flashlight off.

"Hurry up, Gracie," Baxter whispered. "Or we'll never get there. We have a lot more to go."

When still she hesitated, Baxter said, "You can do it, Gracie. Trust me."

Gracie looked over at the boy, a small black figure against the deeper dark of the woods. He was asking her to act counter to every instinct, to relinquish all control to a boy less than a third her age. "Tall order, Bax," she said, then took in a deep breath, lifted her right foot as high as she could, stepped over the wire, and planted her foot on the other side.

With a foot on either side of the wire, she froze.

"Don't stop, Gracie! Keep going!"

Gritting her teeth, she lifted up her left foot and brought it over the wire, hopped sideways on her right foot, wind-milled her arms, twisted her body, and fell backward onto the ground. With an "oof," she landed on her back in the wet duff, the toe of her right boot an inch from the wire.

She slid her foot up close to her body.

"Ha ha! Way to go, Grace," Baxter said. "Do you get it? Grace? Gracie?"

"Got it, Bax," Gracie said as she pushed herself to her feet again and brushed herself off. "Hardy har."

Baxter touched her elbow. "That's okay. You'll get the hang of it. We have a lot more to go."

"Terrific."

In all, there were twenty-two trip wires.

One by one, Gracie and Baxter approached each wire and stopped. Baxter stepped right over it. Gracie lit it up with her flashlight for a split second, stepped over the wire with deliberate care, and moved on.

Finally, when Gracie had been worn to a frazzle from the effort of trying not to end up a tossed salad, Baxter stopped behind a ponderosa tree trunk two feet in diameter and whispered, "We're here."

Gracie crept up behind him. "Thank God!" she breathed into the boy's ear and peered out from behind the tree.

Across a wide, large dirt clearing stood two buildings.

Pointing at the building on the right, Baxter said into Gracie's ear, "That's the house. Looks like everyone except Grandpop Martin is asleep."

The house was an unusually large, two-story brick house with a metal roof and attached triple garage. Pickup trucks and cars were parked in a neat line facing outward. A single window on the second floor glowed yellow like a Cyclops's eye.

"Big day tomorrow maybe," Gracie whispered back.

Baxter's finger moved left to a large metal industrial building with three large bay doors and one smaller one. "That's the garage. That's where the bunker is. Underneath it. And the Inner Sanctum." He pointed even farther to the left. "We'll go around to over there so we end up at that end. That way no one should be able to see us."

"No one *should*?" Gracie whispered, irritated that Baxter's voice was animated, breathless, as if he was having the time of his life. Which most likely he was. "I'm not liking this at all, Bax," she hissed. "This is a bad idea."

"We'll be on the cameras for a little while, but no one will see us. I promise. Come on." At a crouch, the boy ran to the next tree. A flash of a hand told Gracie he was waving her on.

Slipping from tree to tree, Baxter and Gracie circled the yard until they stood opposite the long end of the garage.

Then Baxter said suddenly, "Okay, go!" and, without a sound, sprinted across the yard to the garage.

Shit.

Gracie ran.

GRACIE stepped into the garage, black as pitch, and waited as Baxter closed the door behind them.

He flipped on a switch on the wall. Bright white light from fluorescent ceiling fixtures flooded the room.

Gracie spun around. "Bax! They'll see the light!"

"No, they won't. No windows in here. See?"

Gracie did see, but standing in the room with all the lights on made her feel like a flea in the glare of a circus spotlight. "Turn them off anyway," she said. "We'll use my flashlight."

Baxter flipped off the switch, plunging them back into complete darkness.

Gracie turned her flashlight on and ran the stark, white beam across the near end of the room. The light slid past row after row of brown padded-seat folding chairs, a long metal conference table in front, stopping at a line of white teddy bears, all wearing blue shorts and red suspenders, with one paw held up as if in salute.

"Bizarre," Gracie whispered.

The circle of light lifted and stopped again, illuminating

an enormous flag hung at the front of the room—a white circle on a field of bright red. At its center—a black swastika.

Gracie slid the beam left, hovering it over a Confederate flag, then moved it right again, past the Nazi flag to another, white and black on red, the flag of the Ku Klux Klan. The beam glided around the room to the back wall papered floor to ceiling with flyers and leaflets spewing intolerance and hatred toward every race and religion imaginable, toward law enforcement, advocates for animal rights, pro-choice, gun control, environmentalists.

The hair on the back of Gracie's neck prickled as if a wraith had glided by in the darkness, running skinless fingers along the top of her head. "They hate anyone who isn't just like them," she whispered. Her eyes moved across the wall. "Or maybe they just hate. Period." She felt Baxter standing next to her. "You've seen all this before?"

"Oh, sure," he said, matter-of-factly. "We have meetings here every Monday afternoon. Everybody comes. Even the little kids."

"Starting the indoctrination early. Let's get out of here. I can't breathe."

"The bunker's this way," Baxter said, gesturing across the room. "Through the garage."

By flashlight, they crossed the cement floor, footsteps echoing. "Right here," Baxter said and pulled a door in the metal partition open.

Standing in the doorway, Gracie swept her flashlight beam around the large garage, over ATVs on trailers, gigantic tanks of fuel, three shiny, bright red generators, a green and yellow tractor with a shovel on one end, backhoe on the other. Along the wall on the right was a stainless steel, deep-basin sink and a long wooden workbench with every kind of power tool imaginable: drills, batteries, chargers, saws—band, reciprocal, circular. Above, neatly arrayed on pegboard hooks, were hammers, screwdrivers, wrenches, saws, tape measures, levels.

"C'mon," Baxter whispered. He led Gracie along the back wall to a wide door at the far end and pulled it open.

The flashlight lit up a wooden landing with a ramp leading belowground.

"A ramp?"

"Grandpop Martin's in a wheelchair."

"I forgot."

Closing the door behind them, Baxter led the way down the ramp, circling around and down to another heavy steel security door at the bottom. Feeling as if she were an archaeologist exploring an ancient Egyptian tomb, Gracie followed Baxter into the first of a series of long, narrow rooms with low ceilings and cement-block walls painted white.

The first room was a living area with a comfortable looking sectional couch in cocoa-brown velour. On the wall above a long row of cupboards holding puzzles and board games and an impressive library of DVDs, a flat-screen television had been mounted. In the next room, Gracie's flashlight scanned a full kitchen with two refrigerators, six-burner stove, two-basin sink, and an entire wall of floor-to-ceiling cabinets. Down one side of the room ran a long wooden table with bench seats.

The adjoining room held shelf after built in shelf of canned goods, some store-bought, some home-canned. On the floor sat plastic tubs labeled RICE and WHEAT FLOUR. Freezers lined the far wall. Gracie opened the lid of the first one and shined her light inside. Plastic packages with neatly hand-printed labels. "Meat," she whispered.

She opened one freezer after the other and looked inside. "This one's all . . . vegetables. This one . . . more vegetables. This one is fruit, I guess. Looks like cherries. Peaches. This is a big operation. Huge."

"There's supposed to be enough for all of us to live here for three years."

I wouldn't last three days down here, Gracie thought.

They crossed into the next room containing sleeping

bunks, neatly made up with sheets and blankets and pillows with starched, white cases. Next along was a bathroom with stainless steel sinks and toilets and showers.

The following room was half the size of the others—a medical dispensary with a short examining table and glass-door cabinets filled with medical supplies.

"Like a mini–MASH unit," Gracie whispered.

"What's that?"

"Mobile Army Surgical Hospital."

"I don't think we need to whisper anymore, Gracie," Baxter said in a normal voice. "No one can hear us. The ceilings are soundproof and reinforced." He pulled open the next door. Gracie shined the beam of her flashlight around the room and gasped.

The room was an arsenal, walls loaded with assault weapons, shotguns, handguns, knives, hand grenades. Shelves on the opposite wall were filled with box upon box of ammunition.

"Holy . . ." Gracie said, turning a complete circle in the middle of the room. "There must be thousands of rounds. Looks like they're getting ready for World War Three."

"I *told* you."

Gracie tried the handle of the door leading to the next room. "Why's this one locked?"

"That's the Inner Sanctum," Baxter said. "Only Uncle Win and Grandpop Martin have a key."

"What the heck, Bax. We came all this way and now . . ."

Something dangled in front of Gracie's eyes. She swung the flashlight beam up. "What's that?"

"The key." Baxter's grin looked ghoulish in the glow of the flashlight.

"Do I dare ask how you got that?"

"Uncle Win takes it off. I snuck in and took it while he was sleeping."

"Bax!"

"Auntie Kimberly doesn't like the chain hitting her in the face."

Gracie coughed to hide her laughter. "How'd you get it copied so fast?"

"Oh, there's a key maker in the garage. Didn't you see? They have everything in there. Anyway, Uncle Win never woke up."

"Thank God. So let's open the door already."

Baxter inserted the key, turned the knob, and pulled the heavy door open.

"There are no windows in here, right?" she asked.

"Right."

"Turn on the light."

Baxter snapped on the overhead fluorescents. Light filled the room.

Gracie stepped into the Inner Sanctum.

A waist-high shelf ran along the wall on the left.

Gracie stepped over and looked down.

She thought she might not be able to recognize a real bomb if she saw one.

She was wrong.

The table was covered with dozens of pipe bombs, arranged in a neat line. There was no mistaking what they were—multiple brown wires and a little black box attached to four steel cylinders clamped together and capped on both ends. Four identical black backpacks sat at the end of the shelf, unzipped, ready for packing and transport.

Gracie blew out a breath. She had no idea whether or not the bombs were armed and ready to blow. With no wish to say hi to Saint Peter at the pearly gates this early in her life, she felt the sudden need to be silent and move very, very slowly. She leaned over and said in the barest breath of a whisper into Baxter's ear, "Let's get the hell out. I've seen enough."

She turned around, eyes catching on a metal clothing

rack pushed against the opposite wall. Orange shirts hung next to woodland camouflage pants folded neatly over hangers. On a wire shelf above sat floppy-brimmed hats and pairs of leather gloves. Below, cotton ragg socks had been stuffed into neatly aligned pairs of hiking boots.

But Gracie's attention was riveted on the shirts. Orange. Search and Rescue orange. With orange and yellow Sheriff's Department patches on the shoulders. Stuffed into the breast pocket of each shirt was a lanyard.

She stepped over and drew one out.

Clipped to the end was a Search and Rescue ID. The name she didn't recognize, but the person in the picture she did.

It was Winston.

Gracie pulled the lanyard from the pocket of the next shirt. And the next. And the next.

Lee. Boojum. Jordan. And others, men and women, whose faces Gracie didn't recognize.

"Gracie—" Baxter began.

She held up a hand. "Wait. I have to think."

She reconstructed the chronology in her head.

Winston driving up to camp, ostensibly to apologize. The Ranger unlocked, parked in front of the Gatehouse. Gracie's Search and Rescue uniform hanging behind the driver's seat, clearly visible through the side window. The lanyard around the hanger, ID stuffed in the breast pocket. Gracie walking down to the maintenance shop for another paint roller, leaving Winston alone in the front yard, steps from her truck.

Understanding hit her like a brick to the head.

She hadn't lost her Search and Rescue ID.

Winston had taken it and used it to make exact replicas.

"Fu—," Gracie started.

"Ha ha, Gracie!" Baxter said. "You almost used the F-word. You must be really, really mad."

"I never needed to use it before."

Sheriff's Department IDs gave the Edwards/Ferguson clan access to the Sheriff's Office substation.

Gracie shook her head.

No. Something larger, more deadly. Like . . .

Her breath caught in her chest.

Like a large-incident Command Post.

The perfect target.

Firefighters, Command personnel, law enforcement, Search and Rescue, more than a hundred people, all grouped closely together for the morning briefing at 6 a.m.

Beside her, Baxter pulled a door open. "Hey! This is the tunnel! This is cool!"

Stepping over, Gracie peered down the dark corridor, tall and narrow, walls built with cement block and lumber, floor hard packed dirt—rough, but reasonably flat. A cool breeze lifted her hair, slightly musty, not altogether unpleasant.

"I've never seen the tunnel before," Baxter was saying. "I've seen where it comes out on the other end."

"Where does it come out?"

"There's a hole in the side of the hill. At the creek. You climb up the gully to the road. This is cool!"

Gracie eased the door closed and stepped back in front of the metal clothing rack, staring at the row of orange shirts. Then she lifted the hanger of the first shirt, grabbed the lanyard, removing it from the hanger, then hung the shirt back up. One by one, she moved down the line, removing the lanyards, rehanging the shirts.

Baxter turned to a large chest freezer standing alone against the wall next to the door. "Why's this one in here?"

With a single overhand knot, Gracie tied the ends of the lanyards together, unclipped her belt, threaded the end through the lanyards below the knot, and reclipped it, the IDs dangling from her waist.

Baxter opened the freezer lid, stood on tiptoe, and looked inside. "Ahh!" he yelled, stumbling backward and falling onto the floor. The lid slammed closed.

"What!" Gracie breathed.

Face devoid of color, eyes the size of dinner plates, Baxter stretched out a hand and pointed. "B . . . b . . . bodies."

Gracie took in a deep breath, opened the freezer lid, and looked inside.

At the bottom of the freezer lay two torsos, limbless, headless, but obviously a man and a woman, encased in heavy, clear-plastic contractor bags.

They had found the two missing antiracist activists.

Gracie's mouth filled with the taste of metal and her stomach lurched. She let the freezer lid bang shut, hauled Baxter to his feet, and snapped off the overhead light. "We have to get out of here. Now."

Dragging Baxter along behind, Gracie ran back through the bunker, light from her flashlight bouncing crazily ahead of them.

From room to room they ran, Gracie flinging open each heavy door, running through, letting the door swing closed behind them. Past weapons and boxes of ammunition, through the mini–MASH unit, past showers and bunk beds and freezers of fruits and vegetables, through the kitchen, the living area, up the wooden ramp, and out through the garage.

Gracie flung open the door leading into the meeting room and skidded to a stop. She put up a hand, blinking against the sudden bright light. Baxter ran headlong into her from behind.

The overhead fluorescents blazed, lighting up the entire room.

Next to the table at the front of the room stood a little girl, barefoot, dressed in pink, gray, and black camouflage pajamas. In her arms, she clutched one of the white teddy bears, holding its soft fur up against her cheek.

Gracie recognized her from the training. The girl with the pink whistle.

Winston's daughter.

Heather.

"Hi, Baxter," Heather said. "What are you doing here?"

Too stunned to move, to even think, Gracie stood in the doorway as if her hiking boots had been glued to the cement.

"I thought you were with Gran Sharon," the girl said. "That's what everyone was saying. Daddy and Grandpop and Uncle Lee were really, really mad."

Baxter came to life before Gracie did, stumbling past her and into the room. "H . . . Heather," he said in a high voice. "You're not supposed to be in here."

"Auntie Brianna yelled at me. I needed a teddy." Her eyes moved to Gracie, still frozen in the doorway. "What's she doing here?"

Baxter glanced over his shoulder at Gracie, then back to the girl. "She's my friend."

"Is she going to be a new mommy?"

"I don't know. Yes." He reached out to take the girl's hand. "Come on. You need to go back to the house."

Hugging the teddy bear, Heather turned away, avoiding his grasp. "I don't want to."

"Come on, I'll go with you."

"No!" The girl's bottom lip quivered with the possibility of a tantrum. "I want to stay here and play with the teddies."

What sounded like a screen door slammed outside. "Heather?" a high male voice called. "You out here?"

Winston.

Panic grabbed Gracie by the throat. "Bax!" she hissed.

Baxter turned and pointed in the direction from which they had just run. "I'll stay here. It'll be okay. You go. The tunnel."

Without argument, Gracie backed out of the room and closed the door. Then she ran back through the garage, down the ramp to the bunker, and from one room to the next.

Outside the door to the Inner Sanctum, she stopped.

The door was locked and Baxter had the key.

"Shit!"

She shined her flashlight beam on the knob.

The key was still in the lock.

She turned the knob and opened the door. Pulling out the key and putting it in the side pocket of her pants, she closed the door, testing the knob. Locked.

In two strides, she was across the room and pulled open the door to the tunnel.

She hesitated.

As opposed to the other door locks which were keyed, this door had a push-button combination lock.

She tested the knob.

Locked.

When she closed the door, it would lock behind her.

There would be no returning the way she had come.

She prayed that Baxter was right, that the tunnel led out into the open air, a hole in the side of the embankment, and that she wasn't sealing herself into a cement tomb.

Gracie stepped into the tunnel, eased the door closed, and plunged herself in absolute darkness.

Flicking her flashlight on, she trained the beam on the ground. Her breathing sounding abnormally loud, she trotted down the narrow corridor and around the first corner.

"Ah!" Something grabbed at her hair, her face. Sharp pain pierced a lower eyelid, eyebrows, an ear, her lip.

She jerked to a stop and threw up the hand holding the flashlight to sweep away whatever was afflicting her.

More pain. Sharp and needlelike. The tips of two fingers caught, held.

The flashlight dropped to the ground and rolled at her feet in an arc of light.

Gracie froze. "What the hell is that?" She inched her left hand up her body, slowly, carefully, sliding the fingertips past her chin, up her face to her eye, brushing filament, a tiny metal shaft.

Easing her eye closed and cupping her hand over the lid, she tipped her head back and looked up.

By the dim light of the flashlight, she could just make

out a rain shower of heavy-gauge monofilament suspended from the ceiling.

No fancy gadgetry.

No loud explosions.

Simple and terrifyingly effective.

By the lower lid of her right eye, the top of her left ear, both eyebrows, the upper corner of her lip, her hair, and the third and fourth fingers of her right hand, Gracie had been caught as easily as a trout in a caddis fly hatch, snared by a booby trap of fish hooks.

"*SHIT!*" Gracie fluttered her fingers across her eyelid, feeling where the point and the tiny barb of the fishhook had pushed through the soft skin directly below her eye. For the moment, at least, the point lay harmlessly in the space between her lid and the eyeball itself. As long as she didn't move, there was no danger of damaging her eye.

As long as she didn't move.

She walked her fingertips up to her left eyebrow. The hook there had barely penetrated. She pulled it loose and tossed it up so that it tangled in the other lines.

The third hook was a midge hook, catching the top of her ear, hook and barb embedded in the skin. If need be, she could rip that one free with what she figured would be a lot of pain, but minimal damage.

Her right hand, caught in the air above and behind her head, was already growing tired. Unless she acted fast, things were going to get really ugly.

If she could pull the line down far enough, she might be able to gnaw through it with a canine, like an animal in a trap.

Gracie tipped her head back slightly and looked up to where the lines of filament were attached to eyebolts in the ceiling.

She tugged down on the line connected to her ear. It stretched a millimeter, but held. She hauled on it until the filament cut into her fingers. Nothing.

Her mind flashed to the jackknife she had found the day before, the blade she had used to free the Rottweiler from its strangling collar.

Where was it?

With her left hand, she patted her breast pocket, then those on her pants. Left hip. Left back. Lifted her left leg. Felt the side pocket. Nothing but a pad of paper, a pencil, and the door key. She felt around to her right hip pocket. The right back. Lifted her right leg and felt a PayDay candy bar in the side pocket.

"Where the hell is it?" she whispered.

Then she remembered.

The jackknife was safely zipped inside the pocket of her Search and Rescue fleece jacket, left behind in the truck.

And the gun she so wisely and confidently had obtained for her own protection was completely useless to her. A bullet would probably ricochet back and forth off the walls and ceiling as if in a cartoon until it nailed her. Right between the eyes.

The fingers in her right hand were losing sensation. And with every passing minute, the chance increased that someone would discover her there.

She swallowed back the fear, gently tipped her head back again and examined the fingers of the snagged hand eight inches above and slightly behind her head.

From what she could see, the points of both hooks had pushed into the skin, but the ends of the barbs were still visible. If she could somehow back out each of the barbs, she could release the hooks and free her right hand.

Reaching up with her left hand, not daring to breathe,

she pulled the hook free of her third finger. Her hand moved to the second hook. She wobbled and overcorrected, put a hand on the wall to steady herself, yanked her right hand up reflexively, tugging on the hook, pushing the barb in the rest of the way and anchoring the hook in place.

"Dammit!"

There was a trick to backing out a barbed hook. But even if she could remember exactly how to do it, she would need two hands.

She was caught.

She pushed back the despair that threatened to well up inside of her.

Maybe Baxter would wonder if she had made it through the tunnel and come to look. She instantly felt better at the thought.

Except his key to the Inner Sanctum was in her pocket.

If anyone else came, they wouldn't be friendly.

She thought of the solo hiker who, when trapped by a boulder and faced with the choice between dying or freeing himself by cutting off his own arm, had sawed off the arm. The media had made a hero out of the man and the film industry a movie. Gracie and other rescuers had simply considered him irresponsible and reckless, his predicament self-inflicted.

Maybe when . . . maybe *if* the time came, in order to escape, she would find the will, the inner strength to rip the fish hooks free.

She just wasn't prepared to do that.

Yet.

Gracie stood in the tunnel, arm raised above her head.

On her watch, she kept track of the passing minutes.

Fifteen. Thirty. Thirty-one. Thirty-two.

She tried alternately resting her right arm on top of her head and letting her arm hang from the filaments, systematically changing position, putting weight on her left leg first, then the other, bending and straightening them.

An hour passed. Two hours. Two hours five minutes, ten minutes, fifteen.

Gracie's throat was parched, her tongue dry. It was hard to swallow.

She tried reaching around her back for her water bottle with her free hand, but was unable to actually withdraw it from its sling.

The battery in the flashlight drained down, its light dimming gradually from white to yellow to brown, finally fading out altogether.

Every second became excruciating. Every minute infinity.

Tears spilled from the corners of her eyes, trickling down her cheeks and onto her neck.

Her legs and the raised arm quivered with fatigue. She shivered with both shock and cold, jerking the lines which tugged at her skin.

Her neck had a kink in it. Her shoulders tightened, spasming.

Unbearable.

"I can't do it," she said aloud, voice echoing in the tunnel. "I can't hold on. I can't last another minute. Another second."

She held on.

A minute passed.

Then another.

And another.

A mind-numbing exercise in willpower.

Her mind blanked out.

Legs buckled.

Filament pulled taut.

Pain snapped her awake. She straightened her legs again, releasing the tug on the lid, ear, eyebrow, lip.

She closed her eyes again. Her mind floated. Darkened.

Her eyes flared open.

She had heard voices.

Behind her.

Men and women yelling. Angry. Cursing.

Wide-awake again, Gracie listened.

Someone was in the back room—the Inner Sanctum.

Winston, Lee, their wives, their buddies.

Getting dressed and ready to leave, they had found the lanyards with the Sheriff's IDs missing.

Now, surely, they couldn't follow through with the plan.

Surely, they wouldn't need to use the tunnel.

Surely, they wouldn't find her strung up like a landed marlin on display with the ID lanyards knotted at her waist.

The door of the tunnel opened.

Fresh, cool air whooshed up the tunnel, fluttering Gracie's hair.

Blue string lights strung along the ceiling flashed on, lighting the way.

Footsteps sounded in the tunnel.

Gracie hunched her shoulders and waited.

Someone rounded the corner, almost running into her. Lee Edwards's voice said, "What the f—?"

He slid past, then turned to face Gracie.

Orange shirt. Floppy hat. A backpack slung over one shoulder. An assault rifle over the other. "Who the hell are you?" Over her shoulder, he yelled, "There's a woman here." His eyes took in the filament, the hooks. "Caught."

"Keep going!" Winston yelled from back up the tunnel.

Lee's eyes ran down Gracie's body. "What the—?" He grabbed the bunch of lanyards hanging from her belt. "She's got the goddam IDs!"

"Take 'em!"

In one quick move, Lee slid a knife from a sheath at his thigh, slit Gracie's webbed belt, and gathered up the lanyards. Then he pressed the tip of his knife in the hollow of Gracie's neck, leaned up against her and said, "I should gut you like a mulie right here. Right now."

Over the pounding in her ears, Gracie heard footsteps

approach from behind. Boojum's voice said, "What's goin' on, Lee?"

Lee's eyes flicked over Gracie's shoulder, then back to her face. He leaned even closer so that she inhaled his sour breath. "On down the line, darlin'," he said. "Yer gonna get yers."

Then he turned and trotted out of sight down the tunnel.

Boojum ducked past Gracie, an assault rifle slung over one shoulder. He glanced back at her, eyes widening with recognition. But he gave no verbal indication he knew who she was.

He trotted down the tunnel.

Next, two women slid by, one of them snarling, "You bitch."

The second woman said nothing, but reached up and yanked on one of the fishing lines, tearing the hook from Gracie's ear.

She yelled in pain.

The women disappeared down the tunnel.

Blood, warm and soft, trickled down to pool inside Gracie's ear.

Three more men passed by. Two more women. More backpacks. More assault weapons. All dressed in Search and Rescue uniforms, easily mistaken for volunteers from a neighboring team arriving at the Command Post to help patrol the valley streets, keep the neighborhoods safe.

But they were on their way to commit mass murder and there was nothing Gracie could do to stop them.

If she tore free now, they would shoot her where she stood. Or gut her like a deer.

Gracie felt someone slide past.

Without giving her a glance, he disappeared down the tunnel.

Jordan.

Last in line, Winston ducked past Gracie, his large body scraping hers.

Like his brother, he turned back and stood in front of her. He put his mouth two inches from hers. "I should have known," he said. Then, without warning, he backhanded her across the face so fast she didn't have time to flinch.

Her head jerked back. Filament pulled taut, barbs imbedded, hooks pulled, stretching the skin.

"I'll be back for you," Winston said. "Count on it." He turned and trotted after the others down the tunnel.

Gracie staggered to regain her stance, placed her feet under her, and stood motionless, sucking in air through clenched teeth. Streamers of blood trickled down her cheek, her chin, her neck.

She slowly straightened her back and legs. She licked her lips, tasting blood.

"You bastards!" she screamed. "You won't get away with it!"

The sound died away.

If she didn't free herself, if she didn't somehow get to a phone and call the SO, good and innocent men and women were going to die. Dozens of them. Maybe more.

Gracie backed out the hook embedded in her finger as far as it would go. Then she gritted her teeth, closed her eyes, and took in a slow, deep breath. As if the sound could drown out the pain, she screamed and yanked her right hand down. Hard.

CHAPTER

32

THE hook ripped free from the end of Gracie's finger. Blood poured from the tear.

Tears flowed down her face. She grabbed ahold of the hook attached to her right eyebrow, backed it out as far as it would go, yelled again and tore it free. Blood slid into her eye.

With both hands, she grabbed the line attached to her lower eyelid.

Her body was shaking uncontrollably. She closed her eyes, opened her mouth, inhaled, and froze.

She had heard something.

She held her breath and listened.

Footsteps were returning up the tunnel. They crunched to a stop in front of her.

A flashlight swept her face.

"Holy mother of—" a male voice whispered.

Gracie opened her eyes. Saw nothing, but red. Blinked. Boojum stood before her.

"Boojum . . ." Gracie gasped. "Bombs. They're . . ." She

stopped again. "You already know," she said. "You're one of them."

Without a word, Boojum slung his assault rifle over his shoulder, moved around to Gracie's side, and slid an arm around her waist. "Lean against me," he said in a soft voice.

Puzzled, thankful, Gracie sank against his warm body. Knees buckling, she let him take most of her weight.

He slid a tactical knife from a keep on his belt and flicked it open. Then he studied the hooks attached to her mouth and the tender skin below her eye. "Okay," he said in a voice so gentle, so comforting, Gracie's eyes blurred with fresh tears. "I'm going to leave the hooks where they are, but I'm going to cut the lines. You'll need to stand up again. Can you do that?"

Somehow, Gracie straightened her legs, putting a hand out to the wall for support.

Boojum let go of her waist, took ahold of Gracie's own hand and placed it on the line attached to the corner of her mouth. "Hold it here."

She wrapped her fingers around the filament.

Pulling the line taut with his hand, Boojum laid the edge of the blade against it.

The sharp steel cut the filament like a warm knife through butter.

"One more," he said. Taking Gracie's hand again, he placed it on the line attached to the lower eye lid.

With his face so close to Gracie's, she could feel his warm breath, smelling faintly of clove, he pinched the end of the hook. Sliced through the filament.

Gracie was free.

Her knees gave way and she sagged to the ground.

Boojum knelt beside her. "Can you feel the barb on your eye at all?"

Gracie blinked once. Blinked again. "No."

"Good. Come on. We need to get you out of here." Putting

his hands beneath Gracie's armpits, he hauled her back to her feet. "All hell's about to break loose."

"Wh . . . what?"

"The place is surrounded by law enforcement. Probably with enough firepower to blow up the Golden Gate Bridge."

"Wh . . . what?" Gracie said again. "I don't . . ."

"The cavalry's outside," Boojum said, taking her elbow and edging her up the tunnel. "If there's shooting, we don't want you caught in the cross fire."

With the back of her wrist, Gracie wiped the blood out of her eye so she could look into Boojum's face. "You're not . . . with them?"

"With them? Yes. One of them? No."

"You're . . ." She dredged around for the acronym. Couldn't focus. Watched inside her mind as her own hand reached out, fingers spread, then closed around it. "ARA."

Boojum stopped, his grip on her elbow tightening. "How d'you know about that?"

"I was one of the searchers who found . . . parts. Out in the desert. There was a tattoo . . ."

Boojum bowed his head, leaned against the tunnel wall.

"You knew them," Gracie said. "Those people."

"My sister." A whisper. "And her husband."

"I'm so sorry." With a sickening jolt, she remembered the torsos in the freezer in the room next to the tunnel entrance.

"Someone killed them both," Boojum was saying. "Possibly one of the older boys—Jordan. I don't have my proof yet." He pushed off the wall, his grip retightening on Gracie's elbow. "Let's get you—"

Twin bangs exploded in the tunnel.

Gracie yelled and dropped to her knees, hands over her ears.

Boojum grunted, turned, lifted his rifle with one hand, and fired three shots in quick succession. Poppoppop!

Then he sagged against the wall, sliding down the cement block until he was sitting on the ground.

A dark, wet flower blossomed on his left shoulder.

Ears ringing, Gracie crawled over to him. "Boojum!"

"Goddammit," he said between clenched teeth.

Gracie peeled back the orange shirt, exposing a neat hole in the hollow beneath the collarbone, above the armpit.

She looked down the tunnel. In the blue cast of the string lights, she could see someone lying sprawled on the ground, a dark pool spreading around the head.

Gracie staggered to her feet and stumbled over.

It was Jordan.

She dropped to her knees and felt for a pulse on the boy's neck.

Waited.

Nothing.

Repositioned her fingers.

Still nothing.

Gracie bowed her head, tamping down the feelings that threatened to push up to the surface, to weaken, and paralyze.

Her head snapped up.

From outside, at the end of the tunnel, came a voice over a bullhorn. An announcement. Unintelligible, but the intent clear. You are surrounded. Drop your weapons. Down on the ground. Hands behind your heads.

Men yelled. A woman screamed.

Then a smattering of automatic gunfire.

Return fire.

The voice over the bullhorn again.

Silence.

More sporadic gunfire.

Then, inside the tunnel, a scraping sound.

Gracie pushed herself to her feet and turned to run.

A groan floated up behind her.

She looked over her shoulder.

A dark figure, hunched over, a hand pressed to his side, limped up the tunnel.

Winston.

She must have made a sound, for the big man looked up and saw her. "Gracie. Come help me. I'm hurt. Help me. I never would have hurt you. I wanted to marry you. I love you."

Gracie turned and ran up the tunnel to where Boojum sat. "It's Winston," she said. "Let's go."

Boojum tried to push himself up from the ground, but fell back with a grunt. "Little bastard got me in the leg, too."

"We have to go," Gracie urged. She draped his arm around her shoulder and, pushing up with her legs, hauled him up to his feet.

Together they limped around the corner, up the tunnel to the bunker door.

Gracie put her hand on the knob. "Locked!"

From back down the tunnel came a hoarse cry of anguish.

"Do you know the combination?" Gracie asked.

"No."

Gracie leaned Boojum against the wall, ran back down the tunnel, around the corner, ducking beneath the fish-hooks, to where Winston sat on the ground, cradling Jordan's head on his knee.

"I need the combination to the door," Gracie gasped.

Head bowed, Winston gave no sign that he had heard her.

"The tunnel door is locked," she said. "I need the combination."

Still no response.

Footsteps entered the tunnel from the creek.

Gracie reached behind her back, unsnapped the holster, and drew out Allen's revolver. Holding it with her right hand, cupping it with the left, she placed the barrel against the side of Winston's head above his ear. "I need the combination," she said. "Now."

Without looking up, Winston said in a voice devoid of emotion, "Four, twenty, eighty-nine."

With the revolver still in her hand and repeating *four, twenty, eighty-nine* to herself over and over, Gracie ran back up the tunnel to where Boojum waited, slumped against the wall.

"Four, twenty, eighty-nine," she said.

Boojum snorted. "I should have guessed."

Gracie stood to one side so the rope lights would illuminate the dial.

"April 20, 1889. Hitler's birthday."

One hand on the handle, Gracie punched in the numbers. Still locked.

She cried out in frustration.

A shout back down the tunnel. Gunfire. The sound of feet running.

Gracie took in a deep breath. Punched in the numbers, more slowly. "Four. Two. Zero. Eight. Nine."

Held her breath.

Turned the handle.

Pulled the door open.

She and Boojum fell through into the bunker. The door slammed behind them.

Leaving lights blazing and a trail of bright red blood in their wake, Gracie and Boojum stumbled through the Inner Sanctum and into the weapons and ammunition room.

Boojum let go of Gracie. "You go. Get out of here."

"No!" Gracie said. "You're hurt. I'm not—"

"I'm slowing you down." With his head, he indicated the mini–MASH unit in the next room. "I can hole up in there." He limped over to the shelves lining the wall and picked up a hand grenade. "No one will get past me. Get the hell out of here."

Gracie left Boojum, running once again past the mini–MASH unit, showers and beds and freezers, through the kitchen and living area, up the ramp, through the garage to the door to the meeting room.

A muffled explosion below shook the entire building, rattling the windows. Dust sifted down from the ceiling.

Gracie threw open the door, flipped on the light, and ran

across the meeting room. With a hand on the knob of the door leading out into the yard, she stopped, falling against the wall.

What the hell *am I doing?*

Running outside at a hundred pumped-up-on-adrenaline-and-testosterone law enforcement guys wearing tactical armor and holding weapons with itchy hair-trigger fingers. They had no idea who she was. That she wasn't one of them. She was dressed in orange and camouflage, just like everyone else.

And you have a gun in your hand, you massively hare-brained IDIOT!

Gunfire sounded again from somewhere nearby. Above her head.

Someone was shooting from the second floor.

She looked up, eyes searching the ceiling as if with X-ray vision she could see who was up there.

Grandpop Martin, she guessed. The Edwards patriarch.

As if to confirm her supposition, she heard the low rumble of a man's voice.

Then another voice, one that made her heart stop.

Higher, younger, pleading.

Baxter.

CHAPTER

33

GRACIE'S eyes darted around the meeting room, stopping at a door near the garage wall.

She sprinted over and pulled the door open.

A ramp led up to the second floor.

Easing the door closed behind her and feeling her way in the darkness with a hand on the wall, Gracie tiptoed up the ramp to a landing, around the corner, and up to a door at the top.

Standing off to one side, she found the knob, turned it and pushed the door open a crack. She peered out into the darkened room.

From the glare of spotlights outside flooding in through the single window off to the left, she could just make out that the room was long and narrow, running the length of the building. Piled high down the center were boxes of ammunition, enough for an entire army for a year.

Barely visible in the shadows to the right of the open window, Martin sat in his wheelchair holding a high-powered rifle, the barrel resting on the sill.

On his lap sat Baxter.

Martin's left arm encircled the boy, a revolver in the hand.

Open boxes of ammunition lay next to the wheelchair, large-caliber cartridges scattered across the floor.

"I swear, Grandpop," Baxter was saying in a voice quivering with tears. "It wasn't me."

"Shut your sniveling mouth, you goddamned little traitor," Martin growled. Without aiming, he fired off a half-dozen rounds of the rifle.

The spotlight went out, plunging the room into full darkness.

"I got a kid up here!" Martin screamed out the window. "You goddam pig cops! Pull back, you sissy cowards! Or I'll shoot the boy! He means nothing to me. I swear to God, I'll shoot him!"

"Goddam sissy cowards," Martin muttered. "They won't shoot now. Afraid of hitting you."

Gracie's breath came in quick whispers through her nose. There wasn't a doubt in her mind that Martin meant what he said, that he would kill his own grandson.

Something caught her eye.

A glowing red dot slid along the boxes of ammunition behind Martin.

A laser sight.

A sniper outside looking for his shot.

Surely, Gracie thought, even a trained sniper wouldn't risk shooting into a darkened room with a child right there.

She thought for a moment. Reaching in from the doorway, she slid a hand up the wall. Couldn't find what she was looking for.

She edged into the room, hand brushing the wall until she felt a light switch.

But if she simply turned on the lights, Martin could and would see to shoot . . . Baxter first, then her.

Gracie knelt down on the floor. Feet lifted, eyes trained on Martin at the window, revolver in hand, she crawled into the room. A shadow among shadows, every movement slow, calculated, stealthy. If she made a sound, any sound, she was dead meat. Literally.

But Martin's attention was laser-beamed out the window. He fired off several more rounds of the rifle. "Come on!" he yelled. "Why don't you shoot? The kid's right here. Shoot the little son of a bitch! I want you to!" He sank back in the chair. "Goddam government sissy cowards."

Barely breathing, Gracie inched past the ammunition boxes, lifting each hand, each knee in turn, then placing it carefully, silently on the wooden floor.

She crawled past the wheelchair, then turned and came up behind it.

Taking in a deep, silent breath through her open mouth, she rose up onto one knee and pressed the end of the revolver against the back of Martin's skull. "Move a muscle and you're dead," she said.

Martin jerked, then froze.

"Gracie," Baxter whimpered.

"Leave, Baxter. Now."

Without hesitation, the boy slid off his grandfather's lap. Footsteps thudding on the wooden floor, he ran across the room, scrabbled around the far wall searching for the door, found it and disappeared.

"Tip the rifle out the window," Gracie said. The hand holding the revolver was shaking so badly, she gripped her wrist with the other hand, trying to hold it steady. "Then raise your right hand over your head."

Martin did as he was told. The rifle landed with a clattering thump on the ground outside. He lifted his hand.

"Higher."

With a grunt, he raised it higher.

"Now throw the handgun after it."

"Goddam, bitch!" Martin yelled without turning. "Who the hell are you?"

"Throw it!" Gracie screamed.

The weapon landed with a thud outside.

Gracie's finger closed around the trigger. She bored the barrel into Martin's skull. "You twisted, hate-filled son of a bitch," she growled, teeth clenched so tightly, her jaw ached. "Good people are dead because of you. Because of your hatred."

Martin's head jerked.

"Don't move!" Gracie yelled. "I have all the reason in the world to kill you and not a single reason not to."

Silence.

Gracie pushed herself to her feet, staggered, regained her balance. "Do not move." Then with the gun trained at the back of Martin's head, she backed slowly across the room to the far wall, found the door standing open, then off to the right, the light switch.

Moving her body as close to the door as she could while reaching out for the switch, she took in a deep breath and flipped on the light.

Gracie dived for the door. Missed. Hit the doorjamb. Bounced off.

Bangbang!

She landed hard on her side, head downhill on the ramp. The revolver flew out of her hand, skittering out of sight somewhere below.

"Gracie!" Baxter was on his knees beside her.

"Go, Bax," Gracie grunted. "Your grandpop . . ."

"I think he's dead. I think somebody outside shot him."

That's okay then. Everything's okay.

The stairwell lights flared on.

Gracie groaned.

"What's on your face?" Baxter asked. "And . . . your leg! Gracie! You're bleeding bad!"

Lifting her head, heavier than a piano, Gracie looked up the length of her body.

Arterial blood, bright and red, spurted like a water fountain from a wound on her thigh

He had another gun, she thought. *Should have thought of that. Stupid.*

Vaguely she knew she needed to stop the bleeding or something bad would happen. *Oh, yeah. I'll die.*

Curling her body, she brought her head up toward her knees, stretched out a hand, clamped it over the wound.

Her body was growing cold. She was shivering. And her teeth were chattering again.

Blood oozed out between her fingers.

"Bax. My belt. S'already loose. Wrap it . . ."

She lifted her head, but couldn't hold it up. Banged it back down onto wood. Her body relaxed. Hand released.

She felt Baxter struggle to pull her belt free from the pants loops. "Gracie," he sobbed.

"S'okay, Bax. Holster."

More pulling, fiddling, then with a final tug, the belt came loose.

"Tie it around . . . leg," she heard her own voice say. "Above . . . wound."

She opened her eyes and watched Baxter knot the belt around her upper leg. "Make it tight."

Tears were streaming down the boy's cheeks. "Don't die, Gracie. Please don't die."

"Not g'nna die," she mumbled in a voice that sounded a long way off. "You're . . . hero, Bax. My buddy."

Her eyes closed.

"Gracie," she heard Baxter say.

Another muffled explosion, this time from outside. Then feet pounding the floor. Men yelling. A door banged open.

"Don't shoot!" Baxter yelled, his voice high, terrified. "Don't shoot!"

More voices. Louder. Footsteps.

The ramp quivered.

"My grandpop shot her," Baxter said, sobbing. "She helped me get away. He would have killed me. She's my best friend. Please don't let her die."

"We're not going to let her die," a male voice said.

Gracie felt someone kneel beside her. Opened her eyes a slit and looked into a masked face. Tried to smile. "Happy to see you," she said, then realized that nothing had come out of her mouth.

Her eyes closed again.

The world faded.

GRACIE leaned on her crutches and stared at the black heaps of charred wood and shingles and twisted metal that had been the Camp Ponderosa Gatehouse.

Allen stood at her side, hands in the front pockets of his jeans, white T-shirt covered with a denim jacket, gray hair in a neat braid hanging down the middle of his back.

The front reception area, the kitchen, the little bathroom, Gracie's office, the maintenance shop, and equipment storage room downstairs were all gone. The only thing remaining of the building was the stone fireplace and chimney, a black sentinel rising up stubbornly against a backdrop of pines and Wedgwood blue sky. Burned to black and ash were the grass and yews in the front yard, and other shrubs and trees surrounding the building and along the path selected by the fire. Trees farther away were singed, leaves and needles scorched to rusty brown. All-pervasive was the stench of wet burned wood.

The cold front that had brought the rain, even several inches of snow at the higher elevations, had stopped the

Timber Creek arm of the Shady Oak Fire, the wind shift blowing the fire back on itself, allowing firefighters to gain the upper hand.

The evening of the following day, the evacuation order had been lifted, and relieved residents and vacationers had poured back into the valley.

But forty-eight acres of Camp Ponderosa had already burned. With typical caprice, flames had claimed most of the giant ponderosa pines comprising the high ropes course, two double-wide mobile homes used for employee housing, and the Gatehouse, but spared other wooden structures—the conference center, Mojave Lodge, the three side-by-side single-wide trailers, the rustic cabins and the little chapel next to the lake. The roof of Serrano Lodge had been singed, but the building itself, of cement block, was undamaged.

A sharp wind was blowing from the northeast, swaying the tops of the trees, spinning ash into pewter dust devils, cutting through the fibers of Gracie's fleece jacket and flannel shirt and straight through to the skin.

"I lost your stupid gun," she said, shivering.

"My stupid gun?"

"Your gun. I lost your gun. I'm sorry."

"Better off without it anyway."

"And, only for a second, I swear . . . I suspected you were a white supremacist. *Suspected* is too strong a word. Wondered. I wondered whether you were. But only for a second. I'm sorry."

"Cutie patootie, you wouldn't believe how much that isn't a problem," Allen said, his arm sliding around her shoulder. He nodded toward the blackened rubble of the Gatehouse. "An improvement perhaps?"

Gracie snorted a laugh. "Yeah."

After all that had happened, Gracie was numb, feeling nothing at the sight of the ruined building. That would come later, perhaps all at once like a sucker punch to the gut, perhaps gradually over time in a series of painful stabbing memories.

But it was the dead zone of the back acreage of camp she couldn't face, the charred skeletons of the giant trees she loved, the ash, the fire-scarred moonscape, once an Eden, unspoiled, teeming with wildlife.

Rebirth would come, she knew. Trees and shrubs would regrow. Squirrels and flickers and coyotes and chickadees would return. But it would take years, eons, to regain its former glory.

And she wouldn't be there to see it.

Gracie turned toward her truck parked in the road beneath the arch, confirmed that Minnie's little face was staring at her from the passenger's seat, and turned back. "I talked to the church this morning," she said. "They're keeping camp closed through the holidays."

"So I heard," Allen said.

"Groups coming in starting in January. They won't start rebuilding anything until next spring." Gracie looked over at Allen. "What are you going to do?"

"Don't worry 'bout me, Rumpy Diddle. I always find something." Allen jumped away in a crouch, feet apart, hands like claws. "I'm a cat. Fast. Land on my feet."

Gracie rolled her eyes and laughed. "You're a strange man, Studley Do-Right."

Allen straightened and grinned at her.

"You gonna come back?" she asked.

"Haven't asked me yet."

Gracie snorted another laugh. "You'll be back."

"What about you?" he asked. "You comin' back? Won't be the same 'thoutchoo."

Gracie studied the charred ruins. "I don't know. I'm . . . tired. Maybe I will." She looked back at Allen. "But then again, maybe I won't."

SEARCH AND RESCUE teammate. A camp coworker. Now Morris. *Too many damned funerals in the past year*, Gracie thought and leaned against the end of the pew.

Oblique streamers of sunlight pouring through stained glass windows bathed the enormous neo-Gothic sanctuary in crimson and saffron and peacock blue. Dark, elaborately carved wooden beams soared overhead. At the front of the cathedral, the coffin was barely visible beneath an ostentatious spray of every imaginable color of gladiola, mum, and lily—Morris's last hurrah.

Evelyn sat in the pew next to Gracie, looking both frail and chic in a neat mourning ensemble of black Chanel suit, stockings, satin pumps, and hat with a heavy veil obscuring her face.

On the other side of Evelyn was Morris's son, Harold, his current wife and his two sons. Then Morris's daughter, Lenora, her husband, her children—a son and a daughter. All in a row, like mannequins, models of perfect behavior, dressed to the nines in black and white and gray with a dash of hot pink here or rebellious red there, staring stonily ahead, not a tear among them, not a single ounce of anything resembling loss or grief or love for the man in the coffin.

The priest's voice echoed throughout the sanctuary, his effusive, yet impersonal praise of Morris and his life ringing hollow and leaving Gracie wondering if the priest had ever even met the deceased. She couldn't imagine Morris having set foot in a place of worship in his entire life.

She considered the possibility that a lack of relationship with the Almighty, or accountability to any power higher than himself, had been one of Morris's problems.

Gracie's sigh echoed throughout the hush of the church.

Why am I here?

For the second time in a month, she had flown two thousand miles to see a man she despised, whom she had wished dead for so many years, and who was now, in fact, dead.

Her thoughts swept back to Timber Creek, to the events of the past few weeks. To Vivian and the two antifascist activists who had lost their lives. To Baxter and Boojum, to John and Acacia, whose lives had been changed forever.

To Winston, who had lost his only son and now sat await-ing trial. To Lee, who had come out of the incident unscathed physically, but who had lost his father, his nephew, and, like his brother-in-law and others in the group, awaited trial.

For what?

She thought about choices. Between light and darkness. Between tolerance and fear. Flexibility and rigidity. Forgive-ness or feeding the beast. God or the absence of God.

She thought about her own life, her unease, her restless spirit, her bulldog tendency to hang on with her teeth and never let go. In some circumstances, in some settings, that was a positive trait. In others, it damaged, spoiled. Over the years she had carefully constructed onion layer after layer of emotional scar tissue, stifling her heart, until she had reached the point of emotional paralysis.

She thought about those she had trusted, willfully or, by virtue of her young age, in innocence.

Others, of course, had hurt her. Strangers, employers, casual friends. But for those with whom she had placed no real emotional trust, there had been no true emotional betrayal.

But Morris.

And her mother. Who had refused to defend her own child against her abuser.

And her own father. Who had left his wife and adoring nine-year-old daughter with no warning, no explanation. For more than twenty-five years, Gracie had waited for him to come back, to contact her, to let her know he had loved her, that he still loved her.

Her mother.

Her father.

And Morris.

These were the thickest, toughest layers, the most diffi-cult to remove.

Gracie looked down at the funeral program in her hand, expensive, tasteful. She opened it and scanned the contents, then closed it.

On the back, centered in the middle of the page, written in Edwardian script, was a scripture passage.

"Get rid of all bitterness, rage and anger, brawling and slander, along with every form of malice. Be kind and compassionate to one another, forgiving each other, just as in Christ God forgave you."— *Eph. 4:31–32 NIV.*

Gracie glanced up at Evelyn, a marble statue, the only sign of life a slight quivering of the black veil.

She looked down again at the passage obviously placed by her mother for her daughter. A message. A plea.

"Get rid of all bitterness, rage and anger . . . forgiving each other."

Gracie could walk through life, lugging on her back a big gunnysack of unforgiveness and anger, eventually turning into a lonely, bitter, shriveled-up shrew.

Or she could forgive them.

All of them.

The choice was there.

The choice was hers.

Someday, she thought.

Maybe.

Gracie looked down at her mother's hands, clenched tightly in her lap as if that were all that was holding her together. In spite of the perfectly applied red nail polish, her hands looked old —thin, liver spotted, bones and blue veins pronounced.

With a start, Gracie recognized her mother's pain, a pain that had probably lasted more than twenty-five years. For the first time in her life, she looked at Evelyn without blame and resentment, seeing her not as someone weak and flawed, a failed mother who, instead of protecting her child, had let her down, hurt her with her silence, damaged her with her defense of her abusive husband. Instead, Gracie saw her mother as a real person, battling demons of her own, dealing with her own mistakes, her own weaknesses, her own regrets, her own private pain.

"Forgiving each other."

Gracie looked up at the high ceiling, the dark wood arching overhead, then to the front of the church, the crucifix. She blew out a long, slow, silent breath, then reached out and placed a hand on top of her mother's.

Startled, Evelyn looked up at Gracie. Tears glittered through the veil.

Gracie smiled down at her mother and slid an arm around her thin shoulders.

CHAPTER

35

"AHHH." Gracie laid her head back on the pillow. "This feels great, doesn't it?" she said to Minnie, who was curled up in her little bed next to her own. "Back in our own little cabin. Feels like we've been gone for years."

Finally back in Timber Creek, too exhausted to unpack the Ranger, Gracie had carried inside a grocery bag of a dozen eggs and a half gallon of low-fat milk, and the trash bag filled with items packed the previous week, pulling out only her clock and toothbrush and paste. Everything else could wait until Allen arrived the following morning to help her unpack and move back into her cabin.

Gracie shifted her hips on the thin camp mattress that had served as her bed for more than ten years. "Maybe it's time I actually bought a real bed. Whaddya think about that idea, Minnie? A real bed."

Minnie watched her with bright eyes and said nothing.

Gracie reached over, turned out the lamp, lay back, and closed her eyes.

She opened her eyes again, seeing nothing in the darkness, unsure of whether she had been asleep or not.

What she was sure of was that she had heard something.

Then she heard it again—a thump. Downstairs. Out on the side deck. Near the kitchen.

She reached out and felt for Minnie. The dog was sitting up.

"Probably that blasted raccoon again," Gracie said, more to reassure herself than anything else. She hadn't forgotten the prank phone calls, the wanted poster.

But that was all behind her.

Wasn't it?

Minnie growled.

Gracie eased herself up into a sitting position, swung her legs off the bed. Hanging on to her crutch, she hauled herself to her feet.

"Guess we better check it out. Don't want 'im eating all that new birdseed, do we?"

From downstairs came the sound of glass smashing.

Gracie grabbed up the phone from the bedside table and dialed 911. "This is Gracie Kinkaid," she whispered in the phone. "Fifteen oh three Arcturus. Somebody's breaking into my house. They just smashed a window." She repeated the address.

She threw on hiking boots, taking precious seconds to lace them up so she wouldn't trip down the loft steps and break her neck.

Then she stopped.

She smelled smoke.

Not from outside.

From inside the cabin.

Leaving the crutch behind, Gracie scooped Minnie up in her arms and hobbled down the steps. Tripped. Almost pitched forward. Fell against the wall, bumping her injured thigh. "Shhht," escaped between clenched teeth. She recovered and stumbled the rest of the way down.

At the bottom, she turned and looked into the kitchen.

Flames already licked the curtains. Heavy smoke billowed out through the doorway.

In two seconds, Gracie was across the living room. She heaved open the sliding glass window, stepped outside onto the deck, and slid the door closed.

Setting Minnie down, she limped down the back steps into the dirt yard. Dialed 911 again on her cell phone. No reception. She left the line open.

She threw open the gate below the house and, with Minnie at her heels, slid down the steep hillside toward the road.

She glanced over her shoulder back up the hill. An orange light danced in the windows of the cabin. The fire was spreading fast.

Somewhere on the road above, on the other side of the house, came the sound of an engine roaring to life, the screeching of tires.

A vehicle with a hole in its muffler was speeding down Arcturus.

"Stay, Minnie," Gracie ordered. Ignoring the pain in her thigh, she slithered the rest of the way down the hill to the road. She landed on the pavement as a small white pickup rounded the corner on the road above, catching Gracie in its headlights.

She picked up a fist-sized rock from the side of the road and heaved it with all her strength, hitting the truck's windshield with a loud crack.

The truck swerved to the left, almost winging Gracie. It veered past her, swerved right, then left again, missing the curve in the road. Plunging straight ahead, it left the pavement altogether, and thudded to a sudden stop against the brush-covered embankment.

The driver's side door opened. The driver fell out, landing on hands and knees on the ground.

In the darkness, Gracie couldn't see who it was.

"Wha' th' . . . ? Wha' jes' happ'n?"

Gracie would know that voice anywhere.

Mrs. Lucas.

Gracie leapt down the road, full-body-slamming herself on top of the smaller woman and flattening her to the ground.

The woman screamed.

In a stunning flash of recognition, Gracie knew the maniacal voice screaming in her ear on the telephone hadn't been a man; it had been Mrs. Lucas, voice lowered by years of chain-smoking.

"Get off . . . !" the woman grunted. Wriggling and writhing, she managed to turn herself partially over. By the light of the open door of her truck, she saw who it was on top of her. "You? You goddam bitch!" She bucked her emaciated body, trying to throw Gracie off. "Cuddlin' up to those . . . those . . ." She let loose with an obscenity-laced string of racial slurs. "In my house! *My* house! Well, I showed 'em, didn't I? And now I'm showin' you!" She cackled. "You won't have nothin' left. Just like me. And there ain't nothin' you can do now to stop it!"

Then she spat and hissed and scratched and fought like a wildcat in a snare.

But Gracie had learned a thing or two over the past few months. Grabbing ahold of Mrs. Lucas's wrists, she muscled them, first one, then the other, beneath the woman's body, trapping them there with her own weight. Sliding her own hands out, she lay on top of Mrs. Lucas like a beached walrus, until finally the woman stopped struggling.

"Ungh," Mrs. Lucas grunted. "I can't breathe."

"Too bad."

"Let me up. I hit my head on the steering wheel."

"You should wear a seat belt."

"I hurt my knee, too. Let me up."

Crackling up the hill drew Gracie's eyes back over her shoulder. An orange halo of light lit up the night sky. Her wooden cabin, old and bone-dry, was burning like a torch.

In the distance, a siren wailed.

Mrs. Lucas's words rang in Gracie's head. *"I showed 'em, didn't I? And now I'm showin' you!"*

Mrs. Lucas had set fire to the Robinsons' house.

Gracie rested her head on her arms. Everything about her ached. Her thigh. Her ankle. Her head. But most of all her heart.

Her cabin was burning.

She had lost everything.

She had nothing left.

Nothing

Something warm and wet tickled Gracie's elbow.

She raised her head.

Minnie sat beside her, licking her arm.

"Hi, little girl," Gracie said and smiled.

CHAPTER

36

"THANK you so much for everything," Sharon said, pulling Gracie into another lavender-scented hug.

"You're welcome again," Gracie said.

Sharon pulled away. Walking around Baxter, she brushed his shoulder with a hand, then climbed the steps up onto the sagging porch and disappeared inside the house.

Baxter stood unmoving at the bottom of the stairs, hands in pocket, head bowed. For the first time since Gracie had met him, he looked like a normal eleven-year-old boy wearing a goldenrod T-shirt and a navy blue hoodie, the ends of new sneakers peeking out from beneath too-long blue jeans. The straw-colored hair was trimmed, washed, and combed. He wore new wire-rimmed glasses. He looked like a little man rather than a boy.

"You okay, Bax?" Gracie asked, easing herself down on the bottom step so that her face was even with his.

A nod.

"You have those books I brought?"

He gestured back toward the house.

Gracie looked at the bent head, the sprinkle of freckles across the nose. "You saved my life, you know."

"You saved my life, too," he said, still without looking up.

"Well, then. I guess that makes us best friends for life, doesn't it?"

"Why do you have to leave?"

"I lost my cabin, Bax."

"But why do you have to go away? You could stay with us."

Gracie smiled. "Gran Sharon might have something to say about that."

She looked out over the dirt yard, past the Ranger parked along the street, the houses beyond, the pines towering behind. "I need to go away for a while," she said. "A little break. You have my cell number. You can call me. Anytime. About anything. I mean it. And I'll write you letters. Will you write me back?"

"Where will I send them?"

"When I get to where I'm going to be for a little while, I'll let you know the address."

"Okay."

"Can I have a hug?"

She had barely finished the words before Baxter wrapped his arms around her, his head on her shoulder.

Gracie hugged him back, pressing her cheek to the still-wet hair until finally she managed, "I love you, Bax."

"I love you, too, Gracie," he mumbled into her shirt. Then, dry-eyed, he let go, walked up the steps, across the porch, and into the house, quietly closing the door.

The boy's tears would come later, in private, Gracie knew.

As, she was certain, they would for her.

GRACIE STOOD BEFORE the metal desk in the empty Watch Commander's office, staring down at the piece of paper in her hand.

Moments before, sitting in the Ranger in the parking lot

of the SO, she had handwritten a note to Sergeant Gardner on a sheet of lined paper torn from a pad in her day pack.

Effective immediately, I hereby resign from Timber Creek Search and Rescue.

She had printed her full name, Grace Louise Kinkaid, in block letters below, then scribbled her signature along the bottom.

Gracie laid the sheet of paper facedown on the desk, printed *Sgt. Gardner* on the back, and swiveled the paper around so that it would be facing the sergeant when he sat down.

Next to it, she laid her Search and Rescue ID, her key to the Sheriff's Office building, and her own copy of *The Complete Idiot's Guide to Recruiting and Managing Volunteers.*

She reached out to align the edges of the paper with the book.

Then she spun around and walked out of the office.

Seconds passed.

Muffled voices from a room somewhere in the building.

Footsteps in the outer hallway.

Gracie burst back into the office, grabbed up her ID, the building key, and the sheet of paper, crumpling it up into a little ball.

She picked up the *Idiot's Guide* and tore out the first page with its incriminating address label in the top-right corner, placed the book back in the middle of the desk, turned, and walked out of the room.

THE RANGER SAT at a stop sign at the intersection of two highways down in the desert.

Minnie lay on her bed behind the driver's seat, warm breath tickling the back of Gracie's neck.

Gracie looked right, then left, then right again.

Eleven years before, she had sat at an intersection in

Michigan, faced with a similar choice. Turn right, turn left, or drive straight ahead.

She had turned right and ended up in California.

Now the highway to the left led to Desertview and points west.

The highway to the right led to Palm Springs.

Straight ahead led to the desert town of Barstow, crossroads of the Mojave and the junction of I-15 and I-40. There the possibilities were endless. The highway west led to Los Angeles, San Diego, and Mexico. North to northern California, Oregon, Washington, and British Columbia. East to Las Vegas, Utah, Colorado, the Great Plains, and eventually all the way to the Atlantic.

The world, figuratively, literally, was at Gracie's fingertips.

I need time, she thought. To do absolutely nothing. To think. And heal. Physically and mentally.

And forgive, she added begrudgingly.

She checked the outside mirrors. No cars fuming behind her.

"Well, Minnie," she said. "Which way should we turn?" No opinion was forthcoming from behind her right shoulder.

She thought about driving to Tucson to Ralph and what waited for her there, to Los Angeles to Rob and what waited for her there, or all the way to Detroit and who and what waited for her there.

She considered somewhere different altogether where no one and nothing waited except a new adventure.

Gracie thought.

Considered.

Weighed.

Then she looked right.

Looked left.

Looked right again.

And pressed down on the accelerator.